THE
POWELL
EXPEDITIONS

THE POWELL EXPEDITIONS

JUBILEE WALKER SERIES **BOOK 1**

TIM PIPER

Book design by The Book Designers
https://bookdesigners.com/

ISBN 979-8-9884186-0-3 (hardback)
ISBN 979-8-9884186-1-0 (paperback)
ISBN 979-8-9884186-2-7 (ebook)

Library of Congress Number: 2023909532

Published by
Sunshine Parade Publishing
1907 Sinclair Ct.
Bloomington, IL 61704
https://www.sunshineparadepublishing.com

To Lee Piper

CHAPTER 1

In late February, while winter still had a grip on the prairie, Jubilee Walker's mother fell ill. She was still able to suffer through her work around the farm, but Jubil lay in bed listening to the sound of her cough, staring at the rafters above his loft. In spite of having spent the day cleaning out the barn and the livestock pens, he was not sleepy. In a few hours he would be at it again, splitting and stacking firewood—a never ending chore. It was not the hard work of farming that weighed on Jubil's soul but the monotony of it, and constantly being at the mercy of the weather. But then again, unpredictable weather was the only thing that broke the monotony of the chores that went on every day of the year, year after year.

He opened the door to his imagination and allowed it to roam as freely as his saddle horse, Star, turned out to graze without halter or bridle. One of these days, he was going to saddle up Star, taking nothing more than his rifle, a bedroll, and whatever he could pack in his saddlebags, and ride west toward whatever adventures lay in his path. Following only his instincts, he would see as much of the world as he could before settling in any one place. How he would earn his daily bread was unclear, but he would hunt, fish, and live by his wits—and take a job now and then to earn a little travel money. That method had worked fine for his uncle Pete for many years, until duty called him to the farm and then to war. Jubil's path would become clearer once he was on it.

His mother coughed again, and his daydreams snagged on reality. He couldn't imagine telling her that he was leaving her to run the farm on her own so he could ride carefree across the country in search of adventure. He would not lie here pining for a life that drew him away from his responsibility to her and to the memory of his father.

The other complication in this imagined life was Nelly Boswell. He had never spoken of his changing feelings for her and was unsure whether he ever would, but even if she didn't feel the same, he was not anxious to live his life alone. It was unclear how he might be a husband to Nelly—or anyone else— and a father to their children while living a life of unfettered freedom and adventure.

He rubbed his eyes and told himself, *Stop these foolish daydreams*. His life was on this farm. If he married, his wife would come to live there with him and his mother, and that was that. He reached for the dime novel atop the stack sitting next to his bed, thinking it might help him sleep, but he had read it, and all of them, more than once. He tossed the book aside and blew out the lantern.

Instead of easing, Jubil's mother's cold persisted, and she grew weaker. By late March she was stricken with chills and fever. For the first time in Jubil's seventeen years, he saw her too sick to get out of bed.

She lay in bed, her teeth chattering despite the heavy quilt, her auburn hair a pile of damp curls. She had developed a racking cough and a wheeze in her breathing. Her normally sparkling hazel eyes were dull and unfocused. She declined any food or drink but allowed Jubil to mop her brow with a folded flannel.

"Mama, I hate to leave you here alone, but I'm going to ride into town and fetch Doc Hill."

"Oh, Jubil, I'll be all right if I can just lie here and rest a bit."

"That may be true, Mama, but it won't hurt for him to take a look at you," he said, trying to sound less worried than he felt.

In the stable, Star greeted him with a whinny and a shake of her head.

"Good morning, Star."

She looked him in the eye as he spoke. Star was a fifteen-year-old mare with a chestnut coat, a flaxen mane, and a white four-pointed mark on her forehead. Ever since Jubil's father had passed away, she had been his horse. "Sorry, but your feed's going to have to wait until we get back. We've got to ride for Doc Hill. Mama's very sick."

Jubil poured a scoop of corn into the feed bucket of the horse in the adjoining stall. "No reason for you to wait on breakfast, Max," he said to the big gray Percheron draft horse, who was three hands taller and half again heavier than Star. Max did all the heavy lifting and pulling around the farm.

Jubil set Star south toward Bloomington at a canter and in less than an hour reached the center of town. He was relieved to find Dr. Hill at home. Based on Jubil's description, the doctor's diagnosis was influenza. He gave Jubil a bottle containing a few blue calomel pills and a small sack of linseed.

"Give her one of these pills," Dr. Hill explained, "and see how she handles it before you give her more. The medicine is a purgative to rid her bowels of any infectious accumulations, so the effect is to be expected. If she weakens, don't give her any more. To ease the cough and congestion, boil up some water along with a fistful of linseed and apply a poultice to her chest. There'll be no ill effect from that, so repeat it as needed if it seems effective. I'll be up your way in a few days to check on her."

The poultice seemed to soothe his mother's cough, but that relief was short lived as the calomel took effect. She was too weak to get to the chamber pot, so Jubil tried to help her manage it while still in bed. The result was a failure requiring a cleanup that was mortifying and exhausting for both of them. Even after Jubil changed the bedclothes, the stench hung in the bedroom, but it was too cold outside to open the window.

In addition to caring for his mother, Jubil had to feed and water the livestock, gather the eggs, and milk the cow. As he carried out the habitual motions of his chores each day, he fought to convince himself her illness would pass. He didn't know what more to do for her. It was a great relief when the doctor came by.

"Loretta," Doc Hill said, "you've developed a touch of pneumonia." He turned to Jubil. "Stop the calomel pills. She's too weak to tolerate any more purging. Continue the poultice if it helps. I'm going to leave you this bottle of laudanum. Give her three drops every eight hours, but no more. It will control the cough and let her rest. I'll be back to check on her next week . . . but come for me sooner if needs be."

The doctor went on his way, and Jubil sat on the edge of his mother's bed to give her a dose of the medicine.

"I'm so tired, Jubil," his mother said. Her eyes had sunken into her face in a way Jubil found distressing.

"You'll be fine in a few days, Mama," he said hopefully. "The medicine will help."

His mother reached for his hand. Her touch was weightless, her hand clammy. Tears welled in her eyes, and he tried to control his own.

"You're a good boy, Jubil. You've looked after me and this farm well. Your papa would be very proud . . . your uncle too."

His father had died seven years ago after a fall off the barn roof. His uncle Pete, his father's brother, had died five years ago in the Battle of Shiloh. Since the day his uncle had left for the war, Jubil had been the man of the house.

"Thank you, Mama." He smiled at her and wiped his eyes. "You need to get some rest." He placed her arm back under the quilt and went out to finish his chores.

The laudanum stilled his mother's cough and allowed her to sleep, and over the next several days, her condition improved. The fever and chills abated, but she still had no appetite or energy. Near dawn on the last day of April, Jubil awoke with a start. He thought his mother was calling for him. He listened for a moment and heard nothing but lit a lantern and went to check on her.

She looked as though she still slept, but her complexion was waxy and ashen, her mouth agape. A chill shook him as he realized he could no longer hear the rattle of her breathing. He put the lantern on the nightstand and sat on the bed beside her.

"Mama?" he said. He took her hands—they were icy cold. He could find no pulse. She was gone. He held her cold hands and wept, for her and for himself. He was alone now. His grandparents had passed away long ago. His mother's only sister went west for Oregon in 1849, the year Jubil was born, but they never heard what became of her or her husband. He had no other family that he knew of.

Jubil stood at the foot of his mother's grave on a warm May day, watching the mourners make their way out of the cemetery. He was grateful all these people had come to pay their respects, but the prospect of making conversation with them at the potluck dinner to follow at the church was daunting. He took one last look at his mother's casket.

"Rest in peace, Mama," he said quietly. "Say hello to Papa and Uncle Pete for me. I love you."

The basement of the First Methodist Church in Bloomington was abuzz with lively conversation, and when Jubil heard it, he realized that for the past few days he had only been going through the motions of living: forcing himself to eat something; sleeping fitfully; tending the livestock; making funeral arrangements.

Nelly Boswell came to meet him at the door with a cup of coffee. Nelly had been Jubil's closest friend since they were children. The Boswells had once farmed near the Walkers, until Nelly's father gave up farming to work as a carpenter for the carriage maker Mr. Ferre, whose company had built the ornate black hearse that had carried Jubil's mother to the cemetery. The Boswells had moved to town five years ago, but Jubil and Nelly still saw each other often.

Nelly was sixteen years old, seventeen months younger than Jubil. He thought the combination of Nelly's long black hair, fair complexion, and crystal blue eyes made her the prettiest girl he had ever seen. He had started to feel he would like to be more than friends, but he didn't know how to tell her as much. Partly he was embarrassed to admit his feelings, concerned that she might laugh—or worse, feel sorry for him—but he also did not have much to offer her. He was bound to help his mother with the farm, and he knew Nelly preferred life in town. He did worry that he might lose her to a suitor, but to date that had not happened, so he had decided to keep his feelings to himself.

"How are you doing?" Nelly asked earnestly as he took the cup and saucer from her.

He was tempted to downplay his feelings of grief and loneliness, but he and Nelly had always been able to share their thoughts about most things, and she would know if he did not answer truthfully.

"I've done some crying," he said, "and a whole lot of pondering. I think the crying has been better for me than the pondering."

"What have you been pondering?" she asked quietly.

"What to do with myself . . . now that she's gone," Jubil replied.

"Do you want to stay on the farm?" Nelly asked. "Isn't it too much land to work alone?"

Before he could reply, Nelly's mother joined them. Mrs. Boswell reminded Jubil vaguely of his own mother, but farm life had not worn so hard on her. She had been well acquainted with Jubil's mother through farming and, later, through church work, and she had always treated Jubil as if he were a member of the Boswell family.

"Have you eaten anything today?" Mrs. Boswell asked, her blue eyes, so like Nelly's, reflecting a motherly concern. Mrs. Boswell presented Jubil with a plate holding a generous slice of her apple pie and a wedge of yellow cheese. Nelly took his coffee and set it on a nearby table. Jubil had always loved her apple pie. It was still warm, and he could smell the cinnamon sweetness.

"No, I haven't, ma'am," Jubil said with a weak smile. "Thank you. And thank you and Mr. Boswell for helping me get the funeral arrangements made."

"You call on us any time. Now you eat that," she said, and went on her way, probably to make sure her sons, Nelly's younger twin brothers, Ike and Eli, weren't eating too much of the food on the heavily laden tables that lined one wall of the room.

Jubil had just taken his first delectable bite of pie when Major John Wesley Powell and his wife, Emma, approached him and Nelly. The Powells had visited the farm several times before the war—Jubil's uncle Pete was a friend of Powell's and had accompanied him on several of his expeditions when Powell was an aspiring young naturalist. Later, Uncle Pete had served under Major Powell in the war. Powell was retired now from the military and was currently a professor of natural sciences at Illinois Wesleyan University.

Powell cut a dramatic figure in the room—he was six inches shorter than Jubil, about the same height as Nelly. His right arm was missing from the elbow down, and the right sleeve of his suit coat was pinned up at the elbow. He had receding auburn hair and thick muttonchops that connected with a bushy mustache, leaving his chin bare. He gave the impression of being made from tightly coiled steel.

Jubil swallowed his bite of pie, and then Nelly took his plate so that he could accept Major Powell's left-handed handshake. He introduced the Powells to Nelly.

"My heartfelt condolences, Jubil, on the loss of your mother," Major Powell said. "She was as fine a person as God ever put on this earth."

"Thank you, Major, Mrs. Powell," Jubil replied. "It was good of you to come today."

"We would not have missed it for anything, Jubil," Mrs. Powell said. "Your mother was a model of kindness and caring, and a good friend to many."

"Thank you, ma'am," he replied.

"It pains me to think," Major Powell continued, "you've lost your family at such a tender age. Your father and uncle were good men. Your uncle was a friend to me and a brave soldier."

During the battle at Shiloh, in which Pete had died, Powell had been hit in the wrist by a mini-ball, resulting in the amputation of part of his right arm, but that did not seem to have hindered him much from doing whatever he set himself to.

"Thank you, sir," Jubil said, "he thought very highly of you."

"Those are kind words, Jubil," said Powell. "Your uncle Pete and I had some fine adventures in our youth. I miss his company."

Jubil thought of all the nights he had spent in Pete's cabin listening to his stories of these adventures and wishing he could escape his humdrum life on the farm to have adventures of his own.

"If there is anything Wes or I can do for you, Jubil," Mrs. Powell offered, "do not hesitate to call on us."

"Thank you, ma'am," Jubil said.

"Have you given any thought to your future?" Powell asked.

"Some," Jubil said, "but I've come to no conclusions."

"Come see me at the university, if you'd like to discuss it," Powell offered.

"Thank you, sir," Jubil said.

"But don't wait too long," Powell said, "or you'll miss me for the summer. I'm taking a group of students and professionals on an exploring expedition out west this summer. I'll be departing by month's end."

Jubil felt a jolt of excitement at this news. Was there any chance that he might accompany Major Powell on such an expedition? The hair on the back of his neck stood up at the prospect. He stared at Powell and tried to bring his focus back to the moment.

"I could come by tomorrow," Jubil said, hoping his enthusiasm wasn't unseemly.

Powell grinned. "That would be fine. You'll most likely find me in the library."

With that Major Powell and his wife took their leave.

"Maybe he'll let me come along this summer and start classes in the fall," Jubil said to Nelly.

"Maybe," Nelly said skeptically, handing his plate of pie back to him.

Jubil had just taken another bite of pie when he was approached by his family's attorney, Mr. Tipton.

"My sympathies, Jubil," Tipton said. "Your mother had her affairs in good order. Come by the office anytime if you have questions or concerns."

"Thank you, sir," Jubil said. "I'm sure I'll have some questions soon." Jubil liked Mr. Tipton, though he didn't really know him. His father had trusted him to draw up his will, which left the farm to Uncle Pete. By the time Uncle Pete went off to war, the Illinois legislature had changed the law preventing women from owning property, and Jubil had seen firsthand how helpful the attorney had been in transferring ownership of the farm from his uncle to his mother and drawing up a new will for her. His mother had made sure Jubil understood the family's financial affairs. They held a clear title to one hundred sixty acres of land; had no mortgage on the farmhouse or loans outstanding; and had a bank balance that varied with the season, but currently held around three thousand dollars. They were not wealthy but, thanks to hard work and weather that cooperated more times than not, they were secure.

Later, after Jubil had accepted as many condolences as he could bear, Nelly handed him a box of food her mother had packed for him and encouraged him to go home. "I'll ride with you if you like," she said, and he nodded his thanks. Eli and Ike, her twin brothers, would come along with them to accompany Nelly home.

"I'd like that," Jubil said.

The group rode to the Walker farm in the Boswells' carriage, pulled by their horse Moses, a smaller version of Max. Star followed along hitched to the rear of the carriage. Eli and Ike were fourteen years old, good natured, energetic, and clever to a fault. They were identical twins but easy to distinguish from one another. Ike was quiet and shy with neatly trimmed blonde hair, the same color as their mother's, while Eli was boisterous and gregarious with an unruly blonde mop. The boys kept up a patter of observations, questions, and silly competitions on the way out of town.

"You didn't have a chance to answer my question earlier," Nelly said to Jubil. "Have you decided whether to keep the farm?"

Jubil sighed. "I'm no farmer," he confessed to her. He had never dared say it before. "I love the place, but when I knew my uncle wasn't coming home, I sometimes wondered how many years of my life would go into working on that farm, but those thoughts felt disrespectful. Now, it turns out I haven't given it nearly as many years as I thought I would . . . but don't take that to mean I'm happy about it."

"I would never think that," she said with a pained expression. "I understand how you feel about farming. It's been better for us in town."

"Speak for yourself," Eli said. "I liked it on the farm." Nelly turned to him.

"Will you hush for a while? Jubil and I are trying to have a conversation."

"I can talk if I want to," Eli said. "You're not the boss of everybody."

Ike punched Eli's arm. "Shut up, Eli," he said. Eli frowned at his brother but stopped talking.

Jubil took the spat between the siblings in stride. He'd witnessed similar ever since he'd known the Boswells.

"The world is changing around us, Jubil," Nelly said. "I expect you could do most anything you set yourself to."

"I wish I knew what that might be," he said. "I suppose I could attend university, but I don't know to what end. It seems pointless to go if I don't know why I'm going. But then Major Powell mentioned that expedition with his students, and I got all fired up. I've thought about heading out West. I don't have much notion what I'd do out there, but I'd sure like to go. I'm going to ask the major about it tomorrow."

Jubil stopped abruptly, embarrassed by his confession. He snuck a look at Nelly's face to see if she was disgusted with him. But she only raised her eyebrows, shrugged, and said, "I suppose he might let you go along, but even if he doesn't, what would be wrong with going to university until you set your mind on a direction? Isn't that part of the point of university?"

Jubil had no rebuttal.

"I'm barely allowed to have a say in my own future," she said curtly. "On Sunday, Papa and Mama sat me down in the parlor and talked to me about what will happen next spring when I'm finished with school. Papa wants to do all my planning for me. His preference would be to see me marry and have a family. But I told them I want to go to the normal school and have a career as a teacher. What I didn't say is how glad I'll be not to have to answer to Papa or a husband or anyone.

Imagine the freedom of it! Mama approves of the part about furthering my education, though she'd like to see me marry and have children someday. We'll see who prevails."

"No need to worry about that," Eli said. "No one will want to marry you anyway!"

Ike shoved his twin. Nelly ignored them.

Jubil's first impulse was to admit that he'd be happy to marry her, but he knew what sport the twins would make of that and held his tongue. He was unsettled by her comments about marriage and by his own surprise at what she'd said. She had talked some about wanting to be a teacher, but he'd assumed it would only be for a little while, until she was ready to marry him—or someone else. He had never heard her say that she preferred to remain unmarried. And he couldn't ask her more about it with her eavesdropping brothers present.

"You just need some time to sort things out," Nelly said with a sympathetic grin. "You think more with your heart than your head. But I generally get along fine with people of that sort." She patted him on the back companionably, and he resisted the urge to put his arm around her.

Jubil realized he had been exaggerating his feelings of being alone. After all, he had Nelly. "Thanks," he said, putting all of the heart he could into that one word.

When they arrived at the farm, as Jubil was unhitching Star, Nelly said, smiling, "Come to dinner Sunday. Mama can feed you properly, and Papa can tell you what to do with your life."

"Thanks," Jubil chuckled. "I'd enjoy that. . . . Your mother's cooking anyway."

Jubil settled Star in the stable for the night, then stood on the porch of the farmhouse, holding his box of food, dreading going inside. The moment he stepped across the threshold, the silence in the house overwhelmed him. In the days since his mother's death, he had been occupied with making funeral arrangements and visiting with well-wishers who stopped by the farm. He had spent his nights alone for the first time in his life, but exhaustion had kept melancholy at bay. Now, as he stood at the kitchen counter alone, there was nothing more to be done and no one else to talk to. Yet he couldn't stop expecting the sound of his mother's footsteps in the next room, the sound of her voice.

He began to unpack the food—two large slices of Mrs. Boswell's apple pie, a block of yellow cheese, a generous stack of sliced ham, and a loaf of bread. As he put it away, the clean kitchen and the efficiently organized pantry reminded him of how hard his mother had worked. Never again would the wonderful aroma of her fried chicken, cookies, cakes, and pies fill the house. Jubil was at a loss as to what to do with himself. Her handiwork brightened every spot it touched—crocheted pot holders and dish cloths in the kitchen, a gingham tablecloth and matching curtains at the windows, shams on the couch pillows, quilts on the beds—and he remembered her sitting by the fire making all of those things.

He stepped into her bedroom. He would have to decide what to do with her personal possessions. She would probably want her small wardrobe of clothing for all occasions donated to charity, once he felt ready to part with them. He opened the jewelry box on the dressing table and found the ring—a faceted rectangular ruby set on a band of gold—that had been a birthday gift from his father the year he died. His father had said when he gave it to her that it was the ring she had deserved for their wedding, but he had not been able to afford it at the time. Tears sprang to Jubil's eyes again. He ached to see her, or hear her, or feel the touch of her hand tucking his hair behind his ears. Until today, her absence had felt strangely temporary, but tonight the feeling of loneliness threatened to crush him. He closed the velvet ring box and put it into his pocket. He would put it away for safekeeping among his own things.

He decided to move into Uncle Pete's cabin rather than stay in the farmhouse. Pete, with Jubil's help, had built the cabin when he had come from Decatur to live on the farm. Pete's willingness to come was the only thing that had allowed Jubil and his mother to remain there. About a hundred yards from the farmhouse, Pete and Jubil built the twenty-by-thirty cabin from roughhewn timbers they'd cut from a grove on the western edge of the farm. In the years since his uncle had passed away, Jubil kept the cabin clean and used it as his private retreat. It contained the basic necessities: a bed, a woodstove, a table with two chairs, two rocking chairs on the wide stone hearth. Jubil stared into the fireplace, which stirred a memory of the wonderful aroma of chicken roasting there on a spit. Pete always said that chicken cooked that way made it taste like the outdoors.

Jubil stepped out onto the porch and sat in another rocking chair his uncle had made. As the shadows lengthened, he thought of all the times he and his mother had sat together, quietly watching the sunset, and the tears came again. He wiped his eyes on the sleeve of his suit, and the gesture conjured up an image of his mother. Her ghost stood beside him, wearing a cotton dress and an apron. Her curly hair was pinned up in an unruly pile, and in her right hand she wielded a wooden spoon. She was threatening to whack him with it, but she had a wry grin on her pretty face.

"Jubilee Walker," she scolded, "don't you dare use your best suit of clothes like it was some raggedy handkerchief!"

Jubil was exhausted by the time he climbed into the bed in Uncle Pete's cabin, and he hoped that exhaustion would bring him sleep. But sleep would not come, and he lit the candle again and chose a book from the stack of Beadle's Dime Novels he had carried over from the farmhouse. *Seth Jones or The Captives of the Frontier* was set in western New York after the revolution. Instigated by the British, a gang of Mohawks raid the frontier and, in the process, capture a settler's daughter. Seth Jones joins the captive's family in a rescue mission full of plotting, trickery, and narrow escapes.

Jubil read far into the night and then put the book back on the shelf, blew out the candle, and lay awake in the dark, his mind drifting through options of what to do next. When he eventually dropped to sleep, he slept soundly for the first time since his mother's death, without dreaming.

CHAPTER 2

The next morning, after a breakfast of pie and coffee, Jubil saddled up Star and set off to consult with Major Powell, the warm spring sun and the cloudless sky lifting his spirits as he went. Just north of Bloomington, he rode through the small community of Normal and past the campus of Illinois State Normal University, one of the two universities in the area, and the college Nelly would attend if her father allowed her to train as a teacher. The university housed the Illinois Natural History Society Museum, which contained many of Major Powell's natural history collections. Uncle Pete had accompanied Powell on several of the expeditions during which the items on display—seemingly every possible variety of animal, bird, insect, rock, shell, and fossil—had been gathered.

Pete had entertained Jubil with many tales of exploring with Major Powell, for instance, the story of how Powell discovered a fossilized bird skeleton embedded in an exposed rock on a riverbank. The rock containing the specimen was large and difficult to excavate, and the two men had worked long and hard to dislodge it while standing knee-deep in the river. They at last managed to wrestle the rock up onto flat ground and spent the rest of the day chiseling out a manageable sized chunk to obtain the specimen. Pete told the story with his usual good humor, but Jubil understood the point: Major Powell was obsessively persistent when he had a mission.

Now, Jubil saw a passenger train coming up the tracks, heading north for Chicago. He wanted very much to be one of them. The furthest he had ever been from the farm was a few miles down the Illinois River, camping with Uncle Pete. It occurred to him that he could purchase a train ticket that moment and go see Chicago, if he wanted to.

He felt guilty about taking pleasure in the freedom of his new circumstances, and he would have gladly traded that freedom for his family. But the truth was that even now he was not entirely free. He could not leave the livestock untended, the fields lying fallow, and the general maintenance undone. He was still a farmer with an active farm. It was May, and he and his mother should have been preparing the fields for planting. If he was going to plant this year, he had to do it before the season got away from him. He had told Nelly that he didn't want to farm, but now he wasn't so sure. What else would he do if Powell wouldn't let him join his expedition?

He caught sight of the ornate cupola on the Wesleyan campus a few blocks away. Up close, the building, North Hall, turned out to be a plain narrow three-story structure of whitewashed brick. Jubil hitched Star under a shade tree and went inside. He followed the sign for the library up the stairway to the second floor and paused at the top. The library occupied the whole second floor of the building, and Jubil was reluctant to enter for fear of disturbing the hushed students who sat in the row of individual desks that ran down the center of the room or who browsed the bookshelves that lined the east side of the library or who read at the large tables that occupied the west side of the room. At one of these tables Jubil spotted Major Powell, poring over a multitude of maps and books. Powell looked up, caught Jubil's eye and waved him over.

"Hello, Jubil. Welcome to Illinois Wesleyan University," Powell said as they shared a left-handed handshake. He said he had been studying some materials for his upcoming expedition. "Let's go outside and take in the spring air. Does that suit you?"

"Yes, sir," Jubil agreed.

Outside, Powell admired Star and rubbed her forehead, and Star nodded as if agreeing with his high assessment of her. Then the two men settled in the shade under the tree.

"On what subject may I offer my advice, young man?"

Jubil fidgeted with his hat, then set it aside. "I'm unsure about what direction to take, sir, now that I have no more family ties. I'd value some discussion on where I might go from here."

"It is a difficult time you find yourself in, Jubil, and I'm honored you would take me into your confidence. Do you find yourself drawn in any particular direction?" Powell asked.

Jubil felt tongue-tied and could not hold Powell's gaze. He was too embarrassed to confess that he wanted to join Major Powell's expedition, for fear of appearing immature and naïve. Finally, he asked if Powell thought he should attend the university, even if he wasn't sure what he wanted to study. When he admitted he did not feel drawn to the life of a farmer, Powell laughed heartily.

"You could not have come to a better mentor on that subject," he said. "When I was twelve years old, my parents moved our family from Ohio to a farm in Wisconsin. My father was a minister and a businessman, and my mother was active in church work and crafting. Too busy to do the farming themselves, they set my brother and me to the job, with no great concern over our opinions. I was unenthused but, like you, a loyal son. I spent many an hour worrying over whether to follow my own feelings, against the wishes of my parents. I farmed until I was around your age, until I couldn't plant one more seed or clean out one more stall. I finally announced that my farming days were over, and I started exploring and collecting. Now, I mean no disrespect, but you have no one to answer to now but yourself."

Jubil felt a weight lifting from his shoulders, as though Major Powell were removing any limits that had existed when it came to Jubil's dreams.

Powell suggested that Jubil could manage the farm as a financial asset, as Powell's own father had done.

"Thank you, Major," Jubil said. "Is it all right to ask, how did you make your decision to pursue natural sciences?"

"I believe I was just born with a passion for it," Powell offered. "That passion eventually pulled me off the farm. I have always been so fascinated by every rock, plant, animal, and natural formation—curious to understand how they came to be, how they survive and adapt, how they help form the world around us—that I have pursued knowledge of them from books and firsthand observation from my earliest years. Nearly to a fault, or so I've been told." He grinned at Jubil. "Which is how I came to be acquainted with your uncle Pete."

"Uncle Pete told plenty of stories about your collecting expeditions."

Powell nodded. "I first met Pete when I was nineteen years old and teaching school in Macon County, near Decatur. I set my mind to use the summer to take a flat-bottomed skiff up the Mississippi River to St. Paul on a collecting expedition for shells and fossils. I went to the livery in Decatur in search of a boat, and Pete was working as a blacksmith there. He heard my tale, and we seemed of like mind, so we decided to make the expedition together."

They had taken the skiff over to the Mississippi, made their way up to St. Paul, then sold the skiff and hiked to the Straits of Mackinac before making their way home.

"A splendid first foray," Powell said.

The next year they floated down the Mississippi to New

Orleans. Two years later, they took a train to Pittsburgh and went down the Ohio, made their way over to St. Louis, and then hiked to Iron Mountain, Missouri.

"All the while as I was collecting specimens, I would tell Pete the scientific background of everything we collected, but I may as well have been talking to Star for all he cared about the science of it. Pete was simply adventuring. Between expeditions he worked at the livery and did carpentry jobs or other labor as he needed money. I tried to convince him to attend university. He was an intelligent man, but he always claimed he just wasn't cut out for it."

In 1858 Powell moved to Cleveland to attend Oberlin College but soon returned to Wheaton to attend the Illinois Institute. A year later, he and Pete had one last summer adventure exploring the Illinois, Des Moines, and Raccoon Rivers.

"That was the summer your father died," Powell said, "and Pete settled with you and your mother. We stayed in touch occasionally after that, but he gave up adventuring until we enlisted in the army. Pete was a good man, Jubil, but he was a man in search of his place in the world. He never could seem to settle on a direction. He did have a sense of duty to you and your mother, and that's why he ended up farming. You seem like him in that respect."

"I always did feel a strong bond with him, Major," Jubil said, thinking he was also like Pete in another respect, and he gathered up his courage. "You mentioned you were planning to lead your students on an expedition to the Colorado Territory."

Powell leaned back against the tree, staring at Jubil. His steel-gray eyes seemed to peer into Jubil's soul, making him feel small and exposed. With Jubil's question, Powell's demeanor shifted from that of a family friend to that of an authority figure.

"Yes," stated Powell flatly, "in a general way that is correct. There are also some members of the community enlisted, and the destination is not firmly set. We'll make our way to either the Dakotas or to the Colorado Territory. General Sherman is stationed at Council Bluffs, and he will have knowledge of recent Indian activity in the region. I plan to seek his advice on the relative safety of each of those destinations before deciding which direction the expedition will head."

"If I were to enroll here at the university," Jubil said in a measured tone, "would I be able to go on the expedition?"

Powell let out his breath slowly. "I am sorry, Jubil, but I do not see that as being possible."

Jubil's spirit deflated, and he dropped his eyes to the ground. He hated to relinquish the hope he'd felt when going on the expedition seemed possible. Powell's response was not a complete surprise, but the finality of his verdict was still a blow. How could Jubil change his future if even a family friend wasn't willing to help him begin a new life of adventure? He had hoped his family connection would count for more. Jubil's stomach churned with a combination of disappointment, frustration, and anger. He struggled to maintain his composure in front of the major.

Powell leaned forward and softened his tone. "You must understand, Jubil," he said, "that all the people going on this expedition have a particular area of expertise: ornithology, entomology, zoology, herpetology, mineralogy. Then there is the matter of funding. I have secured support from various academic, scientific, and governmental sources, but not an adequate amount to cover all expenses. In order to join the expedition, each member is required to contribute three hundred dollars. Also, I have considerable concern about keeping everyone safe, a concern eased somewhat by including only people who are accustomed to responsibility for their own well-being. So, you see, there will be no one in this party who is just adventuring."

Jubil felt embarrassed by his academic ignorance. But on hearing the major's last sentence he also felt misunderstood.

"Well, Major, I wouldn't expect to be going on a lark while everyone else works. I could be useful around camp, with the animals, and hunting and fishing if that needed to be done. I'd attend to the science involved and learn all I could along the way. I'd make it part of my education and my search for my own area of interest." As he spoke, Jubil realized he was letting his passion show. His voice had risen, but he didn't care. He was sure of his feelings now—he wanted to go, more than he'd wanted anything for himself before in his life.

Powell gave him a sympathetic grin, "You make a decent argument, and I admire your spirit, but I don't see that going on this particular expedition is possible for you. The plan is for each member of the party to make his own way by train to Council Bluffs by month's end. Mrs. Powell and I will meet them there to plan the next stage and outfit the expedition. As you said yourself, you have the farm that must be attended to, so it would seem you are not prepared to leave in any event. The financial requirement is also regrettably necessary, and even if you have the funds, I would question the wisdom of using them in this way, at this time."

Powell reached out and gripped Jubil's shoulder firmly. "Don't be too disheartened. I assure you this will not be my last expedition. I'd be pleased to have such an able and eager young man along in the future. In fact, if you enroll at the university, and we mount another trip next summer, your chances for participation would be very good."

Jubil tried to smile at the possibility. He did not want to jeopardize his possible future with Powell by overreacting to the rejection. He picked up his hat and put it on, and he and Powell stood and shook hands.

"Thank you for talking with me, sir," Jubil said, "and for your advice. I wish you the best on your expedition this summer."

"It was a pleasure seeing you today, Jubil. You can always count on me as a friend."

"That means a lot, sir."

On the ride home and throughout the evening, Jubil concocted scenarios of free-spirited travel and how he would deal with the details of the farm to make it possible. Even when he tired of mulling over what he might do with the livestock, whether he would sharecrop the land, where he would go, what he would take with him, how much money he had to spend, how long he would stay gone, the thoughts persisted well into the small hours of the morning.

Jubil considered going to church on Sunday, but he was not feeling he owed God much in the way of thanks these days. He was also out of patience with hearing his mother's death explained as part of God's plan, or an example of His mysterious ways. He was thankful for the Boswell family though, and he knew they wouldn't mind if he dropped in unannounced. With his mother gone, he had more eggs and milk than he could use. He decided to take the excess to Nelly's family, which meant he would need to take the wagon.

Max stood still as a statue while Jubil hitched him into the harness. Jubil tied the full five-gallon milk can down in the wagon bed, then he filled a box with straw, packed four dozen eggs into it, and tied that down as well. He and Max left for town midmorning, to be there in time for dinner at noon.

He had some concern over how the conclusions he reached last night would be received by Nelly and her family, but he was confident of his decisions. He would sell the livestock, leave the fields fallow this year, and take a trip West on his own. Exactly where, and for how long—yet to be determined.

Mr. Boswell had built the family home, a white two-story wood-frame with steeply gabled rooflines with elaborately carved panels along the eaves. A covered porch spanned half the front of the house, with a small gabled roof over the front door. The house displayed the carpentry skills that had secured Mr. Boswell a good-paying job with Lyman Ferre Carriages and Wagons. Looking at the house, Jubil wondered if carpentry would be his calling, if he gave it a chance. He shook off the notion as quickly as it landed on him but noted how the world seemed full of new possibilities.

Ike and Eli came out to greet him and, more ardently, Max.

Eli stood stroking Max's shoulder. "Jubil, did you know that Max is the same kind of horse as King Arthur rode? He was a mighty gray war horse and the bravest in the kingdom, just like Max."

Jubil raised his eyebrows at Eli. "Well," he said, "Max does a fair job of concealing his brave and warlike nature."

Nelly and her parents came out onto the porch.

"Good morning, Mr. Walker," Nelly said with a smile. "You've made a grand entrance into our peaceful Sunday."

"I believe the only grand part of my entrance is Max," Jubil said, removing his hat. "I've come to accept your offer of a home-cooked meal. I brought some eggs and milk."

"How nice of you," Nelly said. "Ike, you and Eli unload the eggs and milk and get them into the kitchen. Do not leave them in the yard!"

Ike moved to the back of the wagon, but Eli ignored Nelly's orders and continued to attend to Max. Mr. Boswell crossed the yard to shake Jubil's hand.

"Good morning, Jubil. Good to see you and Max," he said. He was a big clean-shaven man, topping Jubil's six feet by a couple of inches and outweighing him by at least twenty pounds of muscle. Nelly had inherited her coal-black hair from him.

"Eli!" Nelly called out. "Help your brother with the eggs and milk—please."

"You're not the boss of me," Eli said with a sneer. Jubil waited out their battle of wills.

"Eli," Mr. Boswell said, "mind your sister."

Eli gave Nelly a sullen sidelong glance and slouched over to help Ike.

"I'm so pleased you came, Jubil," Mrs. Boswell said from the porch. "I've got a bit of finishing up to do with the meal. You and Nelly can visit until we're ready."

Nelly and Jubil settled on the porch swing, and Jubil told her that he had visited Mr. Powell the previous day.

"What did he say?" Nelly asked.

Jubil could feel her studying his profile as he stared at the porch floor.

"You asked if you could go, and he said no," she guessed.

Jubil looked over at her and she returned his stare. Why did he even bother to speak when she already knew what was on his mind?

"Yup," he confessed. "But we had a good conversation. He said he would consider having me on his next expedition, if there is one, but not this year."

"Well, that sounds like excellent news," she said.

Jubil sighed. "The minute Powell mentioned that expedition, I knew in my heart I wanted to go. I haven't been able to stop thinking about it."

She reached over and patted his hand. "A year will go by quickly, you'll see, and you'll be far better prepared then." She left her hand resting on top of his, and it felt nice.

"I can't stand to wait a year," he said. "I'm making myself crazy with all the pondering. I'm thinking of going West anyway, without Powell."

Nelly stared at him incredulously, then she pulled her hand back and shot up from the porch swing. Her blue eyes bored holes into his soul.

"You're thinking *what*?" she said emphatically.

"I didn't think you would be angry with me. I just—"

"My being angry should be the least of your worries," she

interrupted. "I know we talked about this kind of thing when we were younger, but those were just stories children tell each other, not something a person actually does! You could easily be killed out there. No. . . you probably *would be* killed out there. I don't see why—"

"Dinner's ready!" Nelly's mother called as she stepped out onto the porch. She stared at Nelly, then at Jubil. "Are you two all right?"

"Yes, Mama," Nelly said, in a huff. "Jubil was only telling me of his grand plans."

Mrs. Boswell's eyes flitted back and forth between them, looking for a clue to the heart of the matter. "Well, that's nice. Perhaps he'll tell us all about it, while we have dinner."

At the table, Mr. Boswell said grace. Then he said, "Jubil, it is mighty good that you could join us today. It's a difficult situation you are in, but you are a strong and capable young man. Have you given any thought to what you want to do in the future?"

He recounted, haltingly, Major Powell's rejection. "So," Jubil said, "I've been thinking I might go see the western territories on my own."

Mrs. Boswell's mouth opened in surprise. Mr. Boswell's fork stopped halfway to his mouth. Ike and Eli stopped chewing and looked at him wide-eyed.

"Take me along," Eli implored, "I'd be handy if you get in a gunfight with Indians."

"Pfft, what'll you do," Ike scoffed, "talk them to death?"

"Hush—both of you," Mrs. Boswell said. "Jubil, go on with your story."

Jubil said he might set a course for the Colorado Territory or maybe the Dakotas.

"That's a far piece to travel," Mr. Boswell cautioned. "Why go so far, son? A fellow doesn't need to go that far just to do some exploring."

"Well, Powell's expedition put Colorado in my head. I figure I'm free to go myself, if I choose to."

"I see," Mr. Boswell said, nodding. "It's a matter of pride for you then? To prove you can do this on your own?"

"Maybe," Jubil said defensively. Did all of them, like Nelly, think he wasn't capable of making such a trip?

"Surely you are aware of the dangers of the West, aren't you?" Mr. Boswell asked. "It's not only Indian encounters that put a man at risk out there but the general lawlessness that abounds, not to mention the hardships of the terrain itself. Mr. Ferre, at the carriage shop, just hired on a new man who moved back here after a stint of hard living in the area you are keen on. If you want to hear true tales of life out West, come by the shop and talk to Orville Gulley. It's a hard and a harsh land out there, son, and not to be trifled with."

"Yes, Papa, thank you for making that point," Nelly said. "That is exactly what I was trying to tell him. If he follows this notion, he could very well get himself killed."

"I appreciate the concern," Jubil said, making an effort not to show any pique at the plentiful critiques of his thinking. "I'm not aiming to get myself killed, but I don't think a person can live in fear of what might be. Bad things happen near and far. I don't have to go any further than my mother, father, and uncle to prove that."

Everyone at the table sat in silence.

Mr. Boswell finally spoke again. "We know you have a good head on your shoulders," he said. "It's not our business to chastise you. We're just concerned for your safety."

"Exactly," Nelly agreed.

Jubil felt his shoulders relax. As the meal went on, they turned to other topics, including Jubil's plans for the farm. Mrs. Boswell asked, "Do you intend to put in a vegetable garden this summer?"

"No, ma'am," he said. "Not if I go traveling."

"It's one thing I miss about farm life," she said, "Our little patch here doesn't produce much."

"You're welcome to put in as much garden as you like out at our place," Jubil offered.

"Would you have any objection to that, Theodore?" Mrs. Boswell asked. "The boys could ride up every few days to tend it. They could keep an eye on the farm for Jubil while he's away. And I'll go myself, from time to time, just to enjoy it."

"I have no objection," Mr. Boswell replied amiably.

After dinner, Mr. Boswell went off to read the newspaper and have a nap. Jubil and Nelly were dismissed to the porch. Nelly sat on the swing, and Jubil leaned against the railing, looking at her.

"Are you still upset with me?" Jubil asked.

"Not as much so," Nelly replied with a sly grin. "I do envy the fact that you can just decide to go off on an adventure, while some of us have our lives governed by others. But that's not your problem," she said, rolling her eyes. "Anyway, it's true I was upset, but now I see it's like Papa said. I'm not trying to tell you what to do with your life. I'm just concerned for you. You're my best friend"—her blue eyes met his—"and I don't want to lose you."

Jubil's heart felt full. "That means the world to me," he said. "I'll be careful. I just don't want to be so afraid of dying that I don't truly live." Even though she spoke of him as a friend, he thought he could feel something more there between them. He sympathized with her desire to not be controlled by others, and vowed to never treat her in that way.

Nelly furrowed her brow. "A thought occurred to me," she said. "Even if you were traveling with Major Powell, I would still be worried about you, but the idea of you being out there all alone is what truly concerns me. What if you could make your own way out to some point along Powell's route and meet up with him and then ask to join his party?"

Jubil straightened up out of his slouch. What if he went to Council Bluffs, where Powell had said he was meeting the other members of his party?

"If you had the grit to show him the trip meant that much to you," Nelly said, "he wouldn't turn you away, would he?"

Jubil shook his head in amazement. "You are a piece of work, Nelly Boswell."

"Why, thank you," she said.

Powell would be in Council Bluffs by the end of the month. If Jubil was really going to go, he had a lot to do before he could get on that train.

"I appreciate your friendship more and more as time goes on," he said sincerely.

She beamed at him. "Well, see that you do," she said.

As Jubil said his good-byes to the Boswells and he and Max started out for the farm, he felt excited and—alive. He had finally stopped pondering and started making plans.

CHAPTER 3

Jubil would not be able to take Star or Max with him to Council Bluffs—there just wasn't time to get there on horseback. The Boswells could most likely board Star, but there wasn't room in their stable for Max. Besides, Max was made to pull with all his might, and these days, all he pulled was the wagon. Jubil realized with a heavy heart that he would have to sell Max. He tried to console himself with the thought that Max would benefit from the sale. And Jubil would need the money to buy another horse in Council Bluffs.

That week, Jubil met with Mr. Weed, of Weed and Toms Real Estate, who bought Jubil's cow, two hogs, and all the chickens for fifty dollars. Mr. Weed also promised he would find a buyer for Max.

Two blocks south of Mr. Weed's office was Lyman Ferre Carriages and Wagons. Jubil walked through the shop looking for Mr. Boswell. He found him and a short, wiry man about Mr. Boswell's age installing the side panel on a new carriage.

"Are you in the market for a carriage for your travels?" Mr. Boswell said with a smile. The man he was working with wiped his hands on a rag.

"No sir," Jubil replied, "but I do have something I could use help with. Could I board Star with you? I don't mind paying for her upkeep and your trouble."

"Certainly, but you don't need to pay us. The boys will look out for her."

"Thank you very much," Jubil said. "That is a load off my mind."

"Glad to help," Mr. Boswell said. "Jubil, this is Mr. Gulley. I believe I mentioned him to you."

Mr. Gulley had a ring of hair around his otherwise bald head and heavy whisker stubble. His dark eyes studied Jubil soberly. He struck Jubil as a no-nonsense man.

"Jubil has decided he needs some adventure in his life, Orville. He's thinking of traveling west this summer. I took the liberty of suggesting your thoughts might be educational."

Gulley looked from Boswell to Jubil. "I'm not sure I am your man," he said. "I moved back here to Illinois because the West did not suit me, so I am not likely to give you much encouragement."

Jubil nodded. "Yes, sir. I'm not looking for encouragement so much as facts—whatever it was, in hindsight, you wish you had known before you set off."

Gulley chuckled sourly. "If you listen to the facts," he said, "you'll just stay home."

Jubil smiled. "Maybe if I ask another way. What strikes you as the most important advice I should heed . . . besides not going at all?"

"Well," Gulley said thoughtfully, "I learned a few things that are easier said than done, but if you can do them, they'll keep a bad situation from getting worse: keep your wits about you, keep your gun handy, and keep hold of your valuables."

"That makes good sense," Jubil said.

Gulley nodded. "The world is a dangerous place. Always will be, I reckon. You got a gun, son?"

"Yes, sir. I have a fine Henry rifle," Jubil replied. The rifle, one of the earliest models made, had been one of his father's most prized possessions. Jubil had his own smaller caliber rifle that his father had given him and taught him to use. After his father's death, Uncle Pete taught Jubil how to handle and clean the larger weapon. He remembered how the gun had felt when his uncle first put it into his hands—smooth and supple, almost like a living thing. Going out into the woods with Uncle Pete, Jubil had soon lost count of how many rabbits they'd shot. He'd also soon tired of having to skin so many of them, not to mention eat so much of his mother's rabbit stew, although it was delicious. He clearly recalled the first deer he shot himself, and the bloody lesson Pete gave him on cleaning and processing the game. Pete had made him a gift of the hunting knife they'd used, which Jubil still had. Jubil and Uncle Pete, and then Jubil alone, had shot at least a couple of deer each fall and salted the venison to eat throughout the winter.

"Do your thinking about how willing you are to shoot someone," Mr. Gulley said, "before you get too far down the trail."

Jubil was shocked by this advice but tried not to show it. He had never seriously considered that he might have to kill another person in order to save his own life. "Do you think it's likely to come to that?"

Gulley shrugged. "If matters do come to that, you'll have no time to think it over. You'll have to point and shoot, or you may not get another chance." Gulley glanced over his shoulder at the carriage he and Mr. Boswell were working on. "I reckon it's time to get back to work," he said, but continued to look at Jubil intently.

Jubil understood from that hard look that what Gulley had told him was not idle conversation; these were hard truths about facing death and living to tell about it. "I understand what you've said, sir. I need to look out for myself," Jubil said. "I'll do my best."

Gulley nodded, and Jubil said good-bye to him and to Mr. Boswell.

On his way to the Chicago and Alton Railroad depot to see

about a ticket to Council Bluffs, Jubil played Gulley's advice over again in his mind to make sure he could repeat it word for word. At the depot, the ticket agent educated him about connections and fares. Jubil would go first to Chicago, where he would catch a train on the Chicago and North Western line that would take him to Council Bluffs. Buying a seat in the third-class car would save him some money, and he figured sitting on a wooden bench for a few hours couldn't be worse than what he would face after leaving Council Bluffs for points west.

He left the depot wondering how he would carry his belongings on his journey. His mother's old carpetbag wouldn't do, nor would the trunk his parents had had since their wedding. His questions led him to Livingston and Company, the dry goods store on the south side of the square, but he found nothing suitable for his trip there. He also came up empty-handed at Mills, Schermerhorn and Company. But at Haggard and Powers Hardware Store, the clerk led the way to a wall where a single trapper's pack hung.

The pack had a large canvas cargo compartment, but the best feature was the wood frame the cargo pack was fitted on. The frame had shoulder straps to allow the whole thing to be easily carried, and attached to the rails of the pack were leather straps to allow other items to be tied to the frame. He could fill the pack with his belongings and carry a bedroll attached to the top or bottom of the frame. His rifle could be lashed to one of the side rails, or the top or bottom rail. It was perfect. The clerk quoted a price of three dollars for the trapper's pack, and Jubil bought it. Outside, he tied it onto his saddlebags across Star's haunches and turned her north to ride to Nelly's house, where he found her helping her mother hang laundry out to dry. He asked if Nelly could accompany him to the train station on Friday, and after gaining Mrs. Boswell's approval, they made their plans.

It was on Wednesday, when Mr. Weed came to collect the livestock, that Jubil realized he was really going to go through with it. He was going West. Mr. Weed had brought along Mr. Williams, the farmer who was interested in Max and who ended up paying one hundred fifty dollars for him, a fair price. It was with more than a little melancholy that he bid Max farewell.

On Thursday, Jubil rode into town to visit the bank. He had two hundred dollars from the sale of the livestock and Max, and had decided to withdraw an additional one hundred— with a promise to himself to pay it back. He could not bring himself to withdraw the additional three hundred Powell required from each member of the expedition party. He was hoping Powell would bring him along anyway and allow him to work off the expense somehow.

He also stopped by Mr. Tipton's office. The attorney was not in, but Jubil left an envelope with his clerk. In the envelope were instructions for how to dispose of his assets in case he did not return.

On Friday morning, Jubil packed carefully. In the bottom of his pack he placed two boxes of ammunition, one hundred rounds. He did not expect to need his gun until he went west from Council Bluffs. Atop the boxes he placed a flint, a box of matches and a tin pot, in case he was caught out on his own and needed to make fire and boil water. He took a couple of changes of clothes and a pair of deer-hide moccasins; his shaving razor; a few sheets of writing paper; a steel pen and a bottle of ink, which he wrapped in a rag and hoped would not leak; and a couple of dime novels to help him pass the time while traveling. He sharpened the hunting knife Uncle Pete had given him and slid it into its leather sheath, placing it on top of all his other belongings in case he needed to get to it quickly.

He considered the roll of money he would be taking along. Mr. Gulley's warning about keeping hold of his valuables echoed in Jubil's thoughts. Carrying three hundred dollars in his pocket seemed foolish, yet putting all the money in his pack seemed equally risky. He decided to split it. He put half in an envelope, which he put in his pack, and carried half in his pocket.

He wrapped his rifle in a length of buckskin to keep the rain out but left it unloaded—it seemed dangerous to carry a loaded weapon on the train. He strapped the rifle to the left side of the pack, his canteen to the right, his bedroll to the bottom, and his rolled-up slicker to the top. Everything he needed, all in one unit.

As he packed, the elation he had hoped to feel about his trip eluded him. Instead, he felt apprehensive. He tried to assure himself that anxiety was normal for an inexperienced traveler. As he and Star drew away from the farm, Jubil's apprehension reached a peak. How could he leave the farmhouse abandoned and unprotected? The thought of Eli and Ike Boswell looking after things brought little comfort. He was also edgy about seeing Nelly. This uncertainty on top of the anxiety about traveling was almost enough to change his mind about the trip. It was all he could do to urge Star forward toward town.

When he reached the Boswell's house, Jubil's uneasy feelings were sidetracked by the talk of practical matters. Nelly assessed his food supply, found it lacking, and made him two large ham-and-cheese sandwiches. She wrapped them in the previous day's *Daily Pantagraph* and put them in his pack.

He wasn't ready to say goodbye to Star yet, so he hitched her to the wagon, and they set off for the train depot. A dismal rain began to fall, but they huddled together on the wagon seat under Nelly's umbrella and arrived only slightly damp. Jubil gave Star's neck a pat. "I'll be back for you, girl," he said low into the horse's ear. "Don't you worry."

Star snorted as if she understood.

On a bench inside the depot, he and Nelly looked at each other but did not speak as a train whistle blew in the distance.

Nelly reached into her handbag and removed a handkerchief while Jubil reached into the inside pocket of his jacket and removed an envelope.

"I left a copy of this with Mr. Tipton," he said, handing Nelly the envelope.

"Should I open it?" she asked. "What is it?"

"It's my will. In case I don't make it back."

The look of shock on Nelly's face was painful for him to see. His palms began to sweat as he realized how upset she was.

"It's just a precaution," he said. "I started thinking about what would happen if something were to happen to me. My father's estate was easier for my mother to deal with because he left a will, and my mother's will is doing the same for me. If something happens to me, I want to make things as easy as I can for you."

Nelly shook her head. "For *me*?"

He swallowed hard before responding. "I'm leaving everything to you. But Mr. Tipton will handle the estate."

"Oh Jubil—no!" she exclaimed, pushing the envelope back into his hand and clutching the handkerchief to her face.

"I know you don't want to think about this," Jubil said, "and I don't want to either, but I owe it to my parents to be responsible with the things they worked so hard for. I have no other family, Nelly—none. What would become of my parents' farm, their money, and my horse if I go off and get myself killed and don't leave any instructions? I can't do that."

"Then stay home," she stated flatly.

"You know I can't do that now," he said as he watched her eyes fill with tears. "I've got to make this trip. My heart is set on it, and my mind's made up. But if something happens to me..."

Nelly gave in to her tears. She covered her face with her handkerchief and wept as Jubil sat there helplessly. He wanted more than anything to put his arms around her and comfort her, but their friendship had never included that kind of affection, and such a public display between them would be scandalous.

She wiped her eyes and composed herself. "I'm not old enough to own property, am I? I wouldn't know how to manage it."

"I trust Mr. Tipton to manage it on your behalf until you're ready. When it comes to you not knowing how to manage things, well, I don't believe that for a minute. I'm the one who benefits from your thinking on most matters."

"You had better come back, or I will never forgive you, for as long as I live," she scolded.

"That's fair," he said.

She narrowed her eyes at him. "You waited until the last minute to bring this up."

"So you wouldn't have time to argue," he said with a sheepish grin.

She shook her head. "You are a piece of work, Jubilee Walker."

The train pulled into the station. A few people disembarked, and those in the depot collected their belongings and made their way through the rain to board. Jubil put on his hat and rain slicker, shouldered his pack, then stood facing Nelly.

"Thanks for coming to see me off," he said. "There's no need for you to stand out in the rain while I board. Good-bye."

"You come home, Jubil," Nelly said. "I don't want a farm. I want my best friend."

"I will." He wanted to kiss her, but he could not. Instead, he offered his hand. He felt a sudden urge to abandon his plan and stay in Bloomington, but another part of him felt more alive than he had ever felt in his life.

"All aboard! All aboard for Chicago!" the conductor cried out.

Jubil forced himself to drop Nelly's hand. "Take care of Star," he said as he backed away.

Outside on the platform, Jubil showed the conductor his ticket then walked to the end of the train as directed, to the third-class cars. Third class was a Spartan affair. Rows of straight-backed wooden benches lined both sides of the center aisle, each bench long enough to hold three people. Perhaps a dozen people were already seated. The first row of benches in the car was unoccupied, so Jubil sat down on the depot side of the aisle.

He took off his pack and leaned it against the wall in front of him, then removed his slicker and stepped back out through the door of the car to shake off some of the rain. He could have put the pack in the baggage car, but he did not want to be separated from it. Half of his money was in it.

His feelings of apprehension faded now that the conversation with Nelly was behind him, but he was still uneasy. As the train whistle blew and the train cars lurched forward, he told himself it was only jittery excitement, not fear. *Last chance*, he thought, to grab his pack and jump off the train. But he made no move to do so. As the train began to roll down the tracks, it passed the open door of the depot. He saw Nelly waving goodbye, and he waved back, but he doubted she could see him through the driving rain.

The train rolled on, and he spotted Star, hitched to the wagon, waiting patiently. She looked sad standing alone in the rain, her head hanging low, her beautiful blonde mane sodden and bedraggled. He waved to his horse, and something in that moment triggered his tears. Suddenly all his losses revisited him. He was leaving Nelly to worry about him; he missed his mother so much that he had launched this trip to avoid the emptiness of life without her; his longing for the company of his father and his uncle in this moment seemed as fresh as the loss of his mother; and he was leaving his horse alone in the rain. He was glad he faced the front end of the train car, so he did not have to hide his tears.

The train rolled past the Illinois Wesleyan campus, and when Jubil spotted North Hall, he wondered what Powell would say when he showed up in Council Bluffs and found Jubil there. As the train skirted Illinois State Normal University, Jubil thought of Powell's collections and Uncle Pete's contributions to them. Pete would be proud of him right now. He smiled to himself at the thought and wiped his eyes. As they reached full speed outside of town, his attention turned to the experience of his first train ride. The landscape passed by faster than riding Star at a gallop, but there was little sense of forward motion, only the side-to-side rocking of the car and the clacking of the wheels as they flew over the rails.

Jubil's mood began to improve. He was moving through the world instead of watching it pass him by. Even if he only went to Chicago and came back home, he would have accomplished something. Just last week he had dreamed of taking the train to Chicago, and here he was making that happen, and more.

As the sun set, the train approached the city. The houses and businesses along the tracks seemed to go on and on, and Jubil wondered why anyone would want to live near so many other people. The train slowed to a crawl, and Jubil leaned against his window to better see forward. A huge building like a castle or fortress loomed ahead with towers at each corner and three gigantic masonry arches on its face. Jubil craned his neck to take it in as the tracks divided and divided again and the train rolled into the darkness of the huge depot: the Great Central Station.

The interior of the depot was the largest indoor space Jubil had ever seen. The ceiling soared far above his head. He was momentarily overcome by the noise and bustle of the crowd, which left him feeling small and meek. Even though his train to Council Bluffs would not leave until midmorning the next day, he decided to orient himself by finding where he would board his connection. Once he had spoken to a ticket agent and located the correct platform, he felt less worried but still out of place. Though city people looked much the same as the people in Bloomington, he saw no one else carrying a trapper's pack with a rifle and a bedroll. He thought he must stick out like a sore thumb. It amused him to think people might see him as a rough and seasoned adventurer.

As he walked around the station to see the sights, the aroma of sausages from a vendor's cart aroused his appetite, but he decided to eat Nelly's ham-and-cheese sandwiches and conserve his money. He found a niche along a wall near some benches in a waiting area, a spot removed from the bustle of the station where he could drop his pack and relax. He set up camp there on the floor, thinking it was a good quiet place to stretch out and sleep. He dug out one of his sandwiches and his canteen and ate as he watched people come and go. After a while, he removed one of the novels he'd brought along, *Malaeska the Indian Wife of the White Hunter*, and read until the crowd thinned out and the station quieted down. When he grew sleepy, he lay down facing the waiting area, with his back to the wall, and covered himself with his slicker. He arranged his pack so that he could use the bedroll lashed to the bottom as a pillow, then he drew his hat over his face and slept.

Sometime later, he came half awake. For a moment he thought someone had shaken him but decided he must have been dreaming. He lay still with his eyes closed and began to drift away again when he felt his pack shake. He brought his right hand up slowly beneath the slicker and with one finger pushed the brim of his hat up enough to peek out. Someone was kneeling next to him, working at the straps that tied his rifle to the side rail. Whoever it was carried a fog of beer along with him. Jubil thought of Mr. Gulley's directives: keep your wits about you; keep your gun handy; keep hold of your valuables.

Jubil pulled in a deep breath and sprang up. In one motion

he threw the slicker over the thief's head and shoved him away. The man fell to the floor and flailed at the slicker that entangled him. The tie at the butt of Jubil's rifle had been untied, but the one around the barrel held fast. He jerked the rifle free as the man threw off the slicker and rose to face him. It was then that Jubil saw the knife the man was brandishing. He held the rifle at his hip, aimed it at the thief, threw the lever to chamber a round, and recalled he had decided not to load the gun.

"Give up the gun, boy," the man growled. "I ain't interested in hurting you, or I coulda stuck you in your sleep. I just aim to have that rifle." He flicked the knife to emphasize his point.

The man's unsteadiness and beer stink led Jubil to conclude he had been out for a night of hard drinking. His overall seedy appearance suggested it may have been a common pastime.

"No sir," Jubil said, "I will not do that. Now you be on your way, and we won't have any trouble." Jubil wagged the rifle. He began to feel his panic subside and his wits return as they stood in a stalemate.

Jubil judged them about the same size, but the man was wirier and likely an experienced brawler. Jubil had been in a few dustups in the schoolyard but never anything like this, so hand-to-hand combat was not likely in his favor. The man took an unsteady step toward Jubil and eyed the rifle trained on him. Jubil took his eyes off the man just long enough to scan the common area for help, but he saw no one. The man took another step forward, pointing the knife straight ahead, poised to slash in any direction. Jubil raised the rifle to his shoulder and aimed down the barrel at the thief. But the man, emboldened by the fact that Jubil had not fired yet, took yet another step toward him.

Before the man could get any closer, Jubil dropped to the floor and rolled sideways under the nearest bench. He came up on the other side with the rifle pointed at the man. He immediately realized the flaw in his evasive maneuver: the bench put a barrier between them, but now Jubil was separated from his pack. If thievery was the man's objective, all he had to do was pick up the pack and walk away. Jubil could not lose that pack. Half his money was in it.

He scrambled around the bench, and when he did, the man lunged for him, but his feet tangled in the slicker and he lost his balance. As the thief fell forward, Jubil clubbed him on the forehead with the butt of the rifle. The man dropped limply to the floor. Jubil moved past him to grab his pack. The straps that held the main compartment closed were untied. He considered stopping to see if anything was missing, but pausing there now, without a weapon, would make him too vulnerable. Why had he thought it was smart to stash the ammunition at the bottom of the pack? Yet another mistake he would never make again.

He crossed the common room and exited onto the nearest platform, where, out of sight, he dug the ammunition out of his pack and loaded his rifle. He also removed his hunting knife and slipped the sheath onto his belt, vowing to wear it as often as he could. He took a quick inventory of his pack—his money was missing. He felt his face flush with anger and embarrassment.

He went back to find his assailant and retrieve his money and his slicker, but while the slicker was, surprisingly, still there, the only sign of the thief was a smear of blood on the marble floor. The money was gone. Jubil scolded himself harshly for underestimating the level of planning and vigilance his travels would require. But when the thought occurred that he might as well just go back to Bloomington, everything in him rose up against it.

The clock hanging in the center of the common room read 4:15 a.m. Jubil's train to Council Bluffs was scheduled to leave at 9:45. Too rattled now to sleep, he found a safer location against a wall near the ticket booth, where foot traffic would be heavier. Sitting against his pack, holding his rifle in his lap, covered by his slicker, Jubil silently considered Orville Gulley's advice. He had managed to keep his wits about him and his gun handy, though the gun was less valuable to him than it should have been. He had clearly failed to keep hold of his valuables, and he reluctantly admitted to himself that the drunken man had been right—he could have stabbed Jubil as he slept, and then his short journey would have come to an abrupt end. He had done the best he could do, but it wasn't good enough. He had been lucky, and he would have to take better precautions for the rest of the trip. The loss of half his funds was a setback, but not necessarily a disaster. He wouldn't be able to afford to buy a horse in Council Bluffs, but he had enough money to continue on and wait for Powell. He would not give up yet.

He pondered whether, even if his gun had been loaded, he would have fired on his assailant. He understood now what Gulley had meant when he said there would be no time for decision-making in the midst of such an event. Now was the time to prime his instincts for action and prepare his mind for the consequences. He wanted to live, and he had promised Nelly he would do his best to come home. If his life was threatened, he would not hesitate to defend himself, whatever it took.

He maintained a vigil in case his assailant decided to return, but, in spite of his intentions, he dozed off sitting up. When someone kicked his boot, startling him awake, Jubil did not hesitate to toss the slicker aside and raise his rifle. The child who had tripped over his outstretched legs stared into Jubil's face, wide-eyed with fear, and then began to shriek, earning Jubil a scornful look from the child's mother.

The big clock said it was 8:30 a.m., and the station was once again filled with people. Jubil retied his rifle to the side of his pack frame but left it uncovered and loaded. Once he reached the platform from which his train to Council Bluffs would depart, he retrieved the second ham sandwich from his pack and ate it for breakfast.

On his bench in the third-class car, which he had to himself, Jubil relaxed into the rhythm of the trip. He bought more ham-and-cheese sandwiches from a vendor at the stop in Clinton, Iowa, and ate them at sunset. They did not measure up to Nelly's but would have to do. He read his novel for a while and then sat looking out the window at the moonlit landscape, pondering his strategy for approaching Major Powell in Council Bluffs.

CHAPTER 4

When Jubil woke at sunrise, the train was approaching Council Bluffs from the north, riding the tracks along the town's western edge, and from that vantage point, he got a good look at the town. It had obviously gotten its name from the row of bluffs to the east that gradually flattened to a plateau sloping west toward the Missouri River. The town sat mainly on the plateau, except for a populated area that ran up a large flat trough into the bluffs. The town looked comparable in size to Bloomington. They pulled in at the depot, near the main east-west thoroughfare, busy with carriage and foot traffic. The town was one of the main jumping-off points for the West and had been since the gold rush days of the 1840s. Jubil supposed it was even busier now that it had become the easternmost terminus of the transcontinental railroad, which was still under construction.

He felt a sense of accomplishment as he stepped off the train. Nelly had been correct about the trip to Council Bluffs being an adventure in itself. Even if he only stayed in town a few days then returned home, he would have gained enough experiences to make the trip worthwhile, but he was not ready to start thinking of going home.

The central business district seemed about the same size as Bloomington's, but there was a bustle about Council Bluffs that Bloomington lacked. Everyone seemed to be going somewhere and in a hurry to get there. The variety of characters making up the crowd was more exotic than what Jubil had seen in Bloomington. The main street, Lower Broadway, featured a cast that seemed to span the entire range of humanity: finely dressed men and women in carriages; moderately well-off families in wagons; dirt-poor families in carts piled high with household belongings; hardscrabble men leading heavily laden pack animals; men in buckskins on horseback with packs much like Jubil's but who were much dirtier and more road worn than Jubil was; every age group and several races. Jubil had almost no personal experience with different races, and he had to drag his eyes away from a Negro man carrying a pack like his and an Indian in a cowboy hat. Bloomington was home to a few Negroes and a handful of Chinese and Mexicans, but Jubil knew none of them directly. He had no preconceived notions about other races, having never heard his parents or uncle speak disparagingly of them. He supposed he would deal with individuals of any race as he always did, on their merits, but experience would tell.

He assumed there would be a hotel in the heart of town, so he walked east on Lower Broadway, toward the cluster of tall buildings, passing a wide assortment of businesses—grocery stores, dry goods and clothing stores, bakeries, drug stores, restaurants and cafes, barbershops, cigar stores, an outfitter, hardware stores, meat markets, dressmakers, saloons, billiard halls, sewing machine stores. Each one seemed to be thriving, and he marveled at the amount of money that must change hands in the district every day.

About six blocks east of the depot, Jubil went into the fancy four-story Ogden Hotel, which took up a city block on the corner of Lower Broadway and Pearl Street. When he learned that the daily rate was three dollars for room and board, he asked the clerk if he could recommend anything more modest.

The clerk gave him a copy of the local newspaper, the *Daily Nonpareil*, suggesting he check the ads.

Over a cup of coffee in a café on Broadway, Jubil found several ads for rooming houses. He walked to Mrs. Zeller's, at Pearl Street and Buckingham, which offered room and board at one dollar and fifty cents per day and was available, the ad said, to "respectable travelers." The house was a plain two-story clapboard that reminded Jubil of the Boswells' place, without the elaborate scrollwork on the eaves. He noticed the Council Bluffs Courthouse across the street. The courthouse here was not the hub of the business district, as it was in Bloomington, but merely a prominent edifice.

A sturdily built gray-haired woman answered Jubil's knock and gave him a quick looking over with an experienced eye. Jubil removed his hat and inquired about a room. She asked his business, and how long he would be staying.

"I'm just in from Illinois and plan to wait here for a group heading out West on a scientific exploring expedition. I don't know how many days I'll be here, but it will not be past the end of the month."

She nodded approvingly. "You'll be a refreshing change from what often comes to my door."

She offered him a comfortable room which smelled of the lemon oil she used to burnish the furniture to a glossy shine. One window looked out onto her back yard and stable, the other onto Buckingham Street, with a view of the courthouse. He paid in advance for a one-week stay.

His next order of business was to work out how to find Major Powell. It seemed likely that Powell would take a room at the Ogden Hotel but unlikely the hotel would tolerate Jubil loitering in the lobby waiting for him every day. Keeping a vigil at the train depot would not work either, since he would have to live there to see every arrival, day and night. Powell planned to meet General Sherman before outfitting his expedition, but

Jubil could not envision any way of enlisting Sherman in his cause. This left the outfitters as perhaps Jubil's best possibility for meeting up with Powell before he left town again. He would pay a visit to the only outfitters he had seen on Broadway. It was almost certainly where Powell would come to provision the expedition.

Jubil found Warner and Company Outfitters loaded to overflowing with clothing, spare wagon parts, sheets of canvas, packs, and every other imaginable piece of equipment needed for hard travel. On the wall, a chalkboard featured a list of available commodities, with prices. Another board listed work animals available, without prices. There were many customers milling about the store, and there was a line three customers deep at the cash register. Jubil wondered how they kept all of these items in stock. He was browsing around the store when a short heavyset clerk near his own age approached him.

"How do you do, sir?" said the young man pleasantly. "What can we do for you today?"

Jubil introduced himself and explained that he was to meet the expedition party in Council Bluffs.

"Sounds like you're in for some exciting times," said the clerk. "You've come to the right place. Warner and Company sells the widest range of high-quality merchandise, at the best prices, of any outfitter there is. I expect we've got about any-thing your party would need. My name is Luke Warner. My pa owns the store." The clerk pointed to a middle-aged man, an older version of himself, talking to one of the many cus-tomers. He had graying wavy hair and small square-rimmed glasses that he wore near the tip of his nose. In spite of his potbelly, he looked hearty enough to heft the heaviest of the store's stock himself.

"It's an impressive store," he said.

"Are you looking for anything in particular?" Luke asked.

"The fact is," Jubil said, "our instructions were to meet up in Council Bluffs by the end of the month, but they were otherwise short on details. I figure they'll turn up here at your store at some point, but even so, I'm not sure I'll catch them." Jubil thought his explanation sounded reasonable. At least it was truthful, mostly. He wasn't exactly a member of the party, at least not yet.

"I see your dilemma," said Luke.

"I don't suppose I could just busy myself around the store for a few days until one of them shows up?" Jubil said with a grin. "You could put me to work. I'd try to be useful."

The young man looked at Jubil strangely, and Jubil began to feel jumpy. Had his approach given the young Mr. Warner the impression that he was disreputable?

"Hold up a minute, all right?" Luke said.

"All right," Jubil agreed. He watched with trepidation as Luke spoke to his father at the back of the store. Luke pointed Jubil out, and both men stared at him as he struggled against the urge to cut his losses and leave the store now before he made an even worse impression. But he didn't know where else he would be able to make contact with Major Powell.

The older Mr. Warner shrugged and then accompanied Luke as he returned to Jubil. Luke introduced them.

"Good day, Mr. Walker," Mr. Warner said. "Luke thinks you seem like an honest, hard-working sort. We lost a stock clerk yesterday, and we are short-handed," Mr. Warner explained. "How would you like to spend a few hours in the afternoon here at the store helping unload shipments and stocking shelves, just until we find a permanent replacement? It pays ten cents an hour, five hours a day."

Jubil couldn't believe his good fortune. Such a job would help offset the expenses of this trip. "I would like that just fine," he said. "Thank you, sir."

"You're welcome," Mr. Warner replied. "Come back tomorrow just after noon, and Luke will get you started."

They shook hands, and Jubil left, amazed by how well things were going on his first day in Council Bluffs. He returned to his boarding house and wrote Nelly a letter telling her of his adventures so far. He even told her about the thief in Chicago but focused more on the loss of his money than the violence. At supper Mrs. Zeller was pleased to hear he had found employment. He enjoyed a sound night's sleep, and the next afternoon was off to his new job.

Luke put him to work unloading supplier's wagons and stocking the shelves of the Warner and Company storeroom. He could not see the clientele coming and going from where he was working, but the Warners were on the lookout for anyone who came in from the Powell party. Jubil settled into a comfortable routine and bided his time. It was hard work, but he enjoyed it. As he was stocking shelves with oilcloth one day, an idea came to him. He imagined himself out West, fording rivers, caught in the rain, and his money a soaking wad in his pocket. He bought a length of oilcloth and some rawhide strips and went down Broadway to the dressmaker. There, the seamstress fashioned him an envelope-sized pouch with rawhide strings on either end. He would store his money in the pouch and tie it around his waist, under his shirt. The cloth, a bit abrasive against his skin at first, was softening up as he wore it, and the discomfort was certainly not as great as worrying about his money. He wore it all the time, except when he was in his room at Mrs. Zeller's.

He worked afternoons at the store eight days in a row, including Sunday, as Warner and Company Outfitters was open every day of the week, except on major holidays. On the eighth afternoon Luke Warner entered the storeroom where Jubil was working.

"Jubil," he said, "a member of Powell's party just showed up. He's talking to Pa right now."

"Did you mention me?" Jubil asked.

"No," said Luke. "Are you hoping to surprise him?"

"He'll be surprised all right," Jubil said sheepishly.

Luke looked puzzled.

"I know the leader, Major Powell," Jubil explained, "but not the other members of the party. The fact is, in Powell's opinion, I'm not prepared to join the expedition, but I took it upon myself to come out here and make my case again before he leaves."

Luke grinned. "Figured he wouldn't turn you away if you showed some spirit?"

"I suppose," Jubil confessed. "I don't want you to think I wasn't being truthful with you and Mr. Warner. I appreciate what you've done to help me."

"You're the one helping us, Jubil," Luke declared. "Pa says you're the best stock clerk we've ever had. You show up sober and work hard. Maybe you didn't tell us the whole story, but that's your own business. We better quit jawing before the man leaves. Mind if I eavesdrop? This could be entertaining."

Jubil smiled at Luke. "Let's go."

The man Mr. Warner was talking to was several years older than Jubil, tall and fit, with wavy black hair.

"There you boys are," said Mr. Warner. "I was just telling this gentleman there was a fellow working here who was look- ing to meet up with his outfit." Focusing his gaze on Jubil, Mr. Warner continued, "He doesn't recall you being a member of the party though, Jubil."

Luke jumped in before Jubil could speak, "Oh Pa, I'm sorry. Jubil told me all about his situation, and I clean forgot to mention it to you."

Jubil looked at Luke, surprised but grateful for his help.

"No, he wouldn't know me, Mr. Warner," Jubil said, turning his attention to the customer. "Hello, sir. My name is Jubilee Walker," Jubil said, offering his hand.

The man looked Jubil over and shook his hand.

"How do you do, Mr. Walker? My name is Lewis Keplinger,"

he said. "How is it that you are here waiting for Major Powell, but I have never heard your quite distinctive name before? Major Powell has entrusted me with his list of participants for this expedition, and I do not find your name on it."

"I'm acquainted with Major Powell, but I'm not an official member of the expedition," Jubil said. He explained Powell's acquaintance with his family.

"I see," Keplinger said. "I'm one of Major Powell's students at Wesleyan. Still, like you, I do tend to think of him as Major Powell, though I never served under him. My service was under General Sherman."

Jubil felt an immediate admiration for Mr. Keplinger. He seemed so self-assured without being arrogant, so observant and calm.

"Luke and I should leave you two gentlemen to your conversation," said Mr. Warner. "We're getting ready to close up the store, but you go ahead with your visit."

"Thank you, Mr. Warner," said Keplinger. "I'll be back in touch in a few days, after Powell arrives. He will have the final say on the requirements for the expedition."

Turning to Jubil, Keplinger said, "I'd be pleased to hear your story, Mr. Walker. Could I interest you in being my guest for supper at the Ogden House?"

"It would be a pleasure," said Jubil, enthusiastically. "Would you mind if I went back to my room and cleaned up first? I've been unloading wagons all afternoon and likely smell like one of the horses."

Keplinger smiled. "Shall we meet in the lobby at seven o'clock?"

At the appointed time, Jubil entered the hotel lobby of the Ogden, feeling underdressed for supper, but thanks to Mrs. Zeller, at least he was clean. Keplinger was waiting on a sofa. He had not dressed for supper, either, and Jubil realized that he, too, had probably packed only for the expedition.

"I confess my curiosity is aroused by your situation, Mr. Walker," Keplinger said once they were seated and had ordered their food.

"Please, call me Jubil."

Keplinger inclined his head. "If you'll call me Lew," he said.

At Lew's urging, Jubil told him of his mother's death and of going to visit Major Powell for advice. Jubil finally reached the point in his story when he had worked up the courage to ask Powell's permission to join the expedition.

"And he said no?" guessed Keplinger.

Jubil nodded. "He wasn't unkind about it. I can't even quarrel with his reasoning."

Lew grinned sympathetically. "So why are you here?"

Jubil looked away and sighed. "I don't agree with his reasoning completely," he said. "And I want badly to be a part of this expedition. I've never wanted to do anything more. I suppose I hoped he might change his mind if he knew I was so intent on making the trip."

Lew shook his head, "Powell is not a man to readily change his mind."

"I know," agreed Jubil.

"So you came all this way to make a point you doubt is likely to be effective?"

"No," Jubil said. Then he found himself opening up to Lew, whose curious but calm demeanor encouraged Jubil to trust him. "I came because I couldn't sit alone on the farm any longer wondering what to do with myself. I had to see some of the world. I've never been anywhere in my life. I just had to come out here, whether Powell agrees to let me join the expedition or not."

Lew sat back in his chair, nodding. "So perhaps you inherited some of your uncle Pete's wanderlust?"

"Maybe," Jubil said.

The waiter brought their food, and they began to eat in comfortable silence.

"You have quite a story, Jubil," Lew said. "I'm pleased to have made your acquaintance. I am sorry to say, however, that I doubt I'll have much influence on Powell. Once he has his mind set, I don't believe anyone has much influence on his thinking, save for maybe Mrs. Powell."

"I understand," said Jubil. "I'm pleased to have made your acquaintance as well. You've heard my whole life's story. I'd be interested in hearing how you came to be one of the Major's students."

Lew was twenty-five years old, and he had grown up in Macon County, Illinois, and attended Illinois College in Jacksonville until the war swept him up. He'd enlisted in the fall of 1861, just as Uncle Pete had. He was assigned to the infantry and saw his first action at Fort Donelson in February of 1862. There, he fell under the command of General Sherman, and he was with Sherman until the end of the war. He was at Shiloh; Vicksburg; the Chattanooga Campaign; the capture of the city of Atlanta; Sherman's march to the sea through Georgia and the Carolinas; and the grand review at Washington after the Confederate surrender. He outlined these incredible experiences with no air of boasting or drama, and Jubil imagined that his observant, calm nature had been crucial in helping him survive the war. Afterward, he had returned to Illinois and chosen Wesleyan as the place to complete his general education before going on to study law.

"It's astonishing," Jubil said, as Lew ended his story, "that you've seen that much combat and survived, and were never even wounded."

"Yes, it is," Lew replied drifting into a reverie, "astonishing."

Jubil could not imagine what terrible memories Lew must have. He was coming to see Lew in the same heroic light as he did Major Powell and General Sherman. They sat quietly for a moment.

"When Powell arrives, I'll have a word with him, if you'd like," Lew offered, "and see if he will give you an audience."

"I would greatly appreciate that," Jubil said, smiling.

"I don't expect him for a few more days," explained Lew. "I'm planning to meet General Sherman tomorrow to discuss the expedition and pay my respects. I'm looking forward to seeing him under peaceful circumstances. Would you like to come with me and meet him?"

Jubil was taken aback by the offer. "Yes," he said, trying to keep his enthusiasm at an acceptable level, "I would, very much. It would be an honor to meet such a legend."

Lew laughed. "I suppose he is a legend, but don't call him that when you meet him. He's a hard man, Jubil, but he's a good one. He may even have some thoughts about how to turn Powell's thinking in your favor."

"I'd never expect him to trouble himself with my small problems," Jubil said, embarrassed. "Surely he's got enough on his mind."

"That's true enough," said Lew with a grin, "but he loves a challenge."

CHAPTER 5

In his upstairs room at Mrs. Zeller's, Jubil was composing a letter to Nelly, when he heard a knock on the front door. He put his pen away and straightened his clothing one last time. As he came out of his room, he heard Mrs. Zeller greeting Lew.

"Is our truant young farmer ready to meet the legendary General William T. Sherman?" Lew said loudly enough that Jubil would surely hear.

"I am," said Jubil as he came down the stairs, "and in your debt for the opportunity."

Jubil was nervous about meeting Sherman and determined to avoid embarrassing himself or his new friend. All he had to do, he told himself, was say hello and speak if spoken to.

Lew grinned. "Better hold your gratitude until we see what kind of humor the general is in this morning."

Sherman's current headquarters were, coincidentally, just across the street from Mrs. Zeller's house, in the Council Bluffs Courthouse. Inside, the courthouse was like a larger version of Wesleyan's North Hall but made of cut stone and marble instead of bricks and wood. On the second floor they approached a door displaying the seal of the United States Army.

Lew opened the door and led the way into the large room, which was furnished with a long conference table along one wall, a map table in the center of the room, several desks where soldiers sat tending to paperwork, chalkboards mounted on the wall, and a large desk in front of the windows, where General Sherman sat studying some papers.

Sherman noticed them and rose as they approached. Like Powell, he carried himself with an air of power and authority. He was a bit shorter than Jubil, middle-aged with an unruly thatch of reddish-brown hair, a scraggly short beard, a rough complexion, a furrowed brow, and dark weary eyes. When he saw Lew, some of the hardness left his face, and his frown lifted into a thin smile.

"Lieutenant Keplinger," said Sherman, coming around from behind the desk to greet them. "By God, it is good to see you."

"It's good to see you too, sir," said Lew. He saluted Sherman and then shook his hand. "Congratulations on your new command."

Sherman held his hands out, palms up. "Welcome to the new headquarters of the United States Army Military Division of the Missouri. Guarding and protecting far too much geography with far too few men and resources. Nothing new in that, is there, Lieutenant? The army life as usual, but these days we face Indians rather than Confederate rebels."

"I'm sure they'll soon see that resisting General Sherman is bad policy," said Lew.

Sherman eyed Jubil. "Who is your associate, Lieutenant?"

"I'm sorry sir, I forgot my manners." Lew signaled Jubil to step forward. "This is Jubilee Walker, General. He is an acquaintance of Major Powell's, and hails from my current home, Bloomington, Illinois."

"How do you do, sir?" said Jubil, shyly.

Sherman offered his hand, and Jubil shook it in a haze of disbelief. General Sherman was the most famous person he had met. He'd seen Abraham Lincoln speak in Bloomington once, before he was president, but he hadn't actually met him.

"Powell is a good man," Sherman said. "You are in excellent company traveling with him and the lieutenant."

Sherman invited them to sit down with him at the conference table.

"Powell's telegram said he would be arriving this Friday the twenty-fourth," he said to Lew, "and that he hopes to meet with me."

"Yes, sir," Lew said. "He wants your advice about which territory would be the safest for our collecting expedition, either the Dakota or Colorado. He hopes to get your assessment of the risks to set our destination."

"Humph," huffed Sherman. "The safest territory would be Illinois."

Jubil grinned.

"That may be, sir," Lew said, "but the major's mind is set on studying natural science in the West."

"Well, I hope he can do his studying without getting himself and his party killed," Sherman said flatly.

"Have hostilities increased, sir?" Lew asked.

Sherman leaned forward. "They ebb and surge in various theaters, all across the Plains. The tribes have gone from resistance in their own territories to forming larger alliances. None of these has lasted or grown, but I believe that the angrier and more desperate they become, the more likely it is they will unify, and the strength of their resistance will increase. We need to convince them of the futility of that effort, before the only course left is to eliminate them."

Jubil became fully aware in those moments of the power Sherman wielded. Jubil had mixed emotions about relations between whites and Indians. He was generally not in favor of resorting to violence to settle differences of philosophy, but he had believed eliminating slavery and preserving the union had been worth fighting for. But with regard to the Indian situation, he was not sure where to lay the blame. He thought whites were wrong for completely taking over the Indians' native lands, but the Indians' warlike nature was making the situation worse. The only solution he could see was greater tolerance and compassion from both sides, but he was not naïve enough to believe that these sentiments would swell among either side any time soon.

"The Dakota and Lakota Sioux in the northern plains have been more aggressive than the Cheyenne and Arapahoe in the Colorado Territory," Sherman explained. "I'd advise Powell to stay clear of the Sioux. That is not to say Colorado is without incident. There are always small bands that may strike out at whomever they come across."

Jubil realized how foolish he had been to think he could travel through the West alone. Sherman was pointing out the basis in reality of Nelly's concerns. If Powell would not allow him to join his party, Jubil would not attempt to go further west on his own.

"I'm sure the major will appreciate your advice, General," said Lew. "Once he has arrived and our objective is set, we'll need to outfit our party. I paid a visit to Warner and Company Outfitters over on Broadway." Lew grinned at Jubil. "They seem like good people. Do you have any advice regarding our logistics, sir?"

"Warner is honest and sells quality merchandise," said Sherman, nodding. "The Department of the Missouri has contracted with them to provide a shipment of materials to our troops at Fort McPherson. I'm bound for the fort myself, escorting Warner's supply train."

"Mr. Walker has been lending a hand at Warner's store until Major Powell arrives," Lew volunteered.

"That's very industrious of you, Mr. Walker," Sherman said.

"Thank you, sir," Jubil said.

Sherman focused his gaze on Jubil. "You're a student of Powell's along with the lieutenant?"

Jubil froze at Sherman's direct question. His brain seemed incapable of forming the thoughts necessary to send words to his mouth. Finally, Lew interjected.

"Jubil has a story you will appreciate, General," he said lightheartedly. "Powell was Jubil's uncle's commander in the war. He was lost at Shiloh. Jubil had the misfortune to be orphaned recently and went to Powell for advice. He tried to sign on for the expedition, but Powell thought he was too green. Jubil decided to make his own way out here, to show Powell he was underestimating him."

"I respect your determination," Sherman offered kindly, "but if I know Powell, he won't change his mind. Doing so just sets a bad precedent."

"Yes, sir," said Jubil, finding his voice. "I expect that may be the case. But I also needed to get off the farm and see some of the world, whether Powell will have me or not."

Sherman squinted as though pondering something. "This is not my business, Mr. Walker," he said, "but a thought occurs to me. If you are out to see the West, perhaps you could sign up with Warner and Company to drive a team to Fort McPherson with the supply train. We leave the twenty-fifth, the day after Powell arrives. Perhaps meeting Powell out there would build an even stronger case for your readiness. In any case, you'll see more of the world."

The idea caught Jubil off guard. He had no idea what such a trip would entail. "Thank you, General," he said. "I'll give it some serious thought."

"Now, if Warner turns you down, and you still want to see the West, I would be happy to enlist you in the US Army." Sherman gave Jubil a faint smile. "We'll give you a real close look at the West."

Jubil went wide-eyed. "I, uh," he stammered, "I don't know if . . . well, I'll give that some thought too, sir."

Sherman's smile widened. "Yes, you give that some careful

thought. Soldiering can bring hard times, but it makes you appreciate good ones." He rose from the conference table. "Well, Lieutenant," he said, "I'm sorry to rush you, but I have commitments. I'll see you on the twenty-fourth when Powell arrives."

"Thank you for your time, sir," said Lew.

"It was an honor to meet you," Jubil said.

He and Lew returned to Mrs. Zeller's, where they sat in the rocking chairs on the front porch in the fine spring weather.

"Which of Sherman's propositions did you like more," asked Lew, "the notion of beating Powell to Fort McPherson, or the one about joining the army?"

"They were both something, all right," said Jubil.

"I thought he might have some views on your situation. The general likes nothing more than developing strategies to get the upper hand," said Lew. "I think he also kind of enjoys the prospect of demonstrating how hardheaded the major can be."

"I'm not sure that helps my case," Jubil said skeptically.

"You're probably right," Lew said with a smile. "By the way, driving a team in Sherman's supply train might not be a bad idea, but you and I should have a serious conversation before you go joining the army."

Jubil nodded. "I'll remember that. Thanks."

Lew grinned. "I need to be on my way. I'm heading down to the depot to meet a couple of members of the expedition. Should I mention you to Powell when I see him?"

Jubil shook his head. He was unsure now if he wanted to approach Major Powell in Council Bluffs. "If I change my mind," he told Lew, "I'll leave a message for you at the Ogden. If I join the supply train, I'll leave a message to that effect also."

"Good luck," Lew said. "I hope to see you again one way or another. If all else fails, maybe we'll see each other back in Bloomington."

Once Lew went on his way, Jubil continued to sit on Mrs. Zeller's porch, pondering his options. Jubil could ask Lew to talk to Powell on his behalf. If Powell rejected him, Jubil could be back in Bloomington in a few days, regaling the Boswells with stories of his trip to Council Bluffs. But then what? He would be right back where he started, sitting at the farm pondering what to do with himself. That prospect held no appeal.

He could ask Mr. Warner to send him out with the supply train to the fort, but why go all the way to Fort McPherson for almost certain rejection? He had one other option: he could join the army. His instincts said army life was not for him, but perhaps he should hear Lew's thoughts before closing his mind to the possibility. To Jubil's way of thinking, soldiering was something a man did as a duty, as his father and uncle had done, not something he would do as a profession. It would also require him to be away from Bloomington and Nelly all of the time.

That afternoon when he went to work, he found Mr. Warner with a customer at the cash register. Luke joined him there just as Mr. Warner completed the sale.

"Hello, boys," Mr. Warner said as he turned his attention to them.

"Mr. Warner," said Jubil. "Lew Keplinger introduced me to General Sherman this morning."

Mr. Warner nodded approvingly. "Well, you are keeping fine company, son."

"Yes, sir," agreed Jubil. "Well, the general is going to recommend that Powell head for Colorado rather than Dakota, so Powell will be heading from here to Fort McPherson."

Mr. Warner replied, "I'm sure the general knows best."

"General Sherman said that he was escorting a supply train out to Fort McPherson and that Warner and Company is doing the outfitting."

Mr. Warner nodded but looked puzzled. "Yes, I gave Luke the manifest this morning, and told him you boys should have the wagons loaded and ready to roll before Saturday."

"Well, sir, the general said I might talk to you about signing on as a teamster and going with him to Fort McPherson," Jubil explained.

Warner looked taken aback. "General Sherman wants you as a driver? I thought you were here to meet Powell and travel with his party. You are a popular fellow, Mr. Walker."

"No sir, I didn't put that right." Jubil shook his head. "I am here to meet up with Powell, but that is kind of a long story. The general didn't ask for me as a driver; he just suggested I might be able to help you out."

"I see," said Mr. Warner, still puzzled. "Well, that's a generous offer, but I already have drivers hired for the trip."

Jubil silently processed the news. *That's the end of that*, he thought, struggling with an almost overwhelming sense of disappointment.

"I can use your help here though," said Mr. Warner. "There's plenty to do to get the general ready to travel."

Jubil shook off his disappointment. He was not ready to give up. Maybe there was a third way to get to Fort McPherson.

"Maybe I could just ride along with the supply train, Mr. Warner?" he asked.

Warner frowned. "You seem like a nice lad, Jubil. Luke speaks highly of you, and Luke is a good judge of character. But I get the feeling I'm not getting the whole story here. I thought you were planning to go with Powell and his party on the expedition."

"I'm making a mess of things," Jubil said and threw up his hands in frustration. "I was just trying to keep from troubling you." He explained his situation to Mr. Warner, and when he was finished talking, Mr. Warner was watching him with raised eyebrows.

"Jubil," he said, "I have heard some stories in my day, but that one is a beauty. First, I'm sorry for the loss of your mother. Grief can make a man change course. What you're doing is . . .

a little foolhardy, which is probably how Powell will see it. But I admire your drive."

"Thank you, sir," said Jubil sincerely. "I'm sorry if I came off as mysterious or dishonest."

"I can't pay you to work your way out with the wagons though," Mr. Warner said. "Those jobs are already taken. But if you want to ride out there and back with the wagons, I see no harm in it. My conscience is telling me to consider your safety, but a fellow can't ask for much more security than traveling with General Sherman."

"Thank you, Mr. Warner," said Jubil. "Thank you very much." Two feelings were now competing inside him—nervousness and enthusiasm.

"You're welcome," Mr. Warner said, looking toward the front door as another customer entered. "I need to get to work, and so do you boys. This ought to light a fire under you two to get the general's supplies sorted out and loaded up."

After work, Jubil went to the Ogden to see if Lew had returned from the depot, but he did not find him there. He left a note with the desk clerk containing the details of his plan, and that night he wrote to Nelly. He made much of traveling under Sherman's protection, hoping to ease her mind. It was easy to be convincing on this point, as he firmly believed it himself. He neglected to mention the Indian uprisings that were influencing their route. He told her she could send mail for him to Fort McPherson. It would surely travel faster than his wagon train. And he promised to write her once he arrived there.

Fort McPherson was about two hundred and fifty miles west of Council Bluffs, and it would take twenty days to get there with the supply train. Once Jubil left Council Bluffs, there was no easy way to turn back. He would have to complete the round trip with the wagons, even though he wasn't quite sure what that entailed. When he left tomorrow, he would be committed to a long and risky trip, but he was going. He was not ready to go back to the farm. After packing his belongings, he tried to read himself to sleep, but he was too tense to concentrate on the words on the page.

In the morning, Mr. Warner introduced him to the men he had hired for the wagon train: Biscuit, the camp cook, who had worked for the Warners before, and drove his own Conestoga wagon; as well as the teamsters for Mr. Warner's freight wagons, Irishmen Murphy, O'Brien, and Flynn. Jubil shook hands with the men as they sized one another up. Biscuit was shorter than Jubil by several inches and heavier by many pounds. He was the oldest of the group, around fifty from the look of his bushy gray beard. He seemed pleasant enough, flashing a snaggle-toothed smile. The teamsters were another story. Jubil wasn't sure what to make of them. Murphy and O'Brien were somewhere between thirty and forty and similarly serious. Murphy had a stern look about him accentuated by his handlebar mustache and slicked-back hair, and O'Brien was a swarthy dark-haired man with a walrus mustache and a blank expression. Flynn, who was not much older than Jubil, had red hair, a face full of freckles, and an air of being slightly lost. But he seemed friendly, which was a relief.

Jubil said good-bye to the Warners. He had come to feel very warmly toward them in a short time.

"Best of luck to you on your expedition with Major Powell," Mr. Warner said. "If you are in Council Bluffs again, you be sure to come see us."

"I'll go that one better, Jubil," said Luke. "I'll ask you to make a point of coming back through Council Bluffs and seeing us. I want to hear how your adventures turn out."

Jubil smiled. "No matter which way my adventure goes," he said, "I'll come back through Council Bluffs."

Then Jubil mounted Biscuit's wagon and set off for points west.

CHAPTER 6

The wind from the west picked up again, and the dust stirred up by the horses, mules, and wagon wheels blew back in Jubil's face. He squinted and pulled his bandana up over his nose. Under the cover of the bandana, he took a sip from his canteen to wash the grit out of his teeth and then spat the water onto the ground, wiping his dust-caked lips on his sleeve. His current position, seated on the freight wagon at the end of the train, did nothing to improve his lot.

Flanking the wagon train was a troop of twenty cavalry soldiers. In front of this procession rode General Sherman and Lieutenant Jenkins. From time to time, General Sherman was joined by a Pawnee Indian scout Sherman and Jenkins called White Man's Dog. Jubil was certain it was not the Indian's true name. Jubil watched him communicate with Sherman using a mix of sign language and speech. It was the closest Jubil had ever been to an Indian. He looked exactly as Jubil imagined an Indian should—shirtless, wearing buckskin trousers and moccasins, his head clean-shaven except for a shock of black hair at the crown that was tied in a ponytail of long braided strands decorated with feathers. He looked to be very nearly Jubil's age. Jubil wondered how the scout felt about working for white men.

They had been on the trail for nearly two weeks, following a main artery of the Oregon Trail across Nebraska, along the course of the Platte River. In the years since 1849, thousands of travelers had worn this part of the route into a wide, flat road as hard packed as a barn floor and as impervious to vegetation as stone. The surface of the trail appeared perfectly smooth, but those seated on a loaded wagon experienced the ride as a constant bumpy vibration. This was the trail Jubil's aunt had ridden in 1849, on her way to Oregon with her family. Who knew if she'd survived the trip, and if she had, where she was now?

"Another hot dry day, eh, Mr. O'Brien?" Jubil observed needlessly. "I'm eating so much dust, I'll be too full for supper."

O'Brien's eyes frowned at Jubil over his own bandana. "Well, you know now," he said, "you'd eat a lot less of it if you'd just shut your mouth once in a while."

"Hey, now," Jubil said, "that's not a very friendly thing to say."

"Oh, don't take me wrong, Mr. Walker. It's not that I dislike you. I'm just not one for prattling on and on like an old hen . . . day after day."

Jubil took a deep breath and resisted telling O'Brien how dull and unpleasant he had found his silent irascible company . . . day after day. "An old hen, am I?" Jubil replied. "That's the thanks a fellow gets for trying to be friendly. Well, maybe I should take my banter up to Flynn's wagon."

"They say it's a free county," Mr. O'Brien retorted.

Jubil pulled a face, which was mostly hidden beneath his bandana, and hopped down from the wagon to walk. He did this from time to time, just to take a break from the constant bounce of the wagon seat, and to be alone for a while.

In his daydreams of adventure travel, he had normally pictured himself galloping on a horse across the plains, or camping in some lush mountain glen. Riding in a wagon train across an arid landscape had never been his dream, though he was still happy to be here. But the slow rate of travel tried his patience. The pace of the mules was not hard to surpass, and he soon caught up with the wagon ahead.

"Mind if I come aboard, Mr. Flynn?" Jubil asked as he drew even with the driver. Flynn had tried without success to keep his fair complexion out of the sun. His freckled face was deep red and even more freckled than it had been when they'd started out.

"Not at all, Mr. Walker," Flynn replied, and Jubil climbed up onto the seat.

"How goes your day, Flynn?" Jubil asked.

"It's a devil of a choice of miseries we've got out here, Mr. Walker. This dust will choke a man until he begs for rain, and then the rain will near drown him when it comes. If it don't rain and the wind don't blow, then the sun beats down. Why, it's only June. Heaven knows what we'll face when we come back through here in July. Thank the Lord we've not had any lightning storms or, Holy Mother of God, one of them tornados. We don't have those things in Ireland, you know. That's God's country there, unlike this uncivilized hellhole."

This was not the first time Jubil had heard Flynn's lament. He seemed to have only two topics that held his interest—griping about the conditions and pining for his homeland. He missed the beauty of Ireland, but not the political environment. Flynn and his friends had left County Cork to find their fortune and freedom in America, and escape the brewing troubles between the Irish Republican Brotherhood and the Irish/English aristocracy. Beyond that, Flynn was uncharacteristically tight-lipped about their history. Jubil was left to wonder whether they had left voluntarily, or fled for their lives.

Jubil steered the conversation to Flynn's recollections of Ireland. Once Flynn got started, he was a good storyteller. Jubil especially enjoyed his tales of the little bearded pixies called leprechauns, who spent their time making and mending shoes and had a hidden pot of gold at the end of the rainbow. If captured, a leprechaun would grant three wishes in exchange for his freedom. Jubil was heartily amused to hear Flynn's stories of how different characters, each with a distinct voice, benefited from or squandered their wishes.

By midday when they stopped to water the animals, Flynn had begun repeating stories Jubil had already heard, and Jubil thought he might switch wagons again to ride with Mr. Murphy. How Murphy managed to keep his handlebar mustache so perfectly groomed was a mystery to Jubil. He never saw him touch it. Murphy preferred a continuous monologue to conversation, and he had a miserable outlook on life. He was preoccupied with making his way to America's gold country, and buying his way out of a life of poverty and injustice. He made Flynn look like an optimist.

Jubil changed his mind about riding with Murphy when the time came for the wagon train to set off again, and one of Murphy's lead mules refused to budge. Murphy engaged in a battle of wills with the animal, calling him names that made Jubil blush. Jubil's father had owned a pair of mules before he traded them for Max. Even his father, a man not given to swearing, had occasionally been frustrated by one of the mule's occasional refusal to work, and he too had on those occasions used language not intended for Jubil's ears. Jubil recalled his father telling him not to repeat those words around his mother. Then and now, Jubil had a sympathetic streak for these poor animals that lived a life of drudgery. Sometimes he talked to the mules as he walked beside the wagons, and enjoyed watching their ears swivel toward the sound of his voice.

"Perhaps you'd allow me to try and reason with him, Mr. Murphy?" Jubil called out.

"You can make stew out of the damn thing for what I care," Murphy growled, spitting tobacco juice into the dust and walking away in disgust.

Jubil approached the animal from the front, took hold of its halter, and calmly reassured the mule it would not find itself in Biscuit's stewpot. The other animals in the team looked his way enviously as he patted the reluctant mule on the neck and purred gently to it. He took a step forward and tugged on the halter and the mule stepped out with him, the team following.

"Climb aboard, Mr. Murphy," Jubil said cheerily. "Your team is headed west." Murphy grumbled and stepped up into the driver's seat and took up the reins.

Jubil approached the cook on his wagon. "If you don't mind, Biscuit," he said, "I'll ride with you. I've worn out my patience with the Irishmen for today."

"I don't mind a bit," the cook replied. "I'm happy to have your company. Nice job with the mule. Climb aboard, or stretch out in the back if you want."

Biscuit was Jubil's favorite traveling companion in the group, and his wagon always rode at the front of the wagon train. Jubil would have ridden with Biscuit all the time but didn't want to wear out his welcome. His Conestoga wagon carried cornmeal, bacon, eggs, potatoes, rice, beans, yeast, dried fruit, crackers, dried meat, any game they shot along the way, grain for the animals, and a large barrel of water tied to the side. Biscuit loved to talk but was also a good listener. The first day of the trip Jubil had volunteered to help the cook in any way he could, so his evenings included building fires and following Biscuit's orders. Jubil was learning a lot from him about tending a camp, cooking for a large group, and caring for the animals.

"How are you holding up, Mr. Walker?" the cook asked good-naturedly.

"Well, this is no cakewalk, but I'm not ready to turn for home just yet," Jubil said, grinning at Biscuit. "How many times have you made this trip?"

Biscuit pursed his lips and studied the horizon. "I never

kept count. I started for Oregon in 1850 but wound up working my way all over the West instead. Been at it ever since."

"I'm thinking this is both my first and last trip bouncing across the plains on a wagon," Jubil admitted, dreading the thought of the return trip, which meant twenty more days with the Irishmen. "In a few months, when the transcontinental railroad is finished, folks will ride out West in style. What will you do after the railroad is finished? There won't be much call for wagon trains after it's done, will there?"

Biscuit shrugged and gave Jubil a yellow-toothed smile. "Maybe not, but I'm getting too old for this anyway."

The Indian scout rode in from ahead of the wagon train, spoke briefly with General Sherman, then rode away again in the direction he had come.

The hot dusty afternoon dragged on until Biscuit pointed ahead toward a patch of trees and bushes.

"That looks like a nice bend in the river," Biscuit said, "I'm guessing the general will pull in there for the night."

Lieutenant Jenkins soon rode back to the wagon train announcing what Biscuit had predicted. Jubil was relieved at the prospect of getting off the wagon and having a cool soak in the river. The Indian scout was already there, watering his horse. But Jubil never got his soak. As soon as the men began to unharness the animals, they were assailed by swarms of black flies and mosquitoes, hatched out from the standing pools by the river. The flies went for Jubil's eyes, the corners of his mouth, and his ears, anywhere they could find some salty nectar. The mosquitoes buzzed in clouds about his head and zeroed in on any exposed skin. The horses twitched their tails and shook their manes in defense, but the mules just closed their eyes and stood like statues. Once Jubil got the campfires burning, the smoke provided some respite, if one didn't mind sitting directly in the path of the smoke.

Every evening along the trail, two fires were built. Biscuit used one fire to cook the meal, and that was the fire where

Jubil, the teamsters, Sherman, and the Indian scout sat to eat their supper, along with any soldiers who chose to join them. The rest of the soldiers sat around the second fire. After supper that night, as usual, General Sherman stood and stretched.

"I believe I'll go have a smoke with the men," he announced and walked away to join the enlisted men.

Jubil was impressed that Sherman spent time each night talking with his men as one of them, not as their commanding officer. He thought of Lew's comment that Sherman was a hard man but a good one.

Jubil watched the Indian scout, who had been sitting next to Sherman silently all evening. The scout had been returning to camp every evening, though sometimes it was late, and he did not eat supper. Jubil wanted to talk to him each time, but the man ignored all of them but Sherman and was clearly not interested in conversation. Jubil could not reconcile such a fierce-looking man allowing himself to be called White Man's Dog, but he theorized it was because the scout cared nothing for what anyone thought. The Indian looked toward him, and Jubil averted his gaze, embarrassed to have been caught staring. The Indian stood and walked away.

"I don't understand why an Indian would work for the army," Jubil admitted, directing his comment to Biscuit. "It seems curious to me they don't mind acting against their own people."

"Well, that depends on who you're calling their own people," Biscuit said. "You know, these Indians are not one big happy family. These tribes have been at each other's throats forever. Sometimes they get in a spat and it blows over, but others are at odds all the time. The Pawnee have decided to take the white man's help fighting their tribe's natural enemies, and to try to get on the good side of the white man to boot."

"Is that working for them?" Jubil asked, remembering the dire fate Sherman had predicted if the Indian tribes ever formed a cohesive resistance.

Biscuit shrugged. "Not as well as they'd like, I expect."

Murphy, who had been listening to their exchange, exploded in a tirade of blistering criticism of the American government's uneven adherence to its treaties and pacts with the Indians, which only seemed to warm him up for detailing similar abuses against blacks, Mexicans, and immigrants, including the Irish. Jubil knew there was some truth in what Murphy was saying. He wondered why the man had troubled to come here but thought better of asking. Who knew what conditions Murphy had escaped in Ireland?

The following day, late in the afternoon, Fort Kearney came into view. Jubil kept an eye out for the flag, which he expected to see waving above a defensive wall manned by soldiers on a catwalk with towers at each end. He was surprised, and a bit disappointed, to find the fort had no palisade wall or towers. Instead, it consisted mainly of two large two-story wood frame buildings with brick chimneys built in the center of some other minor structures. The two buildings stood about one hundred feet apart with one oriented north-south and the other east-west. Each building had covered porches upstairs and downstairs, where sentries stood watch. One of the buildings had an old log cabin attached, which Jubil assumed was a remnant of the original fort. Standing between these two buildings was a tall flagpole flying the Stars and Stripes. Scattered randomly around the central buildings were some smaller buildings and several white canvas tents. A large corral and stable stood off to one side. Soldiers milled about the grounds, but the overall aspect of the fort was sleepy.

General Sherman brought the supply train to a stop about two hundred yards from the central buildings and instructed the men to wait while he and Lieutenant Jenkins, along with the scout, went to meet the post commander. The fort officers came out of one of the central buildings to greet them. The officers saluted each other and chatted, and then Sherman and his entourage mounted up again. Lieutenant Jenkins led the column of soldiers into the fort. Sherman rode to address Jubil and the wagon drivers.

"Welcome to Fort Kearney, gentlemen," said Sherman. "This evening we will enjoy the hospitality of Colonel John Gibbon and his men. We'll be on our way again tomorrow. Pull the wagons up near the corral and unhitch your teams. Lead them into the corral and they'll be fed and watered. You are welcome to sleep with your wagons, or the colonel says there is plenty of room in the bunkhouse, if you would prefer a roof and a cot.

"Biscuit," Sherman said, "you'll have the night off. We have been invited to share in the camp mess this evening. I'll be staying in the central officer's quarters and taking meals with Colonel Gibbon and his staff, but I'm available if you need me." Addressing the group again, Sherman asked, "Any questions?"

Hearing none he continued, "Very well then. Tomorrow we will be up, fed, hitched and ready to roll at dawn. Enjoy your evening of luxury gentlemen." Sherman rode off toward the officer's quarters, and the wagon drivers went into the corral.

The prospect of sleeping under a roof, away from weather and insects, did sound like a luxury to Jubil. He helped the teamsters and the cook with their animals, and then he went to find the mess hall and his cot. The food, the bed, and his overall trail-weariness had combined to give him the best night's sleep he had had since leaving Council Bluffs.

In the morning, the mules were as reluctant to leave their corral as Jubil had been to leave his cot, but his soft-spoken way with them proved much more effective than Murphy's ranting. Under Biscuit's patient tutelage, Jubil also had gained some valuable schooling on harnessing the mules for the wagon and driving a team.

Sherman approached as Jubil and the teamsters were hitching the wagons. "Good morning, gentlemen," he said.

"Colonel Gibbon informs me the Cheyenne Chief, Tall Bull, and his Dog Soldiers, have been stirring up trouble, so we'll be taking extra precautions for the balance of our trip to Fort McPherson. I'm going to post a soldier on each wagon to ride with the driver and a pair of soldiers to ride alongside. We'll keep this arrangement in place for the balance of our trip."

Sherman looked at Jubil. "Walker, I'm going to ask you to give up your place on the wagons and see the camp quartermaster to get fitted out with a horse. You can leave your pack on one of the wagons, but I want you to carry your rifle. Are you all right with this arrangement?"

"Yes, sir," Jubil said without hesitation. The prospect of Indian trouble was unsettling, but the idea of being on horseback and free of the wagons elated him.

He looked over each horse in the corral until he came to one that looked like a smaller version of Max. The stocky dappled gray stallion had a dark mane and dark eyes. Jubil estimated him to be a hand taller than Star and two shorter than Max but muscular like Max, not sleek like Star. The horse looked Jubil in the eye, then dropped his head and pawed the ground.

"I like the looks of this one," Jubil told the quartermaster.

The quartermaster shrugged, "He's a good horse....He's strong. You may have to occasionally remind him who's in charge."

"We'll get along fine," Jubil said, patting the horse on the neck. "What's his name?"

The quartermaster snorted. "Whatever his rider calls him."

Jubil nodded as he admired the horse. "His haunches look like two big gray boulders. I think I'll call him Rocky, like the mountains." He thought the comparison was apt, though all he knew of the Rockies was what he had learned in school.

The quartermaster ignored Jubil's comments. "Pull some tack from the rack and saddle him up."

Rocky stood still while being saddled, and Jubil was again reminded of Max. The horse looked Jubil in the eye as he fit the bridle, and he took the bit without a fuss. Jubil smoothed the horse's mane and mounted up.

"All right, Rocky," said Jubil, "let's head west."

The wagons pulled into a line, and the soldiers took their positions as Jubil rode up to General Sherman.

"Where should I ride, sir?" he asked.

"You stay near me," replied Sherman. "If we run into trouble, you high-tail it to the cook's wagon and shelter in it, or under it." Sherman stared at Jubil, his dark eyes ominous. "I don't want Major Powell or Lieutenant Keplinger crediting me with getting their young friend killed. Do we have an understanding, Walker?"

"Yes, sir, General," replied Jubil earnestly.

Sherman turned his horse and trotted to the front of the column, where he looked back over his shoulder.

"Move out!"

After sitting on a wagon day after day, Jubil felt an exhilarating freedom as he started Rocky across the plains. All of the hardships of travel were left behind as he rocked comfortably in the saddle and scanned the horizon. Rocky seemed to share his exhilaration and champed at the bit to be set running. Though Jubil sympathized, he did as the quartermaster suggested and gently reminded Rocky who was in charge. They landed on a compromise: Jubil let Rocky stamp and prance a bit to burn off energy. The experiences of the past two weeks had convinced Jubil that he would never again ride cross-country on a wagon, but traveling by horseback was an entirely different experience. At the moment, he felt as though he and Rocky could ride clear across America.

For three days the supply train moved along the trail without incident. Even the weather cooperated by serving up dry, partly cloudy days. Jubil noted how the wind, which carried a cloud of dust for the passengers on the supply train, was for him only a clean, fresh breeze. This good fortune was owed to riding at the front of the train, near General Sherman.

For several miles beyond Fort Kearney there seemed to be no water in the Platte River. Jubil rode with a few soldiers to the dry riverbed and helped dig into the sand with shovels. One of the soldiers said the water was in "underflow." A flow of water could always be found within eighteen inches of the surface, no matter how dry the sand appeared to be. They repeated this routine to water the animals several times each day, until they finally reached a point downriver where the flow was once again aboveground.

The flat Nebraska plain would occasionally lapse into a rolling terrain with terraces of hills and ridges of eroded rock. Late in the afternoon on the third day, they spotted antelope near a row of ridges and hills in the distance. The wagon train was short on fresh meat, and the prospects for hunting were too good to pass up.

"We'll hold up here for a while and send a hunting party out," General Sherman announced. "Walker, you're out here for adventure. Would you care to show your skill with that Henry rifle of yours?"

"Yes, sir, General," said Jubil with a smile.

"Lieutenant Jenkins," Sherman said, "take Walker and two men and follow the scout."

The lieutenant chose his men, and the hunting party set out, along with a couple of pack horses, toward the hills a half mile to the south. As they approached, some of the antelope seemed to disappear and then reappear on the horizon. When Jubil expressed his confusion, Lieutenant Jenkins explained there was a canyon ahead that the animals were entering and emerging from. Jubil could see no sign of a canyon until they reached its brink, where the plains suddenly opened into a deep, narrow gorge.

The canyon had been carved by runoff water from the surrounding hills that had poured down the hillside with such force that it had plowed a huge ditch into the plains. The canyon could be entered from its origin at the base of the hills, or at its end point, where the stream finally gave out. White Man's Dog led the hunting party to the brink of the canyon at its far end, and Jubil was amazed to look down into a lush valley containing cedar trees, box elders, hackberry, plum trees, and shrubbery up to the canyon's sides. A thin, shallow stream flowed down the center of the channel, but the watermarks along the canyon walls indicated how high the stream would rise when it rained. Easy access to water and the safety of the canyon explained why they'd seen so many antelope coming and going.

The scout led them single file down the narrow rocky trail into the canyon. Jubil leaned back in his saddle as Rocky made his sure-footed way down. The air in the canyon was cool and smelled of cedar. The men tied off their horses and walked through the thicket looking for game. Jubil was the first to spot an antelope among the trees and was proud when he made a clean kill. One of the soldiers took another one, which gave them enough food for the remainder of the trip. They field dressed the game and loaded it onto the two pack horses.

White Man's Dog took the lead again as the hunting party began their ascent out of the canyon. The three soldiers followed in single file behind the scout with Jubil in the rear, leading the pack animals. The scout raised his hand to signal the line to stop, then he turned and signaled for the men to stay in place. He rode ahead up the trail, but as he reached the rim of the canyon, he turned his horse back toward the hunters and kicked it into a run. Jubil heard him shout, "Dog Soldiers! Go! Go!" and saw him point back down into the canyon.

Jubil tried to turn Rocky and the pack animals but found he was blocking everyone's path on the narrow trail.

The lieutenant shouted, "Let the pack animals go!"

Jubil dropped the pack horses' reins and turned Rocky around. The horse's eyes were wide with excitement, but he did not panic as Jubil stirred him into a gallop. Jubil had no one in front of him as he rode along the stream toward the base of the hills. As he neared the point where the trail led out of the other end of the canyon, he saw a group of Indian riders entering.

"Whoa, Rocky," Jubil said, reining in and turning his horse. "We're boxed in, Lieutenant! They're coming this way too!"

"Dismount and take cover!" Lieutenant Jenkins ordered. "Prepare to engage!"

The soldiers scattered.

"Stay on the same side of the trail," the lieutenant shouted, "or we'll end up shooting at each other."

Jubil took a moment to appreciate the lieutenant's presence of mind.

"Walker," the lieutenant barked, "you stay with me."

Jubil hopped off his horse. "Sorry, boy." He hated to leave Rocky to fend for himself, but he followed the lieutenant through the trees toward the canyon wall, about fifty feet away. The other two soldiers fanned out on either side of them. Jubil had no idea where the scout had gone.

Jubil and the lieutenant reached an outcropping of rock and took up a defensive position behind some boulders. The trail was only visible between the trees. The Indians galloped single file down the trail that ran beside the stream, shooting through the trees in the hunting party's direction. Jubil crouched with his rifle lying flat across the top of one of the boulders, and for the first time in his life, he aimed to shoot someone. Clear shots at the raiders were only available for a second as they rode past, but at least the opposite was also true. As the Indians rode past, Jubil fired until he emptied his rifle, but he did not think he hit anyone. In the moment of quiet before the Dog Soldiers passed again, he fumbled in his pocket for another fifteen cartridges to reload. His hands were shaking so badly, he fumbled a few rounds onto the rocky ground, but he did not have time to find them. The Indians made another pass, and Jubil and the soldiers fired. On the third pass, the lieutenant stood up behind the boulders and aimed through the trees.

"You keep your head down, Walker!" shouted the lieutenant.

Then Jubil heard a shot, and the lieutenant was thrown backward against the canyon wall. Jubil scrambled to help, but he was stunned by what he saw. The lieutenant had been hit in the forehead, and his head had exploded onto the rocks behind him. The contents of Jubil's stomach rose up at the grisly sight, and he turned away and retched. The lieutenant was dead. Jubil fell back against the boulder and sat for a moment, every part of his body shaking. His mind went blank until he heard Mr. Gulley's voice—*Keep your wits about you*. The lieutenant was dead, and the Dog Soldiers were still coming for him. He reached into his pocket to reload again. He only had a dozen cartridges left. The rest were in his pack in Biscuit's wagon. That meant he had to be more cautious with his shots.

He crouched again and laid his rifle over the top of the boulder, rising up just enough to see where he was shooting. As the raiders passed again beyond the trees, he fired a few rounds but saw none of them drop from their horses. He heard firing from his left but none from his right. He wondered if the soldier on his right was dead or just conserving his fire.

Jubil looked around for the scout and spotted him working his way through the trees to get closer to the trail. The next time the raiders came down the trail, the scout stepped out from behind a tree and fired. Jubil saw one of the raiders fall, but at the same time a shot hit the scout's right thigh. The scout spun and fell to the ground. Jubil leapt out from behind his boulder and ran to help while the raiders gathered to make another run. When White Man's Dog saw Jubil coming toward him, he tried to wave him away, but Jubil continued until he reached him.

"Come on, lean on me!" Jubil shouted as he helped the scout to his feet.

White Man's Dog put one arm around Jubil's shoulder, and they hobbled toward the cover of the boulders. Before they could reach safety, Jubil heard the raiders approaching for another pass. He twisted around, pointed the rifle toward the trail with one hand, and fired the one round he had chambered. He could not operate the lever to load another round without letting go of the scout, so he focused instead on getting to the rocks. He heard the buzz of a round passing inches from his head as he and the scout dropped behind the boulder where the slain lieutenant lay.

The right leg of the scout's buckskin leggings was soaked with blood. Jubil pulled his belt off and wrapped it around the scout's leg, just above the wound. He pulled the belt tight, handed the end to the scout, and resumed his firing position. As Jubil peered over the boulder, he felt a wave of relief. Sherman's soldiers were riding down the trail along the stream, two abreast.

Jubil turned and slid down the boulder until he sat leaning against it. "The soldiers," he said to the scout. "They're here."

He and the scout looked at each other for a few silent moments. Then White Man's Dog removed a small pouch that he wore across his torso. Holding the pouch out, the scout nodded at Jubil, offering it to him. Jubil was perplexed but took the pouch.

"Good man," said White Man's Dog. "Save life."

It was true that the scout most likely would have died if Jubil hadn't helped him to safety, but Jubil thought it was the least anyone could have done. "Thank you," he said, looking at the pouch. It was buckskin, about the size of Jubil's open hand, smooth and supple to the touch, with fringe along its edges, a beaded flap, and a braided strap. He put the strap over his head and slung the pouch to his right hip, just as he had seen the scout carry it.

Jubil looked over the boulder again to see General Sherman and a few soldiers waiting for the rest of the troop to return from sweeping the Dog Soldiers out of the canyon. To Jubil's left, one of the soldiers in the hunting party made his way through the trees to rejoin the troop. There was no sign of the soldier on his right. "I'll get the general," Jubil said to White Man's Dog. He rounded the boulder and walked out to meet the soldiers.

"Over here, sir," Jubil called out as he approached. "We could use some help. The scout is shot in the leg, and the lieutenant is dead."

Sherman dismounted and ordered a squad of men to follow him. Jubil led them back to the casualties. Two soldiers went to the scout's aid, and two went to attend to the lieutenant. Sherman looked at the lieutenant's body and shook his head, nodded at the scout, then turned his attention to Jubil. The general's eyes dropped to the pouch that Jubil now wore.

"What happened here, Walker?" asked the general.

"We were boxed in, sir." Jubil explained what had happened.

Sherman looked steadily at Jubil as he absorbed the story. "White Man's Dog gave you that pouch?'

Jubil touched it. "Yes, sir."

"You know what that is, son?" asked Sherman. "That's his medicine bag. He keeps spirit tokens in that bag that protect his life. Most times they hold onto those things their whole life, and are even buried with them. It's generally considered sacrilegious to even let a white man touch it. The only way he can gain another one is to take it from an enemy he kills in battle. Because you saved his life, he's giving it to you to return the favor and protect your life. That pouch is big medicine. He will be your friend and protector for life too, if you want that."

Jubil studied the pouch. He opened the flap and looked through the curious contents—a tiny pine cone, two animal teeth, a claw, a little rock, a few small bones, and an arrowhead. He left everything as it was and closed the flap again. "I'll keep the medicine bag, sir, and honor it, but I don't want White Man's Dog feeling any debt to me. He alerted us to the raiders and kept us all from getting killed in the first place. I'd say we're even."

Sherman pursed his lips and nodded. "Good man, Walker."

"Will we bury the lieutenant, sir?"

"Yes. You four men," Sherman said, pointing out four soldiers, "Give the lieutenant a decent burial." Turning to face more of his troops, the general added, "I don't want the bodies of those dead Indians touched. They're riled up enough without us pouring salt in the wound. Leave them be, and let their people come back for them."

Jubil helped the soldiers clear a patch of rocky ground not far from where the lieutenant had fallen. They piled the rocks to one side and dug a shallow grave. They laid the lieutenant with his bandana over his mortally wounded head, and then they covered his body with the sandy soil.

As one of the soldiers tended to the scout's wounded leg, Jubil heard him tell General Sherman that the shot had missed both bone and artery and gone through the meat of the thigh. The soldier sterilized the wounds with alcohol, stitched them closed, and wrapped the scout's leg in a bandage. The scout did not make a sound at any point throughout this treatment. As soon as he was patched up, while Jubil and the others were still busy burying the lieutenant, White Man's Dog was back on his horse, riding out to make sure the raiders were gone.

To conclude the burial, the soldiers and Jubil piled rocks atop the lieutenant's grave. One of the soldiers recited the Lord's Prayer, and General Sherman praised all men who die in the line of duty. As Jubil stared at the grave, he could not erase the image in his mind of the lieutenant sprawled out, his head shattered by a bullet. He felt numb and shed no tears, but he did feel grateful the lieutenant was getting a respectful burial.

During the ceremony, Jubil spotted the soldier who had taken cover to his right early in the skirmish. The soldier glanced up at Jubil but would not hold his gaze. Jubil was tempted to ask the man why he had stopped firing, but he decided to leave him alone.

Then a few soldiers came down the canyon, leading the hunting party's two pack horses laden with the game. One of the soldiers said that the horses had taken refuge at the other end of the canyon. Jubil went to look for Rocky and found him pacing amongst the trees. When the horse saw Jubil, he dropped his head and pawed the ground, then walked toward him.

"That was a close one, huh, boy?" Jubil said soothingly as he patted the horse's neck. "Probably not the first time you've been shot at though." When Jubil led Rocky back to the group, White Man's Dog had returned and was speaking with the general.

"Form up by twos," General Sherman commanded. "We're moving out."

The group rode out of the canyon and across the plains to rejoin the wagons. General Sherman told them they would find a campsite further down the trail, to give the raiders room to recover their dead. Jubil fell into position behind Sherman. He tried without success to stop his mind from replaying every moment of the fight. The image of the lieutenant's blood and brains splattered on the rocks made his gorge rise again, and he fought to calm his agitated mind and queasy stomach.

The remaining three days of travel to Fort McPherson seemed to pass as one long day. At night Jubil either lay awake or was startled awake by violent dreams. In the worst dream, he saw the lieutenant mortally wounded and spread-eagled on the ground but reaching out and pleading for Jubil's help to get up. Jubil had not previously given the progress of the Powell expedition much thought, but ever since the raid, he worried they might fall victim to the same band of Indians, without the protection of the army. He knew his worry and concern did no one any good, but he worried anyway. He also worried what Powell's reaction would be when he discovered Jubil had come all this way, putting his life at risk over something Powell had clearly told him he was not in favor of. He worried Powell might cite his poor judgment and unwillingness to take orders as reasons to bar him from not only this expedition but any future ones as well.

The long days in the saddle were the only time he truly felt sleepy, but he had not mastered the art of sleeping on horseback. Biscuit produced a stew from antelope meat and staples from his wagon, along with a few dozen of his namesake biscuits, and the soldiers praised his efforts. Jubil had enough appetite to eat, but no enthusiasm to enjoy it.

On the third morning, the general announced they would reach Fort McPherson in the afternoon. That day, White Man's Dog rode alongside Sherman all day rather than out ahead of the wagon train. When he passed Jubil on his horse, the scout nodded to him, which was more than he had done before the skirmish.

When Fort McPherson appeared in the distance, Jubil saw that, like Fort Kearney, it was not surrounded by a palisade or a fence. He supposed there were not enough trees around to supply the timbers. The men who had built Fort McPherson had used the terrain to their advantage: the collection of buildings sat on a stretch of high ground at the mouth of a canyon surrounded by rocky ridges. As the wagon train followed the incline toward the encampment, Jubil could see a spring at the mouth of the canyon that grew as it flowed downhill into a wide flat river and produced a broad valley below. In the middle of the broken and meandering river sat an island of several thousand acres covered with fine grass, scrubby willows, and cottonwoods. The fort had a view of the whole valley.

Jubil was relieved to have reached Fort McPherson alive, but he felt out of his league and far from home. Fortunately, he would have a few days to acclimate himself to life at the fort and develop a strategy for approaching Major Powell.

CHAPTER 7

Jubil entered the Fort McPherson mess hall hoping he was not late for breakfast. He had slept in that morning, following his best night's sleep in several days. He spotted Biscuit and the teamsters at a table and, after collecting his food and coffee, he joined them.

"Good morning, Jubil," said Biscuit, brushing crumbs from his beard. "We decided to leave you sleeping."

"Good morning, gentlemen," replied Jubil. "Glad to be sleeping indoors."

"Yes, sir," Biscuit agreed. "I swear every year older I get, the ground gets harder."

Jubil sat down at the table and focused on his food, but he soon found he much preferred Biscuit's cooking. The scrambled eggs were bland and dry, the bacon was undercooked, and the coffee was beyond strong. As Jubil looked across the table, he saw Murphy staring at him.

"Good morning, Mr. Murphy," Jubil said, braving another sip of coffee. "Something on your mind?"

"Top of the morning to you, Walker," Murphy drawled coldly. "Well, you see, the boys and I were wondering how long you expect us to hang about waiting for your friends to show?"

Surprised, Jubil glanced over at Biscuit, who was looking at Murphy with a questioning frown. O'Brien sat ramrod straight, arms crossed, silently defiant, as usual. Flynn was shaking his head and shrugging his shoulders as though this, like the weather, was something he could not control.

"Powell will be along within a week. Why?" Jubil asked. "Are you in a hurry?"

"Warner pays by the day," Murphy said, "and we're doubting he's going to pay us to sit around and play poker. We'll get back and find we wasted our time here."

"Now that ain't right," Biscuit said angrily. "Warner pays on round trip days. He don't pick nits like that. What are you playing at here, Murphy?"

"You keep out of it, old man," Murphy snarled, "or you'll find yourself driving back alone. Warner's wagons and teams are worth a pretty penny—more than we're even getting paid, now that I think about it."

Jubil felt his temper rising at Murphy's threat. "If this is just about getting paid for the days we wait, I'll pay you. But I'll tell Mr. Warner so he doesn't pay you again for those days." He turned to Biscuit. "How much does he pay you?"

"Two dollars a day for me, and a dollar a day for each of them," Biscuit said.

"We won't wait on our money until we get back," added Murphy. "You got any cash?"

Jubil ran his hand absent-mindedly over his money belt and then scolded himself as Murphy's eyes tracked the movement with curiosity. Jubil was now unsure these men could be trusted if he was forced to ride back with them alone. On the way out he had been safe in the company of General Sherman. Would they hesitate to take his money and leave him and Biscuit beside the trail, dead or alive?

"I'll pay for up to one week's time," Jubil said. "If Powell takes longer than that, I'm tapped out." There was no reason for them to know how much money he was really carrying.

"We'll sit here for one week," Murphy said as he rose from

his seat and O'Brien and Flynn followed suit. "If your friend don't show by then, we'll take our pay and head back." Murphy pointed at Biscuit. "And you best not cause us any problems with Warner."

Biscuit scowled as the Irishmen left the mess hall.

"I'm sorry about that, Walker," Biscuit said. "I never worked with these men before—and I'll not again."

"I'll explain things to Mr. Warner so you won't have to," Jubil said. The Irishmen now seemed more like pirates than teamsters.

Jubil pushed his plate away, his appetite spoiled by the negotiations and the quality of the fare. As he and Biscuit left the mess hall, he could see in the distance a long line of soldiers coming from the valley to the south. The column had a single rider in the lead—the company commander—with a flag bearer riding directly behind him. The main column of soldiers rode four abreast and was several dozen rows long. Jubil estimated there were two or three hundred men. A bugle sounded from the column, and the company eased into a canter as they approached. He watched as they began to enter the parade grounds at the center of the fort.

The commander was a tall thin man with shoulder-length reddish hair. He had a horseshoe-shaped moustache that fell to his chin and a strip of whiskers below his lip. His hat was bent up at a rakish angle on the right side. He wore gauntleted buckskin gloves and a red bandana tied around his neck, the loose ends flapping in the breeze. He sat astride his horse with an air of confidence, authority, and pageantry.

"Say hello to Lieutenant Colonel George Armstrong Custer and his Seventh Cavalry, Jubil," Biscuit said. "Fancy, ain't he?" Biscuit winked at Jubil.

Jubil nodded. He had read newspaper accounts of Custer's exploits in both the Civil War and the Indian Wars, but he had never seen a picture of him. He knew Custer was flamboyant, but now he better understood what flamboyant looked like. "Is he just passing through?"

"My understanding is that Custer there and your pal General William Tecumseh Sherman plan to combine forces and go reason with Chief Tall Bull and his Dog Soldiers."

Jubil had previously known Sherman's middle initial but not what it stood for. Now, he thought Biscuit might be making a joke. "Is that really Sherman's middle name?"

"Yup," Biscuit asserted. "His pa named him after the great Shawnee warrior. Ironic, ain't it? The feller in charge of breaking the back of the Indians is named after one."

"Hmm," said Jubil. General Sherman and a few other officers came out of headquarters to greet Custer. Jubil went along with Biscuit to his wagon to rearrange his supplies. Then he went to find the Irishmen and help them unload. When the wagon train duties were complete, Jubil went to the quartermaster's office to see if any mail had come for him. He was excited to find a letter from Nelly waiting. He returned to the barracks to read it.

Dear Jubil,

I hope my letter finds you safe and healthy. We were all most impressed to hear that you will be traveling in the company of General Sherman and his troops. That brings me some comfort, but I confess to still having a constant concern for your well-being.

Mama, the boys, and I have begun our gardening project at your farm. Thank you for tilling a patch before you left. We always check the house to make sure it is secure, and the boys check the barn to run out any varmints. All is well so far. While I am enjoying gardening at the farm, I don't want to own it. So you need to get yourself back here.

Papa and I had another round of debate over my future with no change of position by either of us. Mama says I should show restraint until the end of the school year, when the decision will be at hand. I suppose she is right. My persistence in trying to get a decision from him now is not helping the situation. I'll do my best to follow her advice.

I hope your encounter with Major Powell goes well. He can't help but be impressed by your determination and bravery. Whether you go on with him or return home, take great care. Write to me once you know your plans.

I miss having my best friend to talk to. This is the longest that we have ever been apart. Please take the greatest precautions, and return home as soon as possible.
Yours sincerely,
Nelly

Her letter lifted his spirits considerably. He read it over several times, and imagined her sitting beside him speaking the words as he looked into her blue, blue eyes. He missed talking to his best friend too. He recalled how, if he leaned in just right while sitting next to her on the porch swing, he could catch the fresh scent of her silken black hair. The thought of that fresh scent reminded him of his own less pleasant aroma. He tucked the letter away in his pack and went to have a bath.

In the morning, his lack of duties in the midst of the busy atmosphere of the fort left him feeling at loose ends. He wanted to take Rocky out for a ride, but the soldier on duty in the stable told him the officers would not approve of him riding out alone. Instead, Jubil groomed Rocky and volunteered to help around the stables. He mucked out the stalls and spread new straw, groomed the horses, and fed and watered the horses and mules. The work reminded him of his chores at home, and it was a far better way to pass the time than playing poker with the teamsters and soldiers. The next day he worked in the stables again. After evening mess, Jubil was in the barracks on his cot reading when a soldier not much older than himself came to find him.

"General Sherman would like a word with you, sir, if you would follow me to headquarters."

Jubil could not imagine what this was about, but he followed the soldier to the headquarters building and into a large open room, arranged much the same as General Sherman's office in Council Bluffs. Standing at the map table in the center of the room were General Sherman, Custer, and a third officer whom Jubil did not know. Standing at the back wall of the room was White Man's Dog and an unfamiliar Indian.

"Come in, Mr. Walker," said General Sherman, waving Jubil to step up to the map table.

"This is the post commander, Captain Arthur MacArthur," said Sherman nodding to the officer. "This is Lieutenant Colonel Custer, commander of the Seventh Cavalry. Gentlemen, this is Jubilee Walker. He is a friend of Major Wes Powell's and the man I told you about."

Jubil wondered what Sherman could possibly have told them about him. "It's an honor to meet you," he said.

"Walker, I'm sending an escort party with the wagon train on the return trip—White Man's Dog and four soldiers," announced Sherman.

Jubil glanced at White Man's Dog. The scout stared back at him without expression, as did the other Indian.

Sherman continued, "They will accompany you as far as Fort Kearney. You'll be fine from there to Council Bluffs."

"Well, thank you sir," Jubil said. "May I ask—has something happened between here and Fort Kearney?" Jubil again thought of Powell and his party, and hoped they had not encountered trouble along the way without benefit of a military escort.

"Not that I know of," Sherman said. "Contrary to his name, my scout sets his own agenda. I give him orders, which he takes into consideration, and then he does whatever he thinks is best. White Man's Dog tells me he intends to get you back to Fort Kearney, so that is the end of that. We've got Custer's scout, Curley, so we'll manage."

Jubil addressed White Man's Dog directly. "Thank you," he said.

The scout nodded at Jubil in reply.

"What if I continue on with Major Powell, sir?" asked Jubil. "Will he . . ." Jubil looked to the scout again but stopped mid-sentence. It felt awkward to talk about White Man's Dog as though he was not present. "Will you—?"

The scout looked at Jubil steadily but did not answer.

"If you go with Powell," Sherman said, "White Man's Dog will not follow you. He'll stay with me."

"Yes, sir," Jubil said.

"That's all then, Walker," said Sherman, "unless you have any questions."

Jubil thought for a moment before replying, "I do have a question, sir. I heard you and Lieutenant Colonel Custer are heading out to take on Chief Tall Bull and his Dog Soldiers. If I can ask, sir, when are you leaving?"

Sherman nodded. "Day after tomorrow we ride west for Julesburg to meet another company, and then we'll head south to find Tall Bull. Why?"

"I was just wondering if you would be here when Major Powell arrives, sir," explained Jubil.

"As much as I might enjoy being present for your meeting with Powell," Sherman said, "unless he shows up tomorrow, I'll be gone. I've explained your situation to Captain MacArthur, and he'll pass my thoughts on to Powell in my absence. You handled yourself well on the trip out, Walker. I'll make sure Powell knows my thoughts."

"Thank you very much, sir," said Jubil, embarrassed that his self-serving intentions were so transparent. "And good evening, gentlemen."

Jubil left the headquarters. He sat for a while on the porch of the mess hall, which overlooked the parade ground, where the officers marched a group of soldiers through drills and inspected their weapons. Another group of soldiers was laboring on the construction of a building near the laundry and the hospital. Though there was considerably more activity here than at Fort Kearney, the life of a soldier seemed dull—long periods of boredom punctuated by brief periods of terror in battle. To that point, Jubil's recent experience told him he had no interest at all in getting shot at, or shooting at others, for a living. While he was willing to defend himself against Indians if attacked, he was not willing to kill them just to drive them off the land. Eventually he went to the stables to check on Rocky.

The big gray horse dropped his head and pawed the ground when Jubil approached.

"Looks like we have ourselves some additional company if we have to go back to Council Bluffs, old boy," Jubil said as he stroked the horse's cheek. It had always calmed him to talk to Star and Max at home. It was a habit he had developed over the years as an only child and perfected while working the farm without his father or uncle to talk to.

"I hate to say so, Rocky, but I'm concerned the Irishmen may be trying to make a grab for my money. Since we don't need to worry about traveling alone now, I think I'll just keep the news about our escort to myself for a while. That may be a tad spiteful, but I can live with it. I'll wait and see how long it takes Powell to show up, and whether he allows me to go on with him. Then we'll settle up on our plans for heading home."

Star had always seemed to listen to him attentively and even respond to whatever he said, but Rocky was a bit more stoic, like Max. Jubil missed Star and Nelly. It was difficult, though, to think about what Nelly's reaction would be if she knew what had happened to him so far along the trail.

The afternoon of the next day, Jubil was working in the stables when Biscuit came to find him.

"Jubil," said Biscuit excitedly. "There's a wagon train coming into the fort. It's likely your friend."

Jubil decided he would not surprise Powell by walking into the parade ground to meet him. General Sherman was still here, so Jubil would rely on him to inform Powell of his presence. Jubil left the stable and went to get cleaned up. When he returned to the barracks, Lew Keplinger was standing by a cot sorting laundry.

"Hello, Lew," said Jubil. "Welcome to Fort McPherson."

"Jubil! It's good to see you." Lew clapped Jubil on the shoulder as they shook hands.

"It's good to see you too. I'm glad you made it."

"It was a long, boring trek out here, but we made it with no special hardships," said Lew, good naturedly. "How about you?"

"Long and boring, same as yours," agreed Jubil, "except for one afternoon. We got into a skirmish with a band of Tall Bull's Dog Soldiers between here and Fort Kearney."

Lew looked Jubil over. "Looks like you got out of it in one piece."

Jubil nodded. "I did, but Lieutenant Jenkins was right beside me and took a bullet to the head," Jubil added pensively.

"I'm sorry to hear that," Lew sympathized. "It must be weighing on your mind."

Jubil looked at Lew and thought of all the death he must have seen in his years of following Sherman through the war.

"A fellow never gets used to seeing people die around him," Lew said, as if he knew what Jubil was thinking, "or ever stops wondering why it wasn't him instead."

"Thanks," Jubil said.

"How did you come by that?" Lew asked, pointing at Jubil's medicine bag. Jubil told the story. "That was bold of you," Lew said.

"I'm sure you'd have done the same," Jubil said, proud to have impressed his friend.

As Lew made his preparations to leave in the morning, he and Jubil exchanged stories about their trips. Jubil was already packed and ready to go either direction: farther west with Powell or back east with Warner's teamsters. As they talked, a soldier came for Jubil again.

"Mr. Walker," the soldier said. "General Sherman would like to see you, sir."

Jubil's heart leapt into his throat. He got up to follow the soldier.

"Would you like me to come along?" asked Lew.

Jubil thought for a moment. "How do you think it will sit with the major to learn you and I met in Council Bluffs, and you've neglected to mention it to him?"

Lew replied with a grin, "He'd probably send me home with you."

Jubil chuckled. "I got myself into this situation. I'll stand alone to explain it."

Jubil followed the soldier into the headquarters building, where Sherman sat at the head of the conference table. On his right sat Major Powell, and on his left sat Custer and Captain MacArthur. White Man's Dog and Custer's Indian scout, Curley, stood against the wall behind Sherman.

"Come in, Mr. Walker," Sherman said. "I believe you know everyone here." He gestured to a chair at the end of the table, and Jubil pulled it out, but before he could be seated, Major Powell rose and approached him.

"It's good to see you, Jubil," said Powell, shaking his hand and smiling broadly. "It's quite a surprise, I must say, but not an unpleasant one."

Jubil was taken aback by Powell's good-natured greeting. For weeks he had anticipated this moment, always imagining Powell's reaction as stern, and possibly even angry. Jubil felt relieved but wary, as though this pleasant atmosphere might suddenly change.

"Thank you, Major," said Jubil. "It's good to see you too, sir."

Powell clapped Jubil on the shoulder and returned to his seat, and Jubil took his place at the table.

"Mr. Walker, until I know the disposition of my scout," Sherman said, "Lieutenant Colonel Custer and I can't finalize our strategy, and my scout's plans depend on which way you are headed. I've already filled the major in about our run-in with the Dog Soldiers. Will you speak with Major Powell here, or would you prefer to speak privately?"

Jubil looked at Powell.

"I don't mind talking to the major here," said Jubil.

Sherman prompted, "Speak your mind, then, son."

"Well, Major," Jubil said, "after we talked, I couldn't get the idea of going West out of my head, and your expedition was what I set my mind on. I understood why you thought I wasn't prepared to come with you, but I hoped you might see me differently if I struck out on my own and met up with you along the way. I went to Council Bluffs and met Lew Keplinger, but I asked him not to mention me to you. Lew introduced me to General Sherman, and I learned he was headed to Fort McPherson. I'd been working at Warner and Company, the outfitter who put the supply train together, so I came along on the wagons. And here I am, hoping to travel with you to Colorado."

"You've had an impressive summer so far, Jubil," said Powell. "I can confirm you have accomplished at least part of your mission. I do see you differently than when we last met. You've shown real commitment and fire by striking out alone to travel west. General Sherman spoke highly of your uncomplaining nature on the trail and your presence of mind under fire. Your father, mother, and uncle would be proud of you."

Jubil sat a little taller as a result of this praise and the mention of his family.

"I can see there is no need to be concerned about your

ability to look out for yourself," Powell added, "but I still have other concerns. As we discussed back in Bloomington, this is primarily a scientific expedition, and all the members of the party bring some depth of knowledge to our explorations. I must also be conscious of our supplies. We've planned for a set number of people, and I can't risk stretching those supplies. So I'm sorry to say I can't allow you to go on with us."

There it was. The answer he had expected but hoped not to hear.

"Yes, sir, Major," Jubil said. "I'm disappointed, but I can't say I'm surprised."

Jubil waited for someone to speak, but the room was silent. He couldn't help asking, "Is there anything I can say to change your mind? I think I've proven myself handy on the trail . . . and I don't eat all that much."

Powell smiled but shook his head. "I'm sorry, no."

Jubil wanted to continue to press the issue, but he knew Powell would not give in. He struggled to accept Powell's answer, his spirits dipping. But then he had to laugh at himself a little for expecting the situation to turn out like a story. He wasn't the hero in a dime novel, and Major Powell's decision seemed based more on practical details than on any character flaws he might have detected in Jubil.

"I hope you have a safe trip, sir," he said.

"Thank you, Jubil," replied Powell, "and I hope the same for you."

Sherman looked around the table. "All right, Walker. White Man's Dog and the detachment will be ready to ride at dawn. It's been a pleasure to make your acquaintance."

Jubil rose to take his leave. "Thank you, General. I appreciate everything you've done for me."

Sherman rose along with Jubil. "Are you sure we can't make a soldier out of you Walker? We can always use good men."

For the first time, Jubil saw some expression on the faces

of the other officers: Custer and MacArthur smiled and looked to Jubil expectantly.

"No thank you, sir," said Jubil without hesitation, "but it's an honor to be considered."

"Godspeed, then, Walker," Sherman said.

"I think I'll walk Jubil out, if you don't mind, General," said Powell. "I'll only be a minute."

On the front porch of the headquarters building, Powell said, "We should meet in Bloomington when our travels are over, Jubil. We can exchange stories of our adventures."

"That is something I will look forward to, Major," said Jubil sincerely.

"You know Mrs. Powell is along with us?" said the major. "She is in our rooms at the officer's quarters. She will be greatly surprised to see you here, but very pleased. Stop and see her."

"Mrs. Powell is traveling with you, sir?" said Jubil.

"She is our ornithologist, Jubil, and a knowledgeable one at that. Emma is as hard on the trail as any man here," boasted Powell.

"I'll stop and say hello to her," Jubil said. "I may want to talk to you about Wesleyan again when we get home, sir."

"I'd be glad to talk to you about your education, Jubil, but you won't find me at Wesleyan this fall. I'm taking a position at Illinois State Normal University. I may not return until the spring term though. It depends on the circumstances I find once we reach Colorado."

"Well, that is news, Major," said Jubil. "Congratulations. They'll be fortunate to have you, sir. Are you still thinking you'll mount another expedition next year, or will this change your plans?"

"I hope to make another expedition next summer," said Powell. "I believe I'll have the support of Normal University, and some other patrons, but nothing has been finalized."

"I'd like to be a part of that expedition, Major," said Jubil.

"I'm not sure I'll ever make a scientific contribution to your efforts, but I hope I can prove useful."

Powell studied Jubil's face. "I do believe you have Pete's spirit. We'll discuss the next expedition when we are closer to it. For now, I need to return to General Sherman and the other officers."

They wished each other well again, and when Jubil left the headquarters building, he went to pay his respects to Mrs. Powell, who was amazed to see him at Fort McPherson. She would not let him leave her side until he had accounted for every day since his mother's funeral. After hearing his story, Mrs. Powell understood his disappointment, but she was not surprised at the major's decision. Jubil was only able to take his leave after promising to see her at home. The major's comments about Mrs. Powell's trail-hardiness and his visit with her made Jubil wonder whether Nelly would ever be willing to trek into the wilderness with him. She would probably never seek it out as Mrs. Powell had—she didn't really even like to ride horseback—but if he could make it comfortable enough for her, he thought she would enjoy it.

Jubil returned to the empty barracks and realized the men were at supper. He opened his shirt and removed ten dollars from his money belt and stuffed it in his pocket. In the mess hall, he found Biscuit sitting alone at one table and Lew and a few members of Powell's party at another. He got a tray of food and walked over to the table where Biscuit sat.

"Are you going on with your friend?" Biscuit asked.

"No. He's sending me home," Jubil said.

Biscuit nodded.

"Where's Murphy?" Jubil asked, reaching into his pocket. "I'm ready to pay up."

"You can hold your money," Biscuit said. "He and his countrymen have absconded."

"Gone?!" Jubil exclaimed.

"Yep, snuck off in the night," Biscuit said, scratching his beard. "I went to the livery to check on the teams and found one of Warner's freight wagons missing, along with two mules and a set of harness tack…gone."

Jubil sat down across from Biscuit.

"Where do you think they headed?" Jubil asked.

"He was always talking about gold country," Biscuit said. "I reckon he meant either the Black Hills up in Dakota Territory, or maybe around Virginia City in Montana."

Jubil said. "We should put the law on them."

"I wouldn't expect much from that," Biscuit said with a shrug. "It's a big wide world out here."

"Mr. Warner will be upset," Jubil said.

"Maybe some," Biscuit said. "But he'll about break even since he don't have to pay them. That rig and two mules is worth about what he would a paid the three of them."

"Hmm…" Jubil said, pondering the situation. "Well it still was a lowly thing to do."

"It's going to be a long, lonely trip home," Biscuit said.

"Fortunately not," Jubil said with a shake of his head. "We'll be riding back in the company of Sherman's scout and a small detachment of soldiers."

Biscuit looked surprised. "Well, that's good news."

"Yes," Jubil said. "We'll be on our way tomorrow. What about the other wagons? Do I need to drive one back?"

"We'll ask the soldiers to drive them back to Fort Kearny. The post commander will get them back to Warner in short order. They run back and forth to Council Bluffs all the time."

Jubil was pleased he would not have to ride a wagon all the way back, and especially pleased he would not have to tolerate Murphy, O'Brien, and Flynn's sour company.

He finished eating at the table with Biscuit, and then noticed the other members of Powell's party had finished their supper and were leaving their table, but Lew remained seated. Jubil joined him, and they walked back to the barracks together.

"I'm going back to Council Bluffs," Jubil said.

"Sorry to hear it," Lew said. "What are you going to do now?"

Jubil sighed. "Head home, I reckon. I may spend a few days in Council Bluffs. I enjoyed working with Mr. Warner and Luke. I'm in no rush to get back to the farm, and I still have a little money, thanks to Mr. Warner and the US Army. But I miss Nelly and Star."

"Are those horses or people?" asked Lew as they went inside.

"One of each," laughed Jubil. "Star is my horse. Nelly is my . . . well, she's my friend. She's my best friend, you know . . ."

Lew laughed. "Yes, I think I do. I'll look forward to meeting them both. You and I will get together and swap stories." He walked to his cot and dug a slip of paper and a pencil out of his pack.

"I'd truly enjoy that," said Jubil. "I was surprised the major said the same thing."

"He did?" said Lew incredulously.

"Yes," declared Jubil. "He wasn't upset with me at all but was very cordial."

"Huh," said Lew. He chewed on the detail as he wrote down the address of his boarding house in Normal and handed it to Jubil, who was describing the circumstances of the return trip.

"I hope it's considerably less eventful than your trip out," Lew said.

CHAPTER 8

On their trip back to Fort Kearney, the only Indian they saw other than White Man's Dog was dead. Jubil was riding Rocky next to Biscuit's wagon when they came across a scaffold made of four poles set into the ground with thongs stretched from pole to pole about ten feet up. The Indian was laid out on the scaffold, wrapped in a buffalo-hide and bound with a horsehair lariat. The stench turned Jubil's stomach.

A few yards down the trail, Jubil dismounted at the sight of the bodies of two white men. When he approached on foot, he saw that they were scalped and bloody. That sight convulsed his guts. He doubled over and retched.

Biscuit walked over and patted him on the shoulder. "First time you seen a scalping?"

Jubil straightened up and wiped his mouth on his sleeve. "Yeah."

"It's a vile practice," Biscuit said.

Jubil agreed. How many times had he read a passage in one of his dime novels about some poor soul falling victim to such a fate? But to see it firsthand—it was unimaginably brutal, worse than seeing the lieutenant shot. Four slices with a sharp knife had carved out a rectangle of scalp from each man's head, and then one long filet cut took the bloody trophy—just like carving out a section of sod. It was this cultural practice more than any other, Jubil thought, that made white people fear and loathe the Indians—although many whites had gamely picked up the sport themselves. But whites generally preferred their mayhem done in a more genteel fashion. A simple shooting, hanging, or stabbing was sufficient. Jubil couldn't help but characterize the mutilation he witnessed there as savage.

The scalped men lay near a wagon, but the harness animals were missing. He assumed the Indians must have taken them. Clothing and other personal belongings were spread around the area. This could have been his own fate, he realized, if he had been foolish enough to set out across the plains alone. He wondered if this was what had happened to his mother's sister and her family along the trail.

The corporal who led the escort said they could not risk staying in the area long enough to dig proper graves for the men, so they hastily dug shallow graves, even though they would likely be dug up by wolves or coyotes. Since the bodies were not yet disturbed by scavengers, the corporal estimated they had been killed that morning or late the previous night. Jubil did not like leaving the men that way, but he knew the corporal was correct. White Man's Dog had already ridden out to scout the hills and make sure the Indians who had killed the men were gone. He hadn't come back, which meant either that he hadn't encountered them, or he had been killed. The party moved on several miles before setting up camp.

As Jubil was working at setting the evening's fire, he was relieved to see White Man's Dog ride into camp. Jubil raised his hand in greeting, and the scout returned the gesture as he dismounted. For the past two nights, White Man's Dog had come back to camp late and gone right to sleep. What he was eating, or when, Jubil did not know, but tonight he joined the men as they sat around the campfire and ate the meal Biscuit had prepared. With no general present, the soldiers felt free to conduct loud and often uncouth conversations, which often detailed their past amorous conquests or future lewd intentions. The scout and Jubil sat silently in this company.

Later that evening, as the men drifted off to their bedrolls, Jubil and the scout sat looking into the fire. Jubil had so many questions, and he finally got up the nerve to ask one.

"You understand more English than you speak, don't you?" Jubil asked.

White Man's Dog met Jubil's gaze. "Yes."

"What's your real name?" Jubil asked.

"Taaka Asakis."

Jubil tried to repeat the name. "TA-yaka a-SOCK-us. What does it mean?"

"White Dog," the scout translated.

Jubil nodded. "Who changed it to White Man's Dog?"

"Soldiers," the scout replied.

"General Sherman started calling you that?"

"Before Sherman," White Dog replied. "All soldiers."

Jubil could understand a lowbrow soldier like the ones telling stories around the fire thinking the nickname was funny, but he was disappointed in General Sherman for perpetuating the insult—it seemed beneath him. But then again, Sherman heaped far greater abuse on Indians than calling them disrespectful names. Still, Jubil found the personal slight uncalled for. The army paid the scout to ride ahead and save its sorry hide, and then they taunted him to his face. It didn't sit well with Jubil.

"Can I just call you White Dog?"

White Dog stared at Jubil for a long moment before saying, "Yes."

Jubil poked at the fire. He remembered Murphy's rant about the government's poor treatment of all manner of people. Jubil had always known this unseemly aspect of human nature existed, but he had never faced it in person before. He was only realizing how sheltered a life he had led before now.

The glimpse he had gotten of White Dog's poor treatment inspired him to show the scout some respect. "I understand how important your medicine bag is to you," Jubil said, "and I'm greatly honored you gave it to me. You're welcome to have it back though . . . if it's not disrespectful of me to offer." Jubil did not take the medicine bag off but held it up in his hand toward White Dog. "Sorry . . . are you understanding me?"

"Yes," White Dog replied. "You keep. . . . Spirits follow you now." The scout rose. "Sleep," he said, raising his right hand and walking away.

"Good night, White Dog," Jubil replied. Then he added wood to the fire and went to bed.

For the next three days the escort moved through Indian country without incident. During that time, Jubil worked up the courage to ask White Dog where he was from and where his family was, but he never got the opportunity. White Dog returned to his usual routine of riding out during the day and returning to camp only to sleep.

When they reached Fort Kearney, the corporal rode in to address an officer standing outside the headquarters. He returned bearing the same welcome they'd gotten from Colonel Gibbon on the trip west. They pulled the wagons up near the corrals and began to tend to the mules. White Dog rode up to where the wagons had stopped. He dismounted and stood watching Jubil tie Rocky off to a wagon.

"Jubilee Walker," said the scout. "White Dog leaves now."

"Thanks for helping us reach Fort Kearney," Jubil said.

The Indian nodded.

Jubil put his hand on the medicine bag. "And for the powerful medicine."

The Indian nodded again.

Jubil offered his hand, but instead of the handshake he expected, the scout grasped Jubil's forearm. Jubil grasped the scout's forearm in return.

"Jubilee Walker," said the scout, "friend."

The only moment Jubil had ever felt greater pride was the day his uncle had asked him to always defend his mother. Now, as then, he accepted White Dog's words with a nod. Then the scout mounted up, and Jubil watched as he rode away.

"Were you talking to that Indian?" said Biscuit. "I didn't know he could say more than two words."

"Yes," said Jubil. "He understands a lot more than you think, and he could say a lot more, too, except I don't think he enjoys hearing himself talk. I wish we could have said as much for Murphy."

Biscuit laughed.

"I've got to find the quartermaster," said Jubil, patting Rocky on the neck. "I reckon I'll have to give Rocky back to the army, but I'll miss him. I'm not all that anxious to ride on your wagon for two weeks."

"You get used to it," said Biscuit dismissively. "The quartermaster was in the stable a few minutes ago. I made arrangements to get Warner's other wagons back to him."

Jubil led the gray horse into the stable. The quartermaster said that the general's orders were that the horse was Jubil's until he was done with him, and suggested he return him to the army post in Council Bluffs. Jubil was very pleased with this arrangement.

The trail had toughened Jubil up, and he was making the return trip to Council Bluffs on horseback—two factors that made it far more pleasant for him than the trip out. But he slept better mainly because the chance of an Indian attack was now unlikely.

Evenings were simple and quiet now that the traveling party was reduced to Jubil and Biscuit. The anxiety of the unknown no longer dominated Jubil's consciousness, and as Council Bluffs drew nearer, he began to think more and more often of Nelly. They had been apart for nearly fifty days, longer than any period he could remember. He would never admit to her that there had been days along the trail when no thought of her or home had crossed his mind. The mind had a way of going numb to cope with the monotony, dread, and loneliness of the trek. He wondered if she had similarly put him out of her thoughts. He had written to her just before leaving Fort McPherson, to tell her of his travel plans and the estimated date he would return to Bloomington. But he worried about seeing her again, worried that his choice to be apart from her might have left her no choice but to learn to not need his company at all.

For two weeks they traveled across eastern Nebraska. At the western bank of the Missouri River, they loaded the team and wagon onto the steam-powered ferry and crossed the river into Iowa.

Then, finally, Jubil and Biscuit made their way up Lower Broadway and pulled the team and wagon up outside the storeroom entrance at Warner and Company Outfitters. Jubil had an odd sense of homecoming in a place that wasn't home.

"Welcome back, Jubil," said Luke heartily. "I'm sorry to see you didn't join your expedition, but I'm glad to see you! I'm anxious to hear your stories."

Jubil dismounted and shook hands with Luke. "It's good to see you too—and good to be back in Council Bluffs." His short residence there had been just long enough for him to develop a fondness for the place. After forty days of trail living, it would be the lap of luxury.

"You bought yourself a horse," Luke said, admiring Rocky as Jubil tethered him. "He's a sturdy fellow."

"This is Rocky," Jubil said patting the horse. "Rocky, this is Luke Warner, the best outfitter in these parts."

Rocky dropped his head and pawed the ground.

Mr. Warner stepped out of the storeroom and welcomed Jubil and Biscuit back to town. He and Luke were both looking around expectantly.

"Where are the other wagons?" Mr. Warner asked.

Jubil explained, and Biscuit apologized for not having been able to stop Murphy.

Mr. Warner sighed, and his forehead creased with displeasure. "No apologies needed," he said. "I imagine nothing short of violence would have stopped him, and it wasn't worth that. I had a feeling Murphy might be a bad apple, but he and the other Irishmen were recommended by someone I trusted. I'm glad you're both back safely." He handed Biscuit a packet containing his pay.

"Much obliged," Biscuit said. "You got a good man there in Walker. He's easy to ride with, a dab hand around camp, a crack shot hunter, and a cool head under fire. Good traveling with you, Walker." Biscuit tipped his hat.

"Under fire?" Luke asked as Biscuit drove his wagon off down the street.

"How about if you and Mr. Warner join me for supper tonight at the Ogden House, to properly repay your kindness?" Jubil said. "I'll tell you about my trip."

"That's mighty good of you, Jubil. How about you save your money and come to our house for supper instead? Mrs. Warner would love to meet you and hear about your adventures."

"It would be a pleasure," Jubil said. "I'm going to ride over to Mrs. Zeller's and see if she has a room available. What time should I come?"

"About seven o'clock," Mr. Warner said.

"I'm really anxious to hear more about Jubil's trip, Pa," Luke said. "If he doesn't mind, I'll tag along with him, then come back to pick you up when you close the store."

Luke came along to Mrs. Zeller's house in his surrey, and Jubil found she did have a room available. He unpacked and delivered some laundry to her, and then he joined Luke on the front porch, where he was sitting in one of two rocking chairs.

"Were you terribly disappointed," Luke asked, "that Powell did not invite you to continue on with him?"

"Yes," Jubil said, "but I wasn't surprised. People are not exaggerating when they say he doesn't change his mind. But he plans to mount another expedition next summer, and said he would consider me for that. I've had a good adventure this summer—especially for my first time ever being away from home."

Luke urged Jubil to recount every step of his trip and listened intently. Through each thread of his narrative, he coaxed out more details of Jubil's experience.

"You should ride with one of your supply trains yourself sometime," Jubil said.

"That's not likely to happen," Luke said flatly.

"Why not?" Jubil asked.

Luke hesitated. "It's a long story…"

Jubil waited for him to explain, but Luke changed the subject.

"What are you going to do once you return home?" Luke asked.

Jubil was curious about Luke's avoidance of the question, but it seemed rude to press him about it. "I'm not sure," he said. He mentioned the possibility of going to one of Bloomington's universities or finding a paying job.

"You could work here," Luke suggested. "You could go back to Bloomington and tell Powell you're moving to Council Bluffs to join us in the outfitting business. He'll be back here next summer. Maybe you can go along with him as his outfitter."

Jubil considered it. "That is a pretty good idea," he said, "but I'm not ready to move away from Bloomington yet. I have someone there who is special to me." He told Luke about Nelly and his hopes that they would someday be more than friends. "Do you have someone here like that?" Jubil asked.

Luke shook his head. "Just Ma and Pa," he replied without elaborating further.

Jubil's curiosity about Luke grew, but he did not want to pry. He enjoyed Luke's company a great deal and didn't understand why Luke, who was a few years older than Jubil, seemed to have no sweetheart and no other friends.

"It's too bad you don't have a store in Bloomington," Jubil said. "I'd be glad to work there. I never thought I'd like working in a store, but I like working in yours."

"I've actually thought about opening a new store somewhere else," Luke said. "But Pa and I haven't talked about it in detail. For most of my lifetime this town has been one of the best gateways to the West, and the only way to get there was overland. But when the railroad is completed, hardly anyone is going to go overland anymore, and the outfitting trade will dry up, except for outfitting men like Powell and Sherman. We're either going to have to adapt to that change or get used to a greatly reduced level of business."

Jubil thought about the discussion he and Biscuit had had on the subject of the transcontinental railroad. Where the impact on Biscuit was obvious, he had not made the broader connection to the outfitting business and the impact on the Warners.

"What will you do?" Jubil asked.

"We need to address the needs of travelers in the age of the transcontinental railroad," Luke said. "When people can move freely around the country, they will travel much more for pleasure and adventure. We could supply them with customized clothing and personal items much better suited for travel than what they would find in a dry goods store."

Luke's face lit up as he talked, and his enthusiasm was contagious. Jubil found himself eager to hear more.

"There will always be outdoor enthusiasts, hunters, fishermen, campers, and hikers," Luke continued, "and they will soon be able to travel to spots that were difficult to access before. We can supply them with outdoor goods that most other retailers don't carry at all."

Jubil thought about the single trapper's pack he was able to find after looking in all the other stores in Bloomington.

"As we lose volume on overland travel products," Luke explained, "we need to make it up in new styles of personal and outdoor travel items. But Pa has been reluctant to change the nature of our store. He would rather try out my ideas somewhere else, and if they work, then change over the Council Bluffs store."

"That all makes sense to me," Jubil said. "Why haven't you done it?"

"Well, there are several factors to consider," Luke explained. "We need a location that is accessible and vibrant, where a potential demand for our products exists, and we need a partner to manage it. The last one is the most difficult to find. I can help start the store up, but I can't run it myself. My parents need me here."

Jubil's curiosity was piqued once more by this comment. He thought Mr. Warner seemed perfectly capable of running his store, but there must be more to the story than that. His manners prevented him from probing for explanations.

"Bloomington would probably be a good spot," Jubil said. "It's a thriving community, has two universities, excellent rail access, affluent citizens, and it's located right in the heart of the country. I'd be glad to work in your store, but I can't run it."

"You shouldn't sell yourself short," Luke said. "I'll bet you could. You aren't the type to sit and wait for things to come your way—you go out and get things done. You're connected to travelers like Powell and Sherman. You're good-natured and likeable—and trustworthy. Biscuit liked you. And Pa's very impressed by your determination and hard work."

"Well thanks," said Jubil, embarrassed by the praise, "but I don't see how any of that qualifies me to run a store. You appear to be very good at it though. You should move to Bloomington and open a store, and I'll work for you."

Jubil's proposal seemed to drive Luke within himself. He looked away and stared into space, as Jubil listened to the squeak of their rocking chairs.

"I wouldn't feel right leaving my folks," Luke said with an air of resignation.

"Your Pa seems healthy and capable of running the store," Jubil offered gently, as an invitation to Luke to explain.

"He is," Luke agreed. "It's Ma that I'm most concerned for. I don't want to burden you with my family situation, but since our conversation has come to it, I'll explain if you want to hear."

"I would," Jubil nodded.

Luke sighed. "I once had a brother named Samuel," he began. "He was three years younger than me, the same age as you are. When he was six years old, he came down with the chickenpox, and it was toxic to his system. He passed away. It was difficult for all of us, but my ma took it especially hard. She was bedridden for months, and for several years afterward, she needed constant care. Pa had to run the store, and I tended to her the best I could, but thankfully we were able to hire good help. Over the years her mental state has improved, and today she seems fine, but I've never felt able to leave her side, or my father's."

Jubil felt an empathetic wave of longing. "I am probably even less qualified to give advice than I am to run a store," he said, "but I have some sympathy for your feelings. Even after my mother passed away, I was still hesitant to give up farming, out of respect for what they left me. But I knew I'd regret it if I didn't follow my heart, and I believe they would agree. I found a compromise by keeping the farm, even though I'm not there to work it, and setting off on my own adventure. I'm not sure what I'll do next, but I feel I'm on the right track. Maybe you could find your own sort of compromise. Maybe you could talk to your ma and see what she thinks about you trying your new store. You can promise her that you'll move back here if things don't work out—for her or for you."

Luke seemed to carefully consider Jubil's suggestion. "Maybe I could do that. . . ." he said. "If I open a store in Bloomington, you'll help me?"

"I will," Jubil said with conviction. "It would be beneficial for both of us."

"Yes, it just might be," Luke said. "After supper we'll talk to Pa about the idea. If he's in favor, we'll talk to Ma. I have one more thing to ask of you though. Please don't mention my brother, Sam, this evening—or ever, for that matter. For years after his death, every mention of his name would send Ma back into despair, so we just don't talk about him anymore."

"All right, I understand," Jubil said.

Luke left in high spirits, and Jubil asked Mrs. Zeller to heat his bathwater and made himself ready for the evening. As he bathed, he pondered what Luke had said about Samuel. Jubil had insisted that he understood that he shouldn't say Samuel's name around Mr. and Mrs. Warner, but he really didn't understand—not fully, anyway. It seemed so sad that they had given up talking about someone dear to them as though he had never existed.

Jubil rode Rocky to the northern edge of town, where a huge two-story Victorian house with two rounded turrets sat atop a hill. Jubil could not imagine what all the rooms in a house that size could be used for. He had understood that the Warner family was financially well off, but the wealth suggested by their house was beyond what he had imagined.

As he rode under the portico, a man greeted him.

"Good evening. I am Mr. Garcia," he said. "I will take your horse to the stable."

Jubil, suddenly nervous, hesitated after handing Rocky's

reins to Mr. Garcia, and the other man gestured toward the front door. Jubil's uneasiness fell away when Luke greeted him at the door, although, in the grand foyer, Jubil had to remind himself not to gawk.

Mr. Warner and Mrs. Warner came to greet them. She was a regal, matronly woman, tall and thin, with salt-and-pepper hair pinned up in a neat pile, pale green eyes, and a faint smile that gave her a wistful air.

"Jubil," Luke said, "I'd like you to meet my ma." Luke's use of *Ma* and *Pa* to refer to his parents struck Jubil as a bit rustic for their station, but he liked it.

"How do you do, Mr. Walker?" Mrs. Warner said. "Welcome to our home. I understand you've been on quite an adventure."

Mrs. Warner was warm and friendly, and Jubil could discern no sign of emotional instability. He detected a slight accent to her speech—she flattened his name to *Wahkuh* and said *advencha*—maybe from an eastern state. He was surprised by how at ease he felt with the Warner family. They sat down for supper right away, which was served by their domestic helper, Mrs. Garcia, the wife of the man Jubil had met outside. Luke said that Mr. Garcia was their stableman and groundskeeper.

"I'm sure it was a disappointment not to go on with Powell," sympathized Mr. Warner. "But was your trip worthwhile?"

"It was," said Jubil, without hesitation, "though there was a fair amount of unpleasantness along the way. I feel like I got my first lesson in understanding my uncle Pete's life philosophy. When he told me stories of his travels, he always had the attitude that the journey itself is the heart of the trip, maybe even more important than the destination."

"That is an excellent perspective," said Mr. Warner.

"We should use an idea like that in our advertising, Pa," Luke said. "Warner and Company Outfitters: The Journey Is the Destination."

Jubil and Mr. Warner laughed.

"It does sound good," Mr. Warner said.

Jubil recounted his trip as they had supper. Mr. Warner and Luke were interested in how all the gear had performed, and they wanted Jubil to suggest any changes that would lead to better products. Mrs. Warner took note of the buckskin pouch he wore, and Jubil told them about White Dog and the Indian raid. He shared both his feelings of irritation about the soldiers belittling someone who was helping them and his concerns over the government's broader mistreatment of the Indians, which brought their conversation to a pensive lull. He mentioned the scene he had encountered on the way back but avoided any of the grisly details. He did not like bringing those memories to mind and chance them returning to his dreams.

"I'm sorry if I've talked your ears off," Jubil apologized.

"I've thoroughly enjoyed your stories," said Mrs. Warner. "What a remarkable trip. You are lucky to be alive."

"Now that you're on your way home," Mr. Warner said, "what are your plans for the future?"

"I've decided to keep my family's farm for now, though I'm not interested in farming," Jubil explained. "Major Powell is going on another expedition next summer, and I want to be on it, but I also need to find a way to make an income."

"If you are not too attached to Bloomington," said Mr. Warner, "there's a job waiting for you at Warner and Company Outfitters any time you want it."

Jubil told them about Nelly. "As far as being attached to Bloomington," he said, "it's not so much the town I'm attached to as it is Nelly."

"You must tell your Nelly," Mrs. Warner said, "that we would love for her and her family to come visit us. I would enjoy that very much."

"I'll be sure to tell her, ma'am. She'll be very excited by the invitation. As far as the job offer goes, I really appreciate it," said Jubil. "If Warner and Company Outfitters had a store in Bloomington, I would truly enjoy working there."

Luke was sipping from his water glass as Jubil spoke, and he choked at Jubil's comment. Jubil grinned as he and Luke exchanged a glance. Mr. Warner stopped drinking his coffee and slowly put his coffee cup down. He looked at Luke and then looked at Jubil.

"Would you really?" he asked carefully.

"Well, sure," said Jubil with a grin.

"Lily," Mr. Warner said as he folded his napkin and put it on the table, "would you mind if the boys and I retire to my office to talk business?"

"That's fine, dear," Mrs. Warner said. "I'll just give Rosie a hand cleaning up." She stood from the table and patted Jubil on the shoulder. "It was a pleasure meeting you, Jubil. When you are in town again, you must stay here with us."

"Thank you, ma'am," Jubil replied. "It was pleasure meeting you." He had to catch himself to keep from reaching for her hand. With a pang, he realized that he was missing his mother's embrace something fierce.

Mr. Warner's office occupied the turret on the west corner of the house. Jubil marveled at the spectacular view of the area afforded by the windows there. He did not recall ever having experienced such an expansive view. The prairie of Illinois offered long flat vistas, but nothing like this. From this vantage point the whole city of Council Bluffs was spread out below him. To the right he could see the lush Missouri River valley stretch for miles, and to his left was the row of bluffs that gave the town its name. It made him wonder what the world would look like from atop one of the Rocky Mountains. When he was able to pull his gaze away from the view, Jubil saw that the office was a combination of museum and library. The built-in shelves displayed carvings, weavings, pottery, paintings, weapons, model wagons and ships, and row upon row of books. A huge desk sat away from the windows, and in front of it was a circle of comfortable chairs and side tables.

"I could give you a short tour," said Mr. Warner, "but to tell the story behind every piece in my collection would take days. Some of these things Luke or I collected, but many were given to me by clients. They are my treasures."

"I could not be more impressed," said Jubil sincerely.

"Thank you," said Mr. Warner. "Have a seat."

Mr. Warner poured a whiskey for himself and Luke, and he offered Jubil a glass. Jubil had never been offered liquor. His father had never touched it, and as far as Jubil knew, Pete only had a beer now and then. He had no real curiosity about it, so he asked for water instead. Mr. Warner took a chair across from Jubil and Luke.

"Welcome back from your adventure," Mr. Warner said, raising his glass in a toast to Jubil. "May it be the first of many successful ones for you."

Luke smiled and raised his glass.

"Thank you, sir," Jubil said, "I hope so too."

"I took an interest in your comment about opening a store in Bloomington," Mr. Warner said, looking knowingly at Jubil and Luke. "Luke and I have speculated about doing such a thing but never pursued the notion. We felt we'd need someone to run it for us, and we haven't done the work of looking for a reliable partner. It's quite a coincidence you would suggest it."

"Not really, Pa," Luke said with a grin, "since Jubil and I talked about the idea this afternoon. I told him our thinking about a new store, and about selecting a location and a partner."

"Good," Mr. Warner said, looking at Jubil. "Then you're interested in becoming our new partner? Running a Warner and Company Outfitters for us in Bloomington?"

"Well, I—" Jubil began.

"I'm going to do it, Pa," Luke interrupted. "I'm going to

move to Bloomington, and Jubil and I are going to run the store together."

Mr. Warner looked surprised. He sat spinning the whiskey in his glass as he looked back and forth between Luke and Jubil. He took a sip.

"You're sure you want to do this?" Mr. Warner asked Luke.

"I am," Luke said, nodding assuredly. "I can always come back home if it doesn't work out, or if you and Ma need me here. If you approve of the idea, I'll go talk to Ma."

Jubil waited for the conversation to turn to concern for Luke's mother, but it did not. Mr. Warner knocked back the rest of his whiskey and set the empty glass on the table. "I think it's a wonderful idea," he said finally. "I'm proud of you, Luke. I'm proud of both of you. I think you should call your new store Warner and Walker Outfitters. We should use your name, Jubil, because it's familiar to people in Bloomington."

"I like that idea," Luke said. "I think Pa's right, Jubil."

Somewhat nonplussed by the whole affair, Jubil was still agreeable. "I suppose if you want to, that's fine by me. It makes me sound loftier than I'll feel though. Hard for me to see myself as a store owner, and I'm not sure I can afford the investment."

"You don't need to risk your savings," Mr. Warner said. "We'll pay you a salary for the time being. If the store is successful, we'll reconsider our arrangement."

"That sounds fair, but I do have one other concern," Jubil admitted. "I hope to be part of Major Powell's next expedition, and any others I have a chance at. Does that change your thinking?"

"Not mine," Luke said. "I think your expeditions will be good for business."

Mr. Warner considered for a moment and replied, "If we outfit your expeditions, then we should continue to pay your salary. We'll call you our field representative. Luke can hire help to cover for your absence in the store, assuming it is doing well enough. If it's not, then we've got a bigger issue."

"Even if Ma is amenable to the plan, I'll have to stay in Council Bluffs until Pa finds a replacement for me," said Luke. "In the meantime, I'll get her prepared for the idea."

Jubil and Luke shook hands with Mr. Warner and left him pouring himself another glass of whiskey.

"That went well," Luke said as they left the study. "It was so much easier than I thought it might be to take such a step. Once you and I started talking about it, I just felt everything fall into place. I hope Ma feels similarly. It's early yet; she's probably in her studio."

Luke led Jubil through the foyer to the east turret and in through the open door, beckoning Jubil to join him.

"Ma," he said, "do you mind if Jubil and I interrupt you for a few minutes?"

Just like Mr. Warner's office, Mrs. Warner's studio had a stunning view. She was standing at an easel that had been set up near the windows. The fine clothing that she had worn earlier had been exchanged for a cotton dress, a well-used painter's smock, and flat shoes. Around the room were tables of art supplies and crafting tools of every sort. The aroma of oil paint, brush solvent, and glue perfumed the air.

"I don't mind in the least," Mrs. Warner said, stepping back from the painting she was working on and placing her brush in the solvent jar. "I was about to quit for this evening anyway. My light is fading."

Jubil and Luke joined Mrs. Warner at her easel. The painting was a landscape of a lighthouse—a white tower with a wide band of red around its middle—that sat on the edge of a brushy bluff facing a calm expanse of ocean. Jubil was admittedly no judge of art, but the work looked remarkably good to him.

"Sankaty Head Lighthouse, on the eastern coast of Nantucket island," Luke said to Jubil. "That's where Ma is from, and we still have family there. Beautiful work, Ma."

That explained her accent, Jubil thought—New England.

"Thank you, dear," Mrs. Warner said, cleaning her brush on a towel. "If you are going to be staying in town longer, Jubil, you should come stay with us here. It's a pleasure having you around."

"The pleasure is all mine, ma'am," Jubil said. "Thank you, but I'm heading home in the morning. I'm anxious to get back."

"Yes," Mrs. Warner said with a slight smile. "I imagine you are."

"Before Jubil goes home," Luke said, "there is something I need to tell you...or ask you ...or explain..."

"What is it, dear?" Mrs. Warner said, looking concerned. "You seem flustered. Let's have a seat."

"Luke, I think I'll wait for you in the parlor," Jubil said, deciding his presence would make things awkward, especially if Mrs. Warner reacted emotionally.

Luke looked surprised, but then nodded his assent. "We won't be long."

Jubil left the studio and took a seat in the parlor. He hoped the plan would not trigger an emotional problem for Mrs. Warner. After a few minutes, Luke and his mother came to find him.

"Luke has told me of your plan. I think it is a grand idea," Mrs. Warner said to Jubil, sounding very impressed and happy. "I'm very proud of both of you." She smiled at him.

Luke took his mother's hand. "Once Pa has hired someone to replace me, we'll get on with the plan."

Jubil and Luke remained with Mrs. Warner for a while, talking about the future. To Jubil's relief, there was no mention of, or sign of concern over, anything that had occurred in the past.

Jubil left the next morning on a train bound for Chicago. He bid Rocky a fond farewell, leaving him in the custody of the Warners, who promised to take him around to the army offices and relinquish him.

If someone had asked him before he left Bloomington whether he had any interest in being a storekeeper, he would have answered with an emphatic *no, sir*, but the store Luke described was unlike any he had ever imagined. In fact, it would be unlike anything in Bloomington or Normal, and it would bear his name. He thought about how proud he would be if the venture succeeded and how humiliated he would be if it did not—especially if its failure were due to his own short-comings as a businessman. He wondered how Nelly would feel about the plan.

CHAPTER 9

The Chicago and Alton Express rolled in to Bloomington in the early afternoon of Saturday, July 13, Jubil's eighteenth birthday. He sat holding his pack, anxious to make a hasty exit. As the train pulled into the depot, he saw Star saddled and ready to ride, hitched to the back of a carriage pulled by the Boswells' horse, Moses. The train pulled to a stop, and Jubil spotted Nelly and her father waiting on the platform. She was clutching a handkerchief and dabbing her eyes, which he found odd. Nelly wasn't someone who cried at the drop of a hat. Jubil found it hard to believe she would be crying because she was so happy that he was coming home. He shouldered his pack and stepped onto the platform. He was several cars down from where the Boswells stood. Nelly saw him and waved.

Mr. Boswell stepped out to shake his hand. "Welcome home, Jubil."

Mr. Boswell's stern demeanor gave him an uneasy feeling. He did not seem at all happy to see him. Nelly displayed a weak smile through her tears.

"It's good to see you, Nelly," Jubil said, reaching to shake her hand, "and good to be home. Why are you crying?"

"Jubil," Mr. Boswell said, "I'm sorry to ruin your homecoming, but we can't pretend everything is fine. I'll just come right out with it. There has been an accident at the farm. There was a fire . . . the farmhouse and the barn . . . well, they've burned down."

Nelly put her face in her hands and sobbed.

Jubil was stunned into silence. In his mind's eye, he watched as the farmhouse and the barn went up in flames. It was a moment before he could form a coherent thought.

"Was anyone hurt?" he asked.

"No," Mr. Boswell replied.

"What happened?" Jubil asked tersely.

Mr. Boswell looked at Nelly as she struggled to regain her composure. "It was Eli and Ike," he said. "They were rough-housing and . . . Nelly and her mother were there when it happened. Are you up to explaining it to him, Nell?"

Nelly's crystal blue eyes looked into Jubil's, and the pain there was hard for him to take.

"Mama and the boys put in a garden at the farm, like we talked about," she said. "We went up last week to weed and water, as we've been doing, and Eli said we should check the root cellar. He went into the house for a lantern to take down there with him, and then he and Ike got into an argument about who would carry it. They started tussling, and before Mama or I could stop them, the lantern fell and broke. Burning oil spread everywhere, and things caught fire so fast, we couldn't stop it. The boys tried carrying water from the animal trough and the well, but the smoke got too thick, and Mama wouldn't let them go back in. The farmhouse started blazing, and embers blew over to the hayloft. We couldn't do anything to stop it. I'm so sorry, Jubil. Those stupid boys!"

Jubil felt his face flush and his fists clench. His empathy for Nelly was overwhelmed by his anger at her brothers, who had taken something irreplaceable from him. He remembered the numerous pranks they had pulled in school—putting a toad in a girl's desk, letting a garter snake loose inside the schoolhouse, hiding a dead mouse in the teacher's desk that was not discovered until it began to reek. Once, they chained their father's wagon axle to a tree, thinking it would be funny to see him pull away and be stopped in his tracks. There was no humor in the situation when the wagon axle broke and the wheels fell off. The rear of the wagon collapsed, dumping the load of hay on the ground and causing their father to fall backward off the seat. Mr. Boswell had let them have it good for that one. Jubil wanted to let them have it for this as well. He was glad they had not come to the station to confess, or he might not have been able to control his temper.

"What about the cabin?" he asked.

"It was untouched by the fire," Nelly said. "The wind was blowing away from it."

"I am sorry for the loss my boys caused," Mr. Boswell said. "There is no excusing that kind of carelessness. I want you to know, I'll pay for the loss of your home."

"Thank you," said Jubil, "but it shouldn't be you that pays for it. Those boys need to see some consequences, but I'm too angry right now to think straight. I want to get home and see what's left. I'll consider what to do with them once I calm down."

"Please, Jubil," Nelly pleaded, "don't hate them. You're right to be mad at them, but it would break my heart to lose my best friend because of my idiot brothers." She started to tear up again.

"I don't hate them," Jubil assured her, "and nothing they do will ever change how I feel about you." Jubil watched for Nelly's reaction to his promise, and she gave him a weak smile.

"I'm sorry to bring you such bad news on your birthday," Nelly said as she looked at her feet. "I know it sounds ridiculous, but happy birthday."

Jubil gave her a half smile. "Thanks."

"I brought Star along," Mr. Boswell said. "I thought you would want to ride straight to the farm."

"Thank you," Jubil said.

"You could come to dinner tomorrow," Nelly offered meekly. "We could celebrate your birthday and hear about your trip."

Jubil thought a moment. "Thanks," he said, "that's very thoughtful. I'm sure you'll understand when I say I'm not sure I'll be up to it yet."

Nelly nodded and wiped her eyes again. Jubil hefted his pack and went to fetch Star. When his horse saw him coming, she pranced and whinnied.

"Hello, girl," Jubil purred at the horse as he patted her neck and rubbed her cheeks. "I missed you, too." He lashed his pack across Star's haunches and set out for the farm.

When they arrived, the scene was bleak. All that remained of the farmhouse was the stone fireplace and pieces of the walls on either side of it. Charred timbers from the burned walls and ceiling lay in heaps on the foundation stones, and among them Jubil could make out the blackened lump that had been the kitchen stove. The barn was only partially burned. The wind must have been blowing from the southwest, because there was nothing left of the north or east walls. The front and the side nearest the house were burned halfway to the ground. The plow and other tools in the barn were blackened remains, and half the corral fence had burned to cinders.

Jubil walked into the ashes of the farmhouse and thought about the effort his father had put into building it. Here was where the front porch had been and on it a rocking chair Uncle Pete had made. Over here was where the kitchen table had sat, the one his family gathered around for meals, back when he still had a family. Here were the charred remains of the ladder that had led up to the loft where he had slept and read about the world off the farm and dreamed of seeing it. There, in that corner, had been his parents' bed, the one he had been born in, the bed that became his mother's alone when his father died, and the one in which she died. It was all gone. Jubil saw there was nothing left but dirt and rubble, and he cried.

In the morning he got up hungry. Star was where he had left her the previous night, grazing in the grass beside the cabin. In his haste, he had left town without eating, and there was no food in the cabin. He was going to have to ride back to town to get groceries.

Any thoughts he had now about selling the farm were going to have to be considered in a new light. The land itself had value, of course, but a farm without a farmhouse and barn would be harder to sell and would certainly sell for less. Even though Mr. Warner had said Jubil did not need to make an investment in the new outfitting store at this time, he had been entertaining the idea. Thinking about his capital loss led him to the germ of an idea as to how the boys could make restitution.

He saddled Star and rode back into town, where he stopped at Mr. Weed's realty office. Mr. Weed confirmed Jubil's suspicions about the value and salability of the farm after the fire and gave him an estimate of the damages. Armed with this information, a plan for the boys, and a cooler temper, Jubil rode to the Boswells' house, where Mr. Boswell answered the door.

"Jubil!" Mr. Boswell said. "I'm happy to see you so soon. Would you like to come in?"

"Yes, sir," Jubil said, stepping inside and greeting Mrs. Boswell. "I have a proposition for the boys I'd like to share with you and with them. Are they here?"

"They're here, all right," Mrs. Boswell said. "I'll fetch them."

She went up the staircase as Nelly was coming down. "Hello, Jubil," she said, smiling at him. "Happy birthday."

"Thank you," he said.

She took his arm, and the two of them followed Mr. Boswell into the parlor.

Mrs. Boswell herded the twins down the stairs and into the room. Ike and Eli stood in front of Jubil, looking down at their shoes—Ike's neatly polished, Eli's scuffed and dirty.

"Hello, boys," said Jubil. He could see how bad they felt. He was feeling less angry about what had happened and was seeing the possibility that some good might come out of the situation, so he felt obliged to tease them. "I have Indian stories to tell from my adventures," he said.

The twins snapped to attention and stared open-mouthed at him.

"But I'll get to that later. Right now, I'm here to give you a piece of my mind," Jubil lectured, allowing his aggravation to show, but not raising his voice. "You two caused a lot of damage at my farm. Even if I was able to rebuild the farmhouse and the barn, they would never be the same. My parents built that farmhouse and that barn with their own hands. My parents are gone, and now those buildings, and all the things inside them that belonged to my parents, are gone. They can never be replaced."

Eli looked up sheepishly at Jubil without raising his head. Ike wiped his eyes. Eli was the first to speak, "We really are sorry, Jubil."

Ike nodded and wiped his nose on his sleeve.

"I appreciate that," Jubil said. "But there is also a dollar value lost, which is a fair amount of money. I have a plan for how you boys can repay that loss."

Jubil explained how the Warners had befriended him in Council Bluffs. "The Warners want to open a store in Bloomington," Jubil said, "and they want me to help run it."

Nelly's eyes widened.

"Well, that is wonderful news," Mr. Boswell said.

"And you want to do this?" Nelly asked, with a hint of disbelief in her smile.

"I do," he answered. "I like the Warners, and I like the out-fitting business . . . well, what I know of it anyway. I said I'd help get it started. Which brings me to my plan," Jubil said, addressing the twins, "for you to make good on your debt."

The boys looked warily at him.

"Whatever sort of help is needed to get this store up and running, I'd say you boys owe me labor that would amount to one thousand dollars."

The boys' eyes bugged out at the mention of such a huge sum.

"I figure if you work for Warner and Walker Outfitters until your eighteenth birthdays, we'll call your debt paid."

Ike and Eli locked eyes with one another, and Jubil watched as they seemed to have an eerie silent conversation. Simultaneously, they turned to him and nodded their agreement.

Mr. and Mrs. Boswell and Nelly were practically beaming at him by this point. Mr. and Mrs. Boswell voiced their approval of the plan and then sent the boys to do some chores while Jubil and Nelly retired to the front porch, where Jubil gave Nelly a full accounting of his adventures. He did not—and thought he never would—tell her about the scalping incident. He could not bring himself to tell that story to anyone. He wished he could forget it himself.

"You seem to have omitted a few details in your letters," Nelly observed, "specifically the parts where you had to fight for your life."

"I didn't see any reason to worry you," he said. "It all turned out fine."

"Hmm . . . so you did almost get yourself killed out there," Nelly said, "twice."

"Really only once," Jubil said. "The thief in Chicago was drunk."

Nelly sighed and shook her head.

"I want to be honest with you," Jubil said. "Store or no store, I'm going to Colorado with Powell next summer . . . if I can."

"I'm not surprised," she said flatly.

Jubil searched her face for a sign that his adventuring was something she could live with, that she wouldn't turn away from him because of it. But the expression on her face was uncharacteristically reserved and difficult to read.

Jubil spent the rest of July and August working around the farm. He wished he still had Max, whose help would have made it easier to pull down the barn, but he did not want to borrow him and then let him go again. He persuaded Star to work in the harness, and they pulled the good boards off the burned structure. Then he sawed down the barn's remaining frame posts and trimmed off the burnt ends. He pulled out some foundation stones around the remains of the farmhouse and cleared a path to clean the rubble and ash out of the interior. He dragged any half-burnt timbers into a pile and burned them to ash, then fashioned a wooden blade that he hitched to Star and used to drag the ashes out from the house interior and spread them around the yard, to dissipate in the rain.

He used the reclaimed barn posts to frame up a new stable, and he used reclaimed barn planks for the roofing and siding. He was pleased with the results of his efforts: two horse stalls, a tack rack, a feed storage area, space for the wagon, and the blackened kitchen stove he had salvaged from the farmhouse. He had to cut a few trees to build a new corral. When he was finished, the only evidence of the house and barn were the lonesome chimney and the foundation stones, which he would leave as a monument to his family and a starting point in case he ever decided to rebuild. Perhaps he had exaggerated by telling Eli and Ike that all traces of his family were gone. It was still the Walker place, just a new version of it.

By the time Luke arrived at the beginning of September, Jubil had arranged an appointment with Mr. Weed, the real estate agent, to see a possible location for the new store. It was a residence, however, not a storefront, and it was for sale, not for rent, but the location was good. It was on Center Street, between Front and Grove, one block south of Ferre's carriage shop.

The building was a square two-story box, with tall windows all around. A covered front porch sheltered the door. Not an attractive house, to Jubil's eye, but as a business it might be fine. He tried to picture a sign mounted over the front door: Warner and Walker Outfitters.

"So no one will mind if I convert the house to a business?" Luke asked Mr. Weed.

"I would expect not," said Mr. Weed. "A neighbor, Mr. Wilmeth, converted his house to a confectionery, and I never heard any fuss about that."

That day, Luke made arrangements to buy the place.

When remodeling began, Jubil and Luke joined in the effort, under the supervision of a carpenter recommended by Mr. Boswell. They took out the walls and opened up the space, except on the second floor, where Luke would have an apartment in the front quarter of the building. Jubil enlisted Eli and Ike to fetch, hold, lift, carry, and clean up.

The Boswells welcomed Luke warmly to Bloomington, and he and Jubil were present at Eli and Ike's fifteenth birthday party in October. During supper, Eli delivered a speech.

"Me and Ike have been talking about our arrangement at the store," Eli directed his gaze to Jubil, "to pay off our debt to you. The original deal called for us working for no wages until our eighteenth birthday, but we can pay off the thousand dollars by our seventeenth birthday."

"Oh, is that so?" Jubil said with surprise. "And how do you figure that?"

Eli looked at Ike. Ike pulled a folded piece of paper from his pocket and opened it on the table beside him. "I've got some figures that make our case." Ike presented his assumptions about the number of hours he expected he and Eli would work per year and the value of an hour's work. "So, you see, based on these projections, it takes two years, not three, to repay our thousand-dollar debt." Ike offered Jubil the paper with his figures on it.

Jubil took the paper and studied the neatly written figures. His own three-year payment terms had not been based on any specific information, as Eli and Ike's had. He looked at Luke and Nelly. They sat poker-faced, waiting for his reaction.

"You make a decent case, boys," Jubil said, hiding his amusement. "If you actually work that many hours, and Luke and I get some value from every hour . . . you've got a deal."

"I'll track our hours carefully," Ike promised.

The boys had worked hard, and without complaint, to get the store ready to open. Jubil's concern now was the success of the store. He needed the income, and his pride was at stake.

CHAPTER 10

Before the Bloomington store could open in December, Luke had to return to Council Bluffs to make final preparations with his father. While he was gone, Jubil looked up Lew Keplinger at Mrs. Norris's boarding house on Graham Street. Jubil wanted to know everything about the Colorado expedition, but Lew's answer was disappointing.

"I don't think you missed all that much," he said.

"How can that be?" Jubil asked. He couldn't deny that he had spent a few nights since returning from Nebraska wondering with envy what adventures Lew and the major were having.

"Well, I suppose if you've never seen the Rocky Mountains, you missed something," Lew qualified. "Or if you are interested in every bird, critter, or rock under the sun, you missed something. If you were hoping for adventure, it was a bust. We started out in Denver, but we didn't stay there long. The passes to Middle Park were snowed in, and that's where the major really wanted to go. Longs Peak is there, one of the tallest unclimbed mountains in the Rockies. Powell's got his eye on climbing it, and I want in on that."

"We ended up going south to Pikes Peak, which has been climbed many times. Then we went up Mount Lincoln. All along the way, the party was collecting every manner of thing, and the wagons got so loaded down it was nearly impossible to get them through the mountains. It was a whole lot of hard work and no adventure. Not my idea of adventure, anyway. Yours either, I'm guessing."

"Sounds like the major got what he went for though," said Jubil. He couldn't decide how to feel about what Lew was telling him. He had been feeling regretful about not going along to Colorado, but now it seemed he should be feeling relieved. He remembered riding the wagon train across the dusty prairie and wondered how many adventures would end up being more tedious than exciting.

"He did," agreed Lew. "Scientifically, it was a success. Lord knows how the major will get the specimens back to Illinois."

"The major hasn't come back yet?" asked Jubil.

"From Mount Lincoln, we went back to Denver, where the party disbanded," Lew said. "I came back here, and Major and Mrs. Powell stayed in Denver. The major was set on somehow making his way to Middle Park."

"When will he be back in Bloomington?" asked Jubil.

Lew shrugged.

Jubil wanted Powell to know about his new store. He hoped it would improve his chance of joining Powell's next expedition. For a moment, he thought of writing him, but then thought better of it.

Lew rode out with Jubil to visit the farm, where he soberly toured the site of the farmhouse and barn while Jubil told him what had happened. He brightened when he saw the cabin and enjoyed hearing stories of how Uncle Pete and the major had explored together in their youth. And he was delighted to hear about the grand opening of Warner and Walker Outfitters in December and vowed to be there.

Mr. Boswell made the sign for the store at the carriage shop: "Warner and Walker Outfitters," it said, and then, in smaller letters underneath, "The Journey Is the Destination." As two workers hammered it up on the front of the store, Luke showed Jubil the front page of the *Daily Pantagraph*, where he had placed an ad that would run all week announcing the store opening.

On the morning of December 11, Luke Warner turned to address his staff: Jubil, Eli, and Ike, who would work the sales floor and keep the shelves stocked while Luke handled the cash sales and accounting for the store. The boys were well-groomed for the occasion, which was not unusual for Ike but was for Eli.

"We've done it, fellows," Luke said. "As fine a store as I've ever seen, and I appreciate all the hard work you've done to make it happen."

They had stocked the shelves on the main floor with clothing and accessories. The travel clothing section included men's and women's clothing and outerwear—some lightweight and some rugged—meant for all sorts of travel. In the section for harsh weather gear, their stock included everything from slickers to fur-lined boots. Among the personal travel aides, they included trunks, valises, shoulder bags, handbags, and small carrying cases. The second floor was devoted to sporting goods: guns, knives, and fishing and camping gear.

Luke turned the sign on the front door from Closed to Open, and, as though on cue, Mr. and Mrs. Boswell and Nelly pulled up in their wagon, followed by Mr. and Mrs. Warner. Everyone congratulated Jubil and Luke effusively, and Jubil could tell they were impressed with the store.

Their grand opening happened to coincide with Nelly's seventeenth birthday, and Jubil shook her hand and wished her many happy returns. He had considered buying her a gift, but they had never before exchanged gifts on their birthdays. He thought she looked especially pretty in a blue dress that set off her eyes, but he didn't have the nerve to tell her so.

Just then, Mrs. Boswell approached and said to Jubil, "I baked some cookies in honor of Nelly's birthday and your grand opening. They're on trays in the carriage. Would you bring them in please, Jubil?"

Jubil stepped out of the store and encountered Lew Keplinger on the sidewalk. He recruited Lew to help carry the platters.

"I found a friend outside and put him to work," he said as they came back into the store. "This is Lew Keplinger. We met in Council Bluffs. He was one of Major Powell's students on the Colorado expedition this summer. Lew's the one who introduced me to General Sherman."

"How do you do, ma'am?" Lew said to Mrs. Boswell. He turned to Nelly. "Happy birthday, Miss Boswell."

Nelly gave a little curtsy. When she looked up at Lew, Jubil was surprised to see she was blushing. He was struck by a flash of jealousy. Did Nelly fancy Lew? Lew knew how Jubil felt about Nelly. Jubil had been more candid with Lew about how he felt than he had been with Nelly herself. Perhaps he should stop assuming Nelly also felt their friendship growing into something more, and tell her exactly how he felt, before someone else stole her away.

"Let me show you around, Mr. Keplinger," said Luke, leading Lew farther into the store.

"Your friend is quite a gentleman, Jubil," said Mrs. Boswell, "and a very handsome young man too. Don't you agree, Nelly?"

"Oh, Mama," said Nelly, her color rising even more.

Jubil suppressed a feeling of desperation. Mrs. Boswell obviously viewed him more as Nelly's brother than a potential suitor, or she wouldn't have said such a thing in front of him. Maybe that was how Nelly felt too. He needed to clarify this issue with Nelly as soon as possible.

The Boswells, the Warners, and Lew Keplinger toured the store to their satisfaction and were clustered about the entrance, intent on leaving, when Major Powell came in.

"Major!" Jubil exclaimed. "What a pleasant surprise."

"Hello, Jubil. Congratulations on the store," said Major Powell, looking around. "Emma saw your advertisement in the *Pantagraph*. She sends her regrets. She wants you to know she will be in soon. I'm duly impressed."

"Thank you, sir," said Jubil.

The Warners and Boswells exchanged pleasantries with Powell and briefly chatted about his recent expedition, and then Powell turned his attention to Lew.

"Lieutenant Keplinger," said Powell. "Doing some shopping?"

"Hello, Major," said Lew. "Welcome back to Bloomington. I just came to congratulate my friend and his partner on their new store. You know, Jubil might be a handy gent to know, if a fellow was ever planning a big trip that needed outfitting." He turned his face toward Jubil so that Powell could not see, and he crooked an eyebrow at him. "Good day, Major," he said, tipping his hat mischievously.

"Good day, Lieutenant," said Powell, giving Lew a knowing look.

"Thanks for coming, Lew," said Jubil, grinning at his friend. The Boswells and the Warners followed Lew out of the store.

"I must say," said Powell. "You've quickly gone from being at loose ends to this."

"I can't take much credit," Jubil said. "This store is a lot more Warner than it is Walker. Luke and his father have been thinking about doing something like this for some time. I just happened to come along at the right moment. Would you like to look around the store?"

"I would," Powell replied. "Lead the way."

"The first thing you will notice," Jubil explained, as they walked around the main floor of the store, "is that this store does not look much like the Warner and Company Outfitters in Council Bluffs. This one is an experiment in adjusting to the changing outfitter marketplace that will result from the completion of the transcontinental railroad. It has none of the overland transportation goods and equipment. It focuses on personal products for business, leisure, and adventure travelers."

Powell slowly nodded. "I must admit, for all the times I've thought of the impact of the railroad, I have never considered the impact it will have on the outfitter business. So does this mean Warner will be closing his store in Council Bluffs?"

"No, sir," said Jubil. "That store will transition to offer more products like those you find here, but it will also offer the same products as always for those in the market for them."

"I see," said Powell. "So, I could order some things from you here, but other things I would have to go to Council Bluffs to get?"

"Not exactly, sir," said Jubil. "You could order everything here and pick it up here, if that's what you wanted. We would have your order shipped here. Or you could order it all here and pick it all up in Council Bluffs."

Powell looked around the store. "What would best suit my needs would be to order everything here and pick it up in Cheyenne, Wyoming. The railroad is now complete all the way to Cheyenne. It took Emma and me forty days to get to Colorado, and it took us four days to get home by train."

"Luke Warner mentioned the railroad's progress to me recently," Jubil said, his mind racing. As nonchalantly as he could, he said, "We could do that for you—take your order here and have it waiting for you in Cheyenne."

"You could?" Powell said, surprised.

Jubil wasn't sure if what he was saying was true, but the idea had proven an irresistible challenge. "Yes, sir," he said. "If you provide a manifest of your needs, I'll arrange to get everything and have it waiting for you wherever you want it." With each new promise Jubil made, he felt his heart beat faster. He had only a vague notion of how he could do these things, but between him and the Warners, surely they would find a way.

"Wouldn't the shipping be costly?" asked Powell.

"We would do all we could to minimize that expense. I would go to your destination in advance and procure as much as I could locally," said Jubil, improvising his reply, "then work with the Warners to ship out anything else that was needed. By the time you arrived, I'd have your order packed and ready to go."

Powell stared at Jubil. "Just to be clear, if I were to give you a manifest and a budget, you could manage the procurement and have it all waiting at my destination?"

"Yes, sir," Jubil said confidently.

Powell considered something for a moment. Then he said, "Since you and I last met, the prospects for an expedition next summer have improved. I have some sponsorship from the university and will be working on acquiring additional funding. If I were able to focus on funding, scientific planning, and staffing, without worrying about logistics, it would be very helpful."

"You can count on Warner and Walker Outfitters, Major," vowed Jubil. "Would you allow me to travel with the expedition?"

Once again, Powell took a moment before answering.

"Yes, Jubil, I'd be pleased to have your assistance with our logistics along the way," Powell stated. "As Lieutenant Keplinger put it, you might be a handy fellow to know."

Jubil felt a surge of energetic enthusiasm so strong it was almost impossible for him to stand still. He wanted to whoop with joy and relief. He expressed what he was feeling through a smile that felt as though it stretched from ear to ear.

"Thank you, Major," said Jubil. "I'll do the best I can for you."

"I know you will," said Powell. "I'm looking forward to it. I can see you are ready. For me, it will be a bit like having your uncle Pete's company again. Did you know this is what he did for me when we went exploring together?"

"Did what, sir?" said Jubil.

"Pete handled the logistics for several of my summer collecting trips," explained Powell. "I would tell him about the terrain I wanted to go collecting in and how long I expected to be gone, and he arranged for proper transportation, supplies, camping gear, everything we needed to move and live along the way. I just paid the bills and did my scientific collecting. It was a great freedom and pleasure for me."

"I did not know that," Jubil said, amazed not only at the coincidence, but that Pete had never mentioned it. "I always thought he was just going along for the ride. He never talked about having any responsibilities. He just told me about the places you went and the things you did."

"In a way, he was just along for the ride," said Powell. "When he worked at the blacksmith shop, he paid his own living expenses. When he went collecting with me, I paid for all of our living and travel expenses, but I couldn't afford to pay him any wages for helping me make all the arrangements and collect specimens. He didn't care. He said his payment was the pleasure of making the journey."

"I'm coming to understand how he felt, Major," said Jubil.

"I believe you are," said Powell, kindly. "I should explain, however, that my ideas for exploration have advanced considerably from when we last spoke. I'm developing an expedition plan that will span a full year's time. Next summer we will explore the Colorado Middle Park area to collect native flora and fauna, survey Longs Peak, then camp for the winter and study Ute culture. The following summer we will make a scientific survey of the entire length of the Colorado River. To do this we have to make the first-ever descent through the length of the Grand Canyon. It will be difficult, and dangerous, Jubil. You should understand clearly what you may face."

Jubil struggled to come to grips with the scope of Powell's plans. He had imagined the expedition roaming over mountainous terrain, collecting scientific specimens. What Powell was describing was collecting scientific information on a geologic scale; making a first-ever scientific survey of one of the last regions of America left unexplored by white men.

"It would not be truthful of me, Major," said Jubil, "to deny being taken aback by the scale of your plans, but I expect I'm not the first person to have that reaction."

Powell laughed. "No, you are not."

"I understand about the difficulty and dangers, sir," said Jubil, but he wasn't sure this was true. The expedition Major Powell was describing might be too much for someone of his limited experience. "I'm willing to face whatever we find, and I'm honored to have the opportunity." He sounded surer of himself than he actually was, but he intended to rise to the challenge. An opportunity like this might never come again. He thought fleetingly of Nelly and what she might think of these plans. Would they scrap any chance he had at being more than her best friend?

"What about the store?" Powell asked. "Will you give up your commitment?"

"No sir," said Jubil. "The Warners and I have already discussed this possibility. They understand I won't be in the store all the time. Mr. Warner is very supportive of my travels. He calls me Warner and Walker's field representative."

"Excellent," said Powell, smiling. "I'll be in touch as plans begin to firm up. Congratulations again on the store. Your family would be very proud."

Jubil appreciated the comment, though it brought a pang of regret. He wished his parents and his uncle could share in his successes, and he wondered what Uncle Pete would say about the store's slogan that he had inspired—The Journey Is the Destination.

The only aspect that did not seem well aligned for the future was his relationship with Nelly. All afternoon, when he was not busy helping customers, he searched for the right words to make his feelings known. His greatest fear was that she would laugh at him for thinking the two of them could ever be involved in a romantic way.

That evening, the Warner family hosted a celebratory supper for Jubil and the Boswells at the Ashley House, the hotel where Mr. and Mrs. Warner were staying. Jubil had never experienced such a feeling of accomplishment, and he reveled in it while also being distracted by thoughts of how to talk to Nelly before he lost his nerve. As the evening came to a close and everyone rose to leave the dining room, an idea occurred to him. He approached Nelly and asked, "May I walk you home . . . if your folks don't mind?" It was only a few blocks, and the weather was mild. "It will give you a chance to test out your new coat." Nelly had admired a fur-lined wool parka in the store, and her parents had bought it in honor of her birthday.

Nelly looked to her parents for permission. Her father frowned.

"Unchaperoned?" he asked.

"It's only three blocks, Theodore," Mrs. Boswell said dismissively.

"Hmph, fine," Mr. Boswell conceded, giving Jubil a stern look.

"Don't dally though," Mrs. Boswell said. "Warm new coat or not, it's chilly out there."

"Thank you. We'll be along in just a few minutes," Jubil said. If he was going to speak his piece, he would not have much time.

"Here, take my arm," Jubil said. "The light's not good, and I wouldn't want you to slip on a patch of ice."

Nelly smiled and took his arm. It felt good to have an excuse to be close to her.

"Have you enjoyed your birthday?" Jubil asked.

"I have," she said. "I love my new coat from your wonderful store. I'm so proud of you. Were you and Luke happy with the opening?"

"We did a brisk trade," said Jubil. "Luke was very pleased."

He was so nervous, and he was sure Nelly would detect his state of mind soon. It was time to speak. "I haven't ever told you how much your friendship means to me, Nelly," Jubil confessed. "We've always been friends, but ever since my mother died, I've felt . . . differently. You've helped me find my way, and I appreciate you very much."

Nelly stopped walking and looked up at Jubil questioningly. "Well, that's the nicest thing I've ever heard, Jubil. Thank you. Your friendship is very important to me as well."

They started walking again. Jubil felt a small thrill of victory at managing to get his words out without stumbling. He had meant what he said, but he had not said everything he meant. "You and I have always been very honest with one another, Nelly," he continued, "so I have to tell you that I've been feeling more for you than the kind of friendship we've always had. I care about you very much."

Nelly stopped again, and when Jubil dared to look over at her, he felt a little wave of panic. She wasn't laughing at him, but she wasn't smiling either.

"You'll be taking another summer trip, next year?" Nelly asked. "With Major Powell?"

"Yes," admitted Jubil, surprised that this was the first thing that came to mind for her when he admitted his feelings. He hesitated to tell her the truth of the matter but then forced himself to speak. "Actually it could be even longer. The major has plans to continue into the following summer. Some of the expedition party will even camp in the mountains for the winter, but it's up to me to decide whether I want to do that or not. Do you not want me to go?"

Nelly looked away. "That's a hard question to answer," she said, "but I'm obliged to be honest with you. When you said you were going West this summer, my first concern was that you would be killed and I'd never see you again. So I didn't want you to go, but for selfish reasons. I tried to put them aside and be happy for you, because I knew how important this trip was to you. Then, once you were gone, I found myself worrying constantly over whether you were still alive. I tried to tell myself to be less concerned, but I couldn't stop. I would never tell you not to follow your own heart, but waiting to know if I would ever see you again was very hard on my heart, Jubil. I care very much about whether I see you again. I'm happy you have the opportunity to have your adventures, but waiting and hoping you will return is not something I am looking forward to."

"So my travels prevent us from becoming more than friends?" Jubil asked.

"I'm afraid if I let myself care about you too much, it will break my heart if I lose you," Nelly said, her blue eyes tearing up.

Jubil had sympathized with every word Nelly said until her last statement, which was not sitting well with him. *Of course it breaks our hearts when we lose the people we love,* he thought, *but we don't let that possibility of future pain stop us from loving them.* How could she think this way? He had lost his whole family, and his heart was broken, but it still worked. They walked along in silence as Jubil tried to form a response that did not sound critical of her. He did not think chastising her was the way to win her heart, and the last thing he wanted was to drive her away.

"I know how it feels to lose people you love," Jubil said. "And don't see how a person can decide to hold back love because it will hurt too much to lose someone. Eventually, we are all lost. You have to just go ahead and love, and then take the hurt when it comes. At least that is my experience."

"You're probably right," she said, pensively. "But that's not the only reason I'm guarding my feelings. It's also about my independence. If Papa thinks you and I are as good as engaged, I'm afraid he won't let me enroll at the university. I'm not ready to give that up, Jubil. I care about you too, more than just as a friend, but I can't give up my other dreams . . . just as you can't."

He wanted to push the matter further, to ask her about their marriage prospects in the longer term, but he decided to let it rest. They had taken one small step forward—she had at least said she felt more than friendship for him—and he would have to be satisfied with that for the time being. As he walked back to the Ashley House, where he was spending the night, his sense of accomplishment was overshadowed by the distinct possibility that he was asking too much to want both a life of adventure and Nelly's love.

CHAPTER 11

Jubil pulled the cinch tighter on the fur collar of his parka and leaned into the February wind. During his daily ride from the farm to Warner and Walker Outfitters in the dead of winter, the prairie was sometimes lashed by windblown snow and enveloped in frigid cold. He actually enjoyed meeting these challenges and testing out some of the gear they offered for sale in the store, but he didn't like to expose Star to the worst of it. With Luke's encouragement, he set up one of their wall tents in the yard behind the store, installed a small camp stove, a cot, and a bedroll, and on the worst nights, he camped there and put Star in the stable behind the store. Luke sometimes sent potential customers out to see the gear in use at Jubil's campsite.

That day at the store, a shipment of cold-weather clothing came in, and Jubil unloaded the wagon and then restocked the shelves where necessary. He assisted a steady flow of customers on the sales floor and covered the cash register when Luke went to lunch. When Eli and Ike came in after school, he left them to work the floor and focused on making a list for Luke of which inventory items were low.

Warner and Walker Outfitters paid Jubil nine dollars a week, which was more than enough to meet his needs. He was grateful to make a living without farming, and he enjoyed the work day-to-day, but he couldn't imagine doing it without something else to look forward to. His mind was always returning to the upcoming expedition with Major Powell. He knew that without the prospect of an adventure in his future, he would soon grow restless working in the store.

He also thought often of Nelly. In spite of what she'd said, he couldn't stop wanting more from their relationship. They spent time together as often as they could manage, but the demands of the new store, and her studies before graduation in May, cut into that time more than he would have liked. She had also reminded him they should not appear to be courting, which stung, but he understood her reasons.

The store did a brisk business the rest of the winter and into the spring. The residents of Bloomington seemed excited to come in to see how the inventory changed with the season.

Nelly graduated from public school in May, and Mrs. Boswell baked a cake and held a little celebration. Nelly's father had still not made a commitment concerning university, and Jubil was impressed by her restraint in not mentioning that at the party.

In June, Jubil met with Powell in his new office at Normal University to review the manifest for the expedition which would leave Cheyenne on July 1. But the meeting left him with a troubled feeling, and after leaving Powell's office, Jubil went to see Lew Keplinger at Mrs. Norris's boarding house.

"How much do you know about the major's plans?" Jubil asked.

"Not much," replied Lew. "He asked me if I'd be willing to take regular altitude and latitude readings along the trip, and I told him I would. The Smithsonian Institute is furnishing a sextant, barometers, and chronometers."

"Did you know he plans to bring twenty people?"

Lew shook his head. "I recall he said his fundraising efforts resulted in commitments to about sixty schools. In return for their support, he is supposed to provide each one some kind of specimen for their natural history collection. He'll need a lot of hands to do that much collecting."

Jubil was still not ready to accept the situation. "He's going to have a lot of hands all right. From what I understand, there will be Major and Mrs. Powell, his brother, eight or nine students, two doctors, three preachers, one of whom is bringing his thirteen-year-old son . . . and you and me."

"More company than you bargained for?" asked Lew with an air of bemusement.

Jubil looked down at the floor. Perhaps he was overreacting. "I don't want to sound petty, but here I've been thinking I'd finally made the grade with the major and earned my way on the expedition, but it seems like he's dragging along everybody under the sun. He sure didn't hold these folks to the same high standard he set for me last year."

"You make a good point about a different standard," agreed Lew, "but this is a different trip. We had a different mission last year, and this year he has different goals. You shouldn't take his decision-making personally. There are a couple of things you need to keep in mind when you work closely with the major. He focuses on his mission and does whatever he must to accomplish his goal. In the process, he is not known to give much consideration for anyone's feelings."

Jubil was embarrassed that he might have belittled himself in front of his friend. Where Lew's viewpoint was based on the requirements of the expedition, Jubil's had been immature and self-serving. He had to show he was mature enough to admit his mistake. "Oh, I'm fine," he said, deflating as Lew watched him carefully. "I shouldn't have taken it as a blow to my pride. I'm just happy to be going."

"Good," said Lew. "I'm sure the major values your contribution."

"He's made that somewhat easier than I expected," explained Jubil. "He got Congress to grant him a year's provisions for twenty-five people and a train to haul it to Wyoming. The scientific equipment, like your gear, is being donated by various institutions. I just have to pull it all together and make arrangements for horses, mules, and camping equipment. I'm going to Council Bluffs at the end of June to work with Mr. Warner on those arrangements, and then I'll go on to Cheyenne. I'll have everything ready by the time the major arrives."

Luke had convinced Jubil not to go alone to Cheyenne to outfit Powell. Instead, he would do it in Council Bluffs, where he could depend heavily on Mr. Warner's help. But he was still worried about meeting the major's expectations. But even more powerful than his worry was his excitement about the trip.

"I'm looking forward to adventuring with you," said Lew. "You and I are going to climb one of those Rocky Mountains."

"Yes, we are," Jubil said, remembering standing in Mr. Warner's office looking out over the city and dreaming of seeing the world from atop a mountain. He was on his way to making that happen.

He decided to stop by the Boswells' house before riding back up to the farm, and found Nelly sitting alone on the porch swing, lost in thought. She gave him a weak smile as he dismounted Star.

"Good afternoon, Jubil," Nelly said.

"You looked troubled," he said as he approached the porch. "Is everything all right?"

"Yes," she said with a sigh. "I'm just out here cooling off. Mama and I had another debate with Papa about my starting university this fall."

"Did you prevail?" he asked.

"Not fully," she said scornfully, "but he's not refused

absolutely. He insists on clinging to his belief that higher education for a pretty young girl such as myself—which he thinks he is being complimentary by saying—is a waste of time and money. That only spinsters are meant to be teachers; that I should find a husband; keep house; have babies; follow God's plan. I've heard quite enough."

Jubil took a seat beside her on the swing and silently offered her his hand. She took it in both of hers for a moment, then patted the back of his hand and let him go.

"You could marry me," he said, surprising himself by speaking his mind aloud. "Then you could go to university, regardless of what your father thought...or anyone else for that matter." Nelly looked surprised and then smiled at him warmly.

"Thank you," she said, taking his hand again. "But I wouldn't want us to marry just so I could get my way. Though I do appreciate the sentiment in your offer."

Her response made his heart swell. She was not entirely dismissing the idea of them being married.

"What brings you here?" she asked.

"I've talked to Major Powell and Lew," he said. "I'll be leaving for Council Bluffs at the end of the week, to get things ready for the expedition. Once I leave there with Powell, I won't have any address for you to write to all summer. It will be the longest we've ever gone without being in touch. I'm sorry about that."

She met his gaze and nodded. "Just do your best to make it home again," she said.

He hoped his absence did not cause a setback in their relationship and wished the old adage—*absence makes the heart grow fonder*—would be true for them, but he was concerned that might not be the case for Nelly. His absence left her home alone, worrying he might never return. His best course of action now was to return home safely and prove she need not worry.

After Jubil arrived in Council Bluffs, he came to regret what he'd said to Lew about 'just' having to pull the expedition together. It turned out he had underestimated the complexity of the job. Even though Congress was funding provisions for the expedition, the supplies all had to be purchased, shipped, and inventoried on arrival. Camping equipment also had to be purchased, shipped, and inventoried on arrival. The scientific equipment did not need to be purchased, but it did require ordering, shipping, and receiving. Mr. Warner mentored him in how to execute each of these steps, but he did not do them for him. Above all, the experience was giving him a fuller appreciation for the skills of Mr. Warner.

He found he had a knack for the detailed work of keeping track of what had been done and what still needed to be done. Reviewing his lists and verifying his inventory helped calm his anxiety about the expedition and helped him anticipate what else they might need. But he was still edgy. He wanted to impress the major and did not want to embarrass himself in front of the expedition party.

By late June all the materials for the expedition, save for the horses and mules, had been collected at Mr. Warner's warehouse in Council Bluffs. In addition to all the camping and scientific gear, they carried enough flour, rice, beans, bacon, coffee, and dried apples to get them from Cheyenne to Denver, where they would replenish their supplies. Once they were in the mountains, they would bolster their diet by hunting and fishing. It was not practical to transport the animals by train and not possible to arrange in advance to purchase them in Cheyenne. Jubil would have to find a supplier and purchase the stock once they arrived. Mr. Warner gave him pointers on finding an honest vendor and paying a fair price, but he admitted that his experience was based on a more civilized environment than Cheyenne. Jubil's greatest worry was handling this responsibility alone, and doing it well.

A short letter from Nelly brought good news, of a sort.

Dear Jubil,

While I am touched by your offer of marriage to enable my attendance at university, we will not need to resort to such measures. Papa has finally relented from his negative position toward my attendance.

I will begin classes in the fall at Illinois State Normal University. He still maintains that the teaching profession is for spinsters, and says I should use my advanced education to secure a better class of suitor. I have won this battle of wills with him, but have not won the war.

Please forgive the brevity of my letter, but that is all the news that I have for now. Do be careful on your expedition. I will try not to overly trouble myself about your safety, but I expect to fail in that effort. I want my best friend back.
Yours sincerely,
Nelly

While he was happy that she had gotten her wish, the letter put a new worry in his head. After graduating from university, would she find him too simple? Would she and her father think Jubil was beneath her? He didn't think Nelly would feel that way, but he wasn't sure about her father.

Near the end of June, Major Powell and the expedition party arrived by train in Council Bluffs. Jubil was relieved as Powell checked the manifest against the supplies and found they were all accounted for. Jubil was a little disappointed that his efforts did not even warrant a thank you from Powell, but he thought of what Lew had said about the major and focused on being satisfied by a job well done. To Jubil's eye, the expedition party did not look like a group setting out for the wilderness. The Powells, with their boots and knapsacks, looked the most prepared. Lew and some of the other students were decently outfitted, but many looked like they were on their way to class. He thought the suits of the doctors and preachers would not wear well on the trail. As they boarded the train for Cheyenne, Jubil was happy to finally be underway. Powell spent most of his time apart from the group, reading, studying maps, and writing, but he was congenial enough at meals. Jubil spent most of his time in Lew's company.

Jubil stepped off the train two days later in Cheyenne, the most ramshackle town he had ever seen. It consisted of a wide dirt street lined with mismatched wood-frame store fronts. Behind the row of stores sat a collection of other wood-frame buildings and shacks, which he assumed were houses. The whole place looked as though a strong wind could blow it over, or a single match could set it ablaze. The members of the expedition party helped unload their supplies, stacking them in a huge pile near the depot.

"I'll go round up some transportation, Major," Jubil said. Each member of the party would need a horse, and they would need mules to carry the rest of the supplies. "I'll be back as soon as I can."

"We'll stay here and keep an eye on our supplies," Major Powell said.

"You want some help, Jubil?" Lew asked.

"No, I'll be fine thanks. The major may need you."

Jubil set off down the street looking for a livery stable. If he had been looking for saloons, he would have had an abundance of choices, as they seemed to comprise at least half of the town's businesses. Halfway down the street he came to a blacksmith's shop.

"Good day, sir," Jubil said to a burly fellow in a leather apron, "I'm looking to buy some horses and mules. Could you help me with that?"

The blacksmith looked Jubil over. "Horses maybe, not mules. How many you need?"

"I've got a party of twenty people, and several hundred pounds of supplies," Jubil replied.

The blacksmith shook his head. "I've got six head of horses in the corral."

Jubil's stomach lurched. "That would be a start. No mules?" The blacksmith shook his head again. "Anywhere else in town I could try?"

"Nope. Some drovers are coming through with a herd of wild Mexican ponies soon, though, maybe tomorrow or the next day."

"Thanks," Jubil said, "I'll check back tomorrow." Jubil left the shop with his stomach in knots. How was he going to face the major? If the expedition had to be canceled because he failed to provide transportation, he would never live it down. He decided that when he returned to the group, he would adopt a confident outlook.

"The local blacksmith is low on stock right now," Jubil explained to Powell. "He's expecting several head of horses to arrive in a day or two. No mules though, so we'll have to use horses." Powell seemed unfazed by the news. Jubil was relieved but not yet vindicated. Those horses had to show up.

Some of the members of the party went to find sleeping rooms while others agreed to stand guard over the supplies and sleep outdoors. Jubil couldn't sleep anyway, so he did not mind standing guard. The next morning, he was relieved to see riders driving a herd of horses into town. Jubil, Powell, and Lew went to meet with the blacksmith. They found him in his shop talking to the foreman of the wranglers.

"We're going to need thirty head of your horses," Jubil said.

"Sí, we can do that, señor," the foreman said. "You know . . . they are not broke."

Jubil's confidence plummeted. He had never broken a horse in his life.

Powell seemed to take this circumstance in stride as well. "We'll do what we must."

Jubil found Powell's acceptance of the situation liberating. His circumstances were as troublesome as any he had feared might occur, and Powell was not blaming him for the delay or inconvenience. The major seemed to view it as simply a challenging situation that had to be dealt with, and so Jubil would view it and future challenges the same way. He was no longer worried about what anyone else in the party might think of him, but he was concerned he might break his neck while breaking the horses.

The foremen led them out to the corral and bargained with Jubil and Powell on the terms of the deal. Powell agreed to a price that included the wranglers helping to break the horses. Each person would select a horse from the herd and the wranglers would bring that animal to accept a bridle and saddle. After that, the riders were on their own.

Powell sent Jubil to fetch the rest of the party. As he explained the circumstances, he did his best to ignore the griping. The Reverend Wood in particular was displeased with Jubil and Powell's efforts to avoid this inconvenient and dangerous situation. Jubil announced matter-of-factly that anyone unwilling to accept this necessary complication could take the next train home. Dr. Vasey, one of the botanists, did just that. The rest came along, willingly or begrudgingly. Powell was unfazed by Wood's complaint, and philosophical about Vasey's departure. Jubil imagined Powell would have reacted differently had a general mutiny threatened the number of hands needed to do his specimen collecting.

Jubil was first to select a horse, preferring to take action rather than wait around, dreading his fate. A herd of roughly one hundred horses milled about in the corral. The horses were smaller in stature than Star, and all were solid colored in various hues. One in particular caught Jubil's attention, a black mare who stood to one side of the corral, perfectly still and staring directly at him, as the other horses swirled around her.

"I'll work with that one," Jubil said to the foreman, pointing to the black horse.

"Ah . . . ella es el diablo," the foreman said.

"Beg pardon?" Jubil asked.

"She is the devil," the foreman replied, "a black horse with a black heart. See how she stands and stares? She will have a will of her own, that one."

Jubil stood by his selection. What came next was the most brutal treatment of an animal he had ever witnessed. The wranglers roped the black horse, brought her to the ground and tied her legs, whipped her with ropes and stood on her head until she lay still and would take the bit and bridle. It was all Jubil could do not to scream at the men and pull them off the horse. He'd had no idea that this was the way horses were tamed. Thankfully, the horse soon conceded, and the men allowed her to stand and then saddled her. Now it was up to Jubil. He approached the horse and tried to calm her.

"Easy girl," he said as he took her bridle and held it close under her chin. "He says you are the devil . . . el diablo . . . I reckon you're my devil now." He patted the horse's cheek and she shied away, wild-eyed. "I'm climbing aboard. I'd appreciate it if you would not break my neck."

Jubil pulled himself into the saddle, and the rodeo began. The black horse bolted and ran around the corral, bucking and spinning, but to Jubil's amazement, he stayed on. After a few minutes, the mare calmed and began to respond to Jubil's command of the reins.

"That's a good girl. We'll do fine, you and me," he said and rode to where Powell and Lew stood watching. The horse was still high-strung and easily spooked but not out of control.

"Well done," Lew said.

"Gentlemen . . . meet Diablo," Jubil said, proud and relieved.

He rode his new mount out of the corral and observed as a few others made their choices, but he and his horse both found the process too disturbing to watch. Jubil told Powell he was taking Diablo for a ride, and he rode off into the countryside around Cheyenne, which calmed both of them.

Breaking and shoeing all the horses took three days. Jubil helped saddle train those who would be used as pack animals, in case they needed to be ridden at any point on the trip. He volunteered to help Powell break his horse and one for Mrs. Powell, but to Jubil's amazement Powell did the job himself, in spite of having only one arm. By the time they were ready to leave for Denver, Jubil was an experienced horse wrangler, though he swore he would learn a more humane method of doing the job.

Finally, the party left Cheyenne and trekked south toward Denver. They were led by Major Powell, his wife, Emma, and Walter Powell, the major's brother. Lew had informed Jubil that Walter Powell had been a prisoner of war during the Civil War, which left him with a disturbed temperament. Lew said Walter might be moody and melancholic at times, but at other times he could be pleasant company.

Jubil and Lew rode behind the Powell group along with Dr. Wing, a physician and member of the Illinois Board of Education. Wing had shed his suit coat and tie, and wryly told them he preferred their company over the preachers. This morning, Jubil had removed White Dog's medicine bag from his pack and put it on, intending to wear it for the remainder of the trip. He was proud of it, and did not mind any protection it might offer. Dr. Wing took notice of it and was impressed by Jubil's story. Jubil wondered how many times he'd have to explain his unique accessory, but he did not mind. Behind them were the rest of the Wesleyan and Normal students, and the group of three ministers that included the Reverend Wood—the chief complainer—and his thirteen-year-old son, Henry. Jubil found the northeastern Colorado landscape starkly beautiful. The mountains were still too far away to be visible, and the plains were rockier and more arid than Nebraska. Occasional brushy trees dotted the landscape, and dried tumbleweeds rolled along beside them. Hugging the ground were small bushy plants and an abundance of small cactus. Major Powell recited the Latin names of several of the cactus, but all Jubil could recall was their common names—the prickly pear, the mountain ball, and the particularly nasty-looking fishhook.

Sunday, the first full day on the trail, brought contention from the ministers. They insisted on observing the Sabbath, which meant no work or travel of any kind. Major Powell was having none of that. He said once the party made significant progress on the trail, he would be more flexible, but he would not abide sitting still only one day into the journey. This soured the ministers' attitude. For several days they griped about the weather, the food, the water, and the sleeping arrangements. Listening to them, Jubil thought fondly of his trip the previous summer with the teamsters. In spite of the hardship, there had been no complaining, beyond the habitual grousing of the Irishmen.

Jubil winced to see the poor horsemanship displayed by some members of the party. The horses required a firm hand, which some of the riders lacked. Jubil wished those people had shown the same wisdom as the botanist and not attempted a ride beyond their ability. On more than one occasion, a rider was thrown, or a horse bolted, rider and all. In either case, the animal had to be ridden down, and Jubil and Diablo took responsibility for the job.

Major Powell suggested the expedition party break into smaller groups to allow for more manageable numbers around the campfire for warmth and cooking. Jubil and Lew set up camp along with Sam Garman, a friend of Lew's from Wesleyan, and two other students. In his role as Powell's outfitter, Jubil doled out rations to each group from the expedition's supplies per Powell's orders, attended to the animals every evening, helped gather firewood and water, and packed the horses each morning. He did not mind the work, and found his experiences with Biscuit had helped prepare him to manage a camp.

One afternoon Reverend Wood's son, Henry, lost control of his horse again, and Jubil stirred Diablo into a gallop to run them down. He caught up with the terrified boy—who remained on the horse only by clinging desperately to the saddle horn—and grabbed the reins just below the horse's chin. When Jubil began to slow Diablo down, the boy's horse began to buck, pulling the reins out of Jubil's hand. Then the horse reared up on its hind legs, and the boy rolled off his back, and when he landed, he screamed in pain so loudly, that Jubil thought he'd certainly broken a bone. He circled back, filled with dread, to find that poor Henry had had the great misfortune to land in a bed of prickly pear. Dr. Wing earned his keep that day pulling cactus spines out of the embarrassed lad's posterior while the rest of the party waited and Jubil chased down the horse. When he returned to the party, Reverend Wood was complaining loudly to Major Powell.

"That young man doesn't know a thing more about horses than I do!" Reverend Wood insisted, even when he saw that Jubil was within earshot. "Anyone knows not to spook a horse that way, and now look at poor Henry!"

Jubil met the reverend's gaze calmly, but it was only with considerable restraint that he managed to keep his temper in check.

"How long has young Henry been riding?" Powell asked pointedly, and Reverend Wood let out an indignant breath and returned to check on Dr. Wing's progress.

Major Powell was not pleased so far with their rate of travel. He was scheduled to meet in Denver with General Ulysses S.

Grant, his former commanding officer and current candidate for the office of President of the United States, and he became concerned that he would miss their appointment. At the next stagecoach station they came to on the trail, the major explained to the group, he and Mrs. Powell would catch a stagecoach to Denver. Once they left, Powell waving happily back at them before climbing into the stage, the gripers in the party focused on their absence as another offense to concern themselves with. In their view, Powell was giving himself special consideration over the rest of the party. Jubil had mixed feelings about the major's having left. He agreed that the pace of travel was annoyingly slow, but he thought the major could have at least pretended to be remorseful about leaving the others behind. This, he supposed, was just another example of Powell's lack of concern for the feelings of others when he was on a mission.

On the fourth day of the journey, Jubil and Lew rode silently side by side. The horses and the disgruntled members of the expedition seemed to have finally given in to their fate. The quiet monotony was a welcome relief.

"What do you make of that, Jubil?" Lew asked, pointing westward toward the horizon.

Jubil looked for anything out of the ordinary. "What . . . those clouds? They don't look troublesome."

"Look again, my friend," Lew said, "and behold the Rocky Mountains."

Jubil felt a touch of lightheadedness as the purple-gray haze transformed from a low-hanging bank of clouds into a line of majestic mountains. A sense of elation rose inside him. He recalled all the hours he had spent daydreaming of an adventure just like this one. He was finally here. He had made it.

"Woo hoo!" he shouted as he swung his hat in the air. Diablo was startled into a prance.

Lew laughed as other members of the party looked on questioningly.

By midafternoon they were close enough that Jubil could see more detail: the foothills rising in front of the mountains, the ridge of peaks making up the line of the Continental Divide, the snowcaps, some still frozen, even in July.

"You see the mountain that rises taller than the others?" Lew asked, pointing as he spoke. "That's Longs Peak. You and I are going to stand on top of that."

Jubil stared at it. He felt an odd combination of excitement and disbelief. He had never felt so small. The idea of standing atop that monstrous peak seemed utterly impossible.

CHAPTER 12

Jubil quietly celebrated his nineteenth birthday on the trail, one day out from Denver. The landscape remained largely the same as the earlier part of the trip, though the mountains now loomed large, only a few hours ride to the west. Powell had made his connection in Denver with General Grant, who was campaigning in the region. Grant was on his way to Central City to visit with the miners, and Powell intended for the expedition party to follow along. Jubil found Grant less congenial than General Sherman. The most memorable thing about him was his aroma—whiskey and cigars. The party traveled west for Berthoud Pass with Grant and bid him farewell when he turned for Central City.

The circumstances at Berthoud Pass were idyllic. The weather was mild, but large patches of snow remained in the shady areas. Pines and aspen covered the landscape, game and berries were plentiful, and the water was clean and close by. It was the most beautiful place Jubil had ever seen. The smell from the pines filled the air with a wonderful perfume, and the water gurgling in the nearby stream was a constant soothing song. Jubil thought that if he ever got the chance, he would bring Nelly to this very spot. The only thing that could improve on the setting was her easy company.

The expedition party set up camp, and the students and

ministers began collecting samples of the flora and fauna. Much to Jubil's relief, the living conditions and the enterprise of collecting seemed to greatly improve the mood of the party. He spent most of his time hunting, fishing, and hiking, sometimes alone. Often he visited with Lew, who, the entire time they were at that elevation, faithfully took barometer readings every hour and recorded them in a notebook. Berthoud Pass, at eleven thousand feet, was a unique location with a variety of weather patterns, so Powell wanted barometer readings every hour of the day and night, including during miserable weather. Lew declined any assistance in taking the readings overnight, and only Powell assisted during the day, so Lew could nap. For the week and a half they were there, Lew drove himself to accomplish the mission. Jubil was astonished when Lew sat up all night on his twenty-seventh birthday, taking readings in an unexpected snowstorm. Jubil was impressed by Lew's determination and endurance, but he was also puzzled by his need to push himself so hard when help was available.

Even though Lew would not accept Jubil's help, he gladly taught him some things about operating the equipment. Jubil found the sextant fascinating. A person skilled in using this device could determine his location on the planet and find the distance to far points, which was obviously highly practical for a traveler. He sat through some basic lessons with Lew, but found that, in order to use the tool accurately, he would have to know astronomy and always carry a Nautical Almanac and maps with latitude and longitude. Ultimately, the trappings seemed excessive for the limited use he would find for the device. Lew's explanation of the barometer's use, not only for determining barometric pressure but also altitude, was another eye-opener for Jubil. In this case, the device was easy to operate, but calculating altitude given the readings required not only basic math skills, which Jubil possessed, but also a gift for using them in original ways, which he did not. Perhaps he would reconsider enrolling at Wesleyan when he got home, though he still found the prospect uninspiring. He thought he must be like Pete in that regard as well.

Specimen collecting for Powell's sponsors had begun in earnest. The biology students captured and killed birds native to the area—the magpie, the Stellar's jay, the Western scrub jay, and more—and placed them in salt boxes. They also caught snakes, such as the prairie rattlesnake and the western hognose. Dr. Wing again earned his keep when one of the students was bitten by a hognose. The hognose was not venomous but delivered a bite that could easily fester. The rattlers were deadly. Dr. Wing disinfected the wound, wrapped the hand, and assured the student he would survive.

The ministers picked alpine forget-me-not, purple fringe, blue columbine, and western fringed gentian, and then they dried and pressed them and stored them in waterproof canvas folios. Jubil sometimes watched Lew and the major catalogue items being gathered but was not involved in the collection. Listening to them cite the proper scientific classification for each specimen gave him some insight into what he'd be in for if he ever decided to study natural science at Wesleyan. The Latin names for the items did not stick in his mind at all. But he did enjoy learning their common names.

In a way, he thought it was a shame to capture and kill all this beauty, but he knew how much he had enjoyed seeing Powell and Pete's collection at the Natural History Society Museum. And each of these items was on its way to be similarly treasured by a sponsor of the expedition. He spent most of his time hunting, fishing, and exploring, and helping attend to camp and the animals. He was enjoying the trip and felt useful, helping to keep the expedition party warm, fed, and moving. After a week they had collected all the samples they needed from that area, and prepared to move northwest into Middle Park to set up a new camp at Hot Springs.

The day they broke camp they were joined by a friend of Major Powell's, William Byers, editor and publisher of the *Rocky Mountain News*. Byers, along with his wife and two children, had been traveling with General Grant but were now on their way to Hot Springs. Byers owned a trading post there operated by his brother-in-law, a self-avowed mountain man named Jack Sumner. The expedition followed the stream down the mountainside until midafternoon, where they finally entered the broad vale of Middle Park, where they camped overnight. Two days later they reached Byer's Hot Springs trading post. There they found Jack Sumner angrily lecturing a ragged group of Indians. Jubil could hear enough to pick out an occasional profanity but not the gist of the issue. When Sumner noticed the riders entering the area, he shooed the Indians away to their camp, a collection of a dozen or so teepees set up in a clearing just west of the trading post, and walked out to meet the visitors, smiling and waving. Byers and Powell dismounted.

"Good day, Jack," Byers said, "I'd like you to meet Major John Wesley Powell. These other folks are members of a scientific exploring expedition the major is leading in his role as professor of Natural Sciences at Illinois State Normal University. They'll be staying in the area a few weeks to do their work."

"Howdy do, Professor," Sumner said, not offering to shake hands until the major offered his left-handed shake, which Sumner accepted.

"Good day, Mr. Sumner," Powell replied.

"Looks like you're leading a pretty green army into your battle with nature," Sumner said with more a smirk than a smile.

Powell did not seem offended by Sumner's comments and demeanor, but Jubil was. He looked at Lew for a reaction and got raised eyebrows and a grin.

Sumner proceeded to give orders to Powell as to where to set up camp and how to avoid the theft of supplies, equipment, and horses at the hands of the Ute Indian tribe camped nearby. Jubil looked at this bedraggled collection of people and thought of his friend White Dog and the humiliation he had faced at the hands of the soldiers, but that seemed small compared to the humiliations these people endured. Rather than the colorful garb worn by the Indians Jubil had seen before, these people were dressed in filthy, worn-out hides or hand-me-down clothes from white people. The buffalo hides covering their teepees were stained and worn, and their naked, unwashed children played while the women busied themselves around the camp. Their ponies were bony and tired looking. These were a completely defeated people. Jubil could see some inevitability in whites and Indians not being able to live side-by-side, but still could not shake his feelings of remorse.

The expedition party established camp near the trading post and found conditions at Hot Springs even more comfortable than they had been at Berthoud Pass. The Hot Springs was a natural wonder, pleasant for bathing and useful for doing laundry, and no one minded the warmer temperatures at this lower elevation. This was another place he could imagine bringing Nelly to visit one day.

They had spent a couple of days in the vicinity of the trading post when Lew said to Jubil with a grin, "I may be jumping to conclusions, but I think Jack Sumner might be pretty proud of himself and his own opinions."

"I have jumped right along with you," Jubil said. "When he first told the major how to set up camp, I was suspicious of that, but after listening to him pontificate for days now, I'm convinced. Jack's pretty sure he knows it all."

The expedition had been camped at Hot Springs for two weeks when Major Powell joined Jubil and the others at their campfire one evening.

"Good evening, gentlemen," said Powell. "Tomorrow morning, I'm leaving with a small party to make an attempt on the summit of Longs Peak. You are all welcome to come along, if you would like." Climbing to the summit of the mountain had no real scientific value, but the major was intent on being the first to accomplish it.

Lew looked at Jubil and the others. Jubil felt what was now becoming a familiar mixture of trepidation and excitement. He had been looking forward to the climb and had hoped for it. He nodded, and the others agreed as well.

"Count us in, Major," replied Lew. "Thank you, sir."

"Finally," said Lew after Powell had left them. "I thought he'd never ask."

Jubil did not feel as intimidated by the idea of standing atop Longs Peak as he had when Lew first pointed out the mountain. He had some apprehension, as he did in any new situation, but he was excited about the prospect of a new experience.

In the morning, Jubil arose to find Major Powell sitting cross-legged, holding a bowl in his lap and mixing biscuit dough with his one good arm.

"Can I give you a hand, Major?" said Jubil. Quickly realizing his blunder, he added, "I'm sorry, sir, I didn't mean any disrespect."

Powell laughed. "None taken, but no, thank you. I'm ready to put them in the pan."

Jubil went off to the springs to wash up while breakfast cooked, then returned to help Lew pack up the horses with several day's rations and camping gear.

After a breakfast of bacon, berries, and the major's biscuits, the men set out for Longs Peak. Powell had brought along his brother Walter, the newspaperman Byers, Jack Sumner, and Ned Farrell, a friend of Sumner's camped at the trading post. These four, along with Jubil, Lew, and Garman constituted the climbing party.

As they rode out, Jubil and Lew fell in together bringing up the rear of the party, as they often did. Lew liked that position for keeping an eye on things.

"Have you decided if you are going with the major down the Colorado River next summer?" Jubil asked.

"I have," Lew nodded. "I'm not going."

"I'm sorry to hear that," Jubil said.

"I'm not saying I'll never go adventuring again," said Lew, "but it will be a long while before I do. I graduated from Wesleyan this spring, and I've been offered a position with Williams and Burr, a law firm in Bloomington. I'll read law there and clerk for them and hope to be admitted to the bar by the end of next year. After that, I'm not sure where I'll practice."

"Congratulations," said Jubil. "I'm glad you'll be in Bloomington."

"What are your plans?" Lew asked.

"I intend to go with the major down the Colorado next year and to help the Warners out with the business, and I'd like to stay in Nelly's good graces, but beyond that, no plans."

"Those sound like plans," said Lew.

"Yes, but not long-term plans, like yours," explained Jubil.

"I'm twenty-seven years old," said Lew. "You're nineteen. Don't be too hard on yourself."

Jubil nodded. He was coming to see Lew as a mentor, and it wouldn't be the same traveling with Major Powell without him.

After two long days of riding, the men camped on the western side of the Continental Divide at the base of McHenry Peak. This spot was west of Longs Peak and slightly north, but in order to access Longs Peak, they would have to first climb over the Divide. According to Sumner—who had so far lived up to Lew and Jubil's opinion of his character by seeming to believe himself the authority on almost everything—McHenry Peak offered one of the most accessible paths. He declared with confidence that the party should go up McHenry, cross the ridgeline of the Continental Divide and continue southeast to Chief's Head Peak, then go east to Pagoda Mountain, and finally northeast to Longs Peak. The men built a makeshift corral for their animals, and in the morning, they set out on foot to make their climb.

While Jubil had hiked every day since they'd set out from Cheyenne, he had never done any real mountain climbing. He was tense as the party set out to ascend McHenry Peak and kept his mind on his footing and on persisting through the hours of exertion, which kept him from dwelling too much on his fears of what might lie ahead. The climb over McHenry and the Continental Divide was a long hard scramble over loose rock, but there were no sheer cliffs to be ascended on their route. On the other side of McHenry, they followed a wide ridge to Chief's Head Peak and then on to Pagoda, but as they traveled northeast toward Longs Peak, they came to a section that stopped them in their tracks. The ridgeline became a flat pathway perhaps fifty feet long but no more than eighteen inches wide. Its most unsettling feature was the extreme angle of slope on either side. It was a narrow pathway through thin air.

"Let's see how Sumner enjoys this," Lew said quietly, as Sumner, leading the way, stood staring at the ridge. Sumner took a few steps out onto the pathway, arms outstretched as if walking a tightrope, and then stopped. He bent his knees and slowly let himself down to sit on the ridge, legs on either side, as if sitting a horse.

"What's the matter, Jack," goaded Lew. "Why don't you go on across?"

"I ain't all that impatient to get where we're headed," declared Sumner.

"Well, I am," said Lew.

Jubil watched in astonishment as Lew ventured out onto the ridge, stepped around Sumner, and walked the length of the path as though it were as wide as a city street. Reaching the plateau on the other side, Lew looked back at the rest of the party.

"By God," Sumner swore, "I can do anything you can do, Keplinger." With that, he began to scoot across the ridge on his tail. Reaching the plateau where Lew stood, Sumner turned to the other members of the party. "It ain't so bad if you stay on your rump . . . and don't look down."

The other members of the party, including Major Powell, scooted across the ridge, leaving Jubil the last to cross. He stood looking across at Lew and heard Gulley's voice remind him, *Keep your wits about you*. That was exactly what had kept Lew Keplinger alive all these years, Jubil thought. Lew did not let fear paralyze his mind or his body. Jubil stepped up to the edge of the ridge.

"That's the spirit," said Lew, smiling. "Just walk across it."

Jubil reached to his hip and touched White Dog's medicine bag, then began to walk across. His life depended on his ability to do something as simple as walk a straight line for fifty feet without falling. He imagined himself with blinders on, like a horse unable to see any of the disturbing reality around him, just the narrow view of what lay ahead. He focused on looking at the narrow ridgeline but not straight down, and took one step after another. Soon he had reached the other side.

"Good man," said Lew, patting Jubil on the back.

"Well done," said Major Powell. "Impressive for a fellow fresh off the prairie."

Jubil smiled and breathed a sigh of relief. He felt a rush of euphoria from having overcome his fear. He laughed to himself as he thought how upset Nelly would be with the risk he had taken, and decided he might, regrettably, have to keep this part of his adventure to himself.

The party continued along, but about five hundred yards on, the ridge was cut by a notch. The drop between the ridge plateaus was precipitous and a hundred feet across. They had no choice but to turn back and look for a new route. Returning to the narrow crossing, Lew walked across first, followed by

Jubil. The rest of the party scooted across as before. Then Major Powell made a decision. "We should abandon the idea of traversing a ridgeline between the mountains," said Powell. "Let's cross over the ridge and descend into that basin," he said, pointing southeast into a wide bowl surrounded by the peaks of the ridge they were standing on. "We can camp down there and look for an approach to the mountain from its base."

By early afternoon they had made their way into the bottom of the basin. They found a hospitable area to camp, near a small lake with abundant trout and a running stream to provide clean water.

"We'll look for an approach up Longs Peak in the morning," Powell said.

"I wouldn't mind going out to have a look yet today, Major," offered Lew.

"I have no objections, Lieutenant," replied Powell, "but for my part, I've had all the mountaineering I need for one day."

The others in the party mumbled their agreement.

"If you don't mind," said Jubil. "I'll go with you."

"I would welcome your company," said Lew.

Jubil and Lew stood a short distance north of their campsite, studying Longs Peak. The whole south face of the mountain was visible, rising from the basin and continuing up to a prominent flat-topped summit.

"It looks like we could just walk up that big trough," Jubil said, pointing, "and then cut over to the top."

Lew laughed. "Well, that sounds easy enough. Let's go have a look. By the way, to impress your friends back home, the proper mountaineering term for that big trough is a couloir."

Jubil and Lew set out, and Jubil learned how deceiving distances are relative to mountains. The hike from the campsite to the base of the mountain took nearly an hour. Lew studied the mountainside for several minutes as Jubil stood beside him, staring at it in awe. What had looked like a gradual incline from a distance now looked to be a slope of at least forty-five degrees, and straight up in some places. Jubil's heart began to race and his palms to sweat as he considered the seemingly impossible heights they faced. He tried to slow and deepen his breathing in order to calm his nerves and hoped his friend did not detect the anxiety he felt. He could not have said exactly what he was afraid of. Falling was of obvious concern, but this feeling was not that specific. It was a more general dread, one that could not name all the ways this huge mountain could kill him. He reminded himself to focus on one step at a time—just like crossing the narrow ledge yesterday.

"See that ribbon of snow curving down the middle of the couloir," Lew asked Jubil, "the one that runs between the ridge on the left and the wall of cliffs on the right?"

"Right there?" Jubil pointed at a line of snow snaking down the mountain.

"Yes," confirmed Lew. "We'll want to stay well clear of that. While the snow is often easier to walk on than the talus and scree, it also creates wet, slippery rocks all around it. It will be hard enough to keep our footing without contending with wet rocks or black ice."

"Talus and . . . what?" Jubil asked.

"Talus and scree," repeated Lew, "more mountaineering terms. Talus refers to the whole slope of loose rocks, scree are the small ones making it up. Those are the remnants of the rock that once filled the couloir."

Jubil nodded.

"We'll go up the couloir from right here," said Lew, "but we'll hold tight against the base of the wall of cliffs on the right to stay clear of that channel of snow. When we get above the wall of cliffs, we'll decide which route to take to the top. Agreed?"

Jubil shrugged. "I suppose."

"Good," Lew grinned at Jubil. "Are you ready?"

Jubil did his best to keep up. The angle of ascent was

not overly steep until they reached the bottom of the wall of cliffs. At that point the slope steepened to over forty-five degrees, and the drop into the couloir was long enough that a fall would result in serious injury. Jubil moved cautiously and tested every handhold and foot placement before trusting his weight to it. Lew, surefooted, did not move hastily but moved constantly upward without pausing to rest. After about three hours of climbing, they had gone past the wall of cliffs on their right. For the first time since they had begun their ascent, Lew stopped to survey.

"Now we need to decide which way is the best route to the summit," said Lew.

Jubil, winded, was grateful for the rest. He marveled at how Lew hardly seemed to be breathing hard, even after that long climb.

"If we traverse to the left, over to the center of the peak," Lew said, "it looks like we could turn and go right up that slope to the top. But if we go straight up from here, toward that notch to the right of the summit peak, it would be a much shorter distance, assuming we can reach the summit from the other side of the notch—it's too steep to go up from this side." Lew considered for a moment before deciding. "Let's go up and have a look through the notch," he said. "If we can't make it, we'll go the other way tomorrow. It will also be easier for us to keep our bearings if we stay on this line instead of traversing the slope. It will be getting dark before we get down. If we stay on this line, it will be easier to find our way."

Lew's comment sent a tingle down Jubil's spine. It had not occurred to him they would be caught on the side of the mountain in the dark, and it certainly had never occurred to him they could lose sight of the path back down. Lew started toward the notch, and Jubil stood watching his friend climb, torn between shouting out that he was going no further and trusting his friend to know what was best. Why would Lew insist on continuing in the face of such risks when they could easily finish the job tomorrow? Jubil considered Lew's dogged determination to take his barometer readings unassisted, and his stroll across the narrow ridgeline. Perhaps Lew thought of himself as invincible. A man who had survived battle after battle without even being wounded might be excused for such thinking. None of this reasoning did anything to quell Jubil's concerns in this situation—for all he knew, Lew might be invincible, but who said Jubil was? —but he refused to give in to his own fears. He touched White Dog's medicine bag, then began to follow Lew up the mountain.

After about four hours they reached the edge of the notch and followed it around to the east side of the summit peak. Behind them, the sun was sinking rapidly.

"Oh, my," said Lew, stopping short and extending an arm back to stop Jubil from advancing further. "Well, we've come to the end of this route."

Jubil could see that Lew's hand was shaking. He craned his neck to see past him, took one look, and moved back several feet. The east face of the mountain was a sheer cliff that dropped hundreds of feet straight down.

"Look, Jubil," said Lew, pointing down to a lake below. "One more step, and we'd be down there in short order."

Jubil did not think much of Lew's humor. He could only think of the consequences of coming across a spot like this in the dark.

"We'd better head down," Lew said.

They began to retrace their steps along the notch as the shadowy light faded to full dark. A shot of fear ran through Jubil when he noticed he could see well enough to place his feet, but not well enough to see the surrounding landmarks. He could not see the wall of cliffs they had followed up the couloir. He could not see the couloir, and he could not even see the summit of the peak. His hands began to shake, and he fought to keep the shaking from taking over his whole body. He had to keep his wits about him.

"Lew," Jubil said quietly. "I'm going to admit to being a little worried."

"I'll join you," agreed Lew.

"How will we find our way down?" asked Jubil.

Lew took a deep breath and exhaled. "If we keep the wall of the notch on our right side, it will lead us back past the couloir. But if we can't see it, and miss it, we'll traverse right across the south face. We have to find the couloir or sit down and wait for the moon. We will have a waxing moon rising around midnight, and the sky is clear, so there will be enough light for us to navigate by."

"Won't we freeze up here?" Jubil asked. Having started out in the warmth of an August day, they had carried no cold weather gear or even a pack up the mountain.

"It won't get that cold," Lew said dismissively. "We can huddle up if we have to. This mountain's not enough to kill the likes of you and me, Jubil."

There it was, Jubil thought. Lew was certain to a fault of his invulnerability. Jubil held his tongue and breathed deeply to calm himself. He was at least grateful for Lew's awareness of the moon's movements and the weather. Jubil would pay closer attention to such things in the future. As they continued to retrace their steps to the couloir, Jubil caught a flicker of light out of the corner of his eye. He stopped and looked again but saw nothing.

"What is it?" asked Lew.

"I thought I saw a light," Jubil replied. He turned and walked back a few steps.

"There it is!" exclaimed Jubil. "There's a light down there!"

Lew looked down toward the base of the mountain. "I think the major has set a signal fire at the base of the couloir," said Lew. "We almost walked right past it."

Jubil's relief at finding their bearings was tempered by the anxiety of making his way down the edge of the couloir in the dark, but they made it to the base of the mountain before the moon rose. Jack Sumner was there, tending the signal fire.

"I never expected to be happy to see your face, Jack," said Lew.

"Damn you, Keplinger, you had the major worried sick over you and that boy. It's about time you showed up," said Sumner. "We need to get some sleep. We've got a mountain to climb in the morning."

As they hiked back to the campsite, Jubil allowed himself to daydream of home. As much as he enjoyed adventuring, he was looking forward to sitting, comfortable and safe, on the Boswells' porch with Nelly. Perhaps climbing a mountain in the dark was not as dangerous as being shot at during an Indian raid, but it could kill him just as dead. Nelly's fears were hardly unfounded: it was possible he would get himself killed out here.

The men were up before dawn, making ready to test themselves against the mountain. Jubil felt more rested than he expected, having gone to sleep as soon as they returned to camp. He had some bacon and berries for breakfast but declined when offered one of the major's biscuits. As he had discovered the previous day, they were firmly textured, to say the least. They set out to hike to the base of the mountain before the sun came up and arrived as the sky was lightening over the mountains.

Lew described to Powell and the others the route he and Jubil had taken the previous day and how it had led to a dead end. Jubil suppressed a shudder remembering the sheer drop on the east side of the notch. "We should traverse across the face of the mountain," Lew said, "to about the center of the peak. From there, we can go straight up to the summit."

Powell studied the mountain and nodded. "Lead the way, Lieutenant."

Jubil came up last as they started their climb, to make sure no one lost their way and to provide help if needed. The climb up the couloir was uneventful, though far slower than the pace Lew had set yesterday. The Powell brothers followed behind Lew and could have kept pace with him, but the major reined Lew in and allowed the slower members to set the pace. Byers, the newspaper man, followed Powell. He was a hearty fellow who moved steadily but slowly. Sumner and Farrell followed Byers and did not seem to mind the slow pace. Garman brought up the rear with Jubil. Once Lew reached the top of the couloir, he stopped and waited for the rest of the party to catch up. Then he pointed out his intended direction of travel up and across the mountain. "We'll have no choice but to walk right up that snowfield," he said, "so watch your footing. We'll come out of the snowfield right at the base of that big mound near the peak. We'll turn there, and go straight up to the summit."

The traverse was unsettling because they were walking across the face of a forty-five-degree slope. This unnatural body position was disorienting and dizzying. Jubil extended his arms for balance and made his way step by step, just as he had done on the ridgeline yesterday. His position crossing the snowfield was the safest, since the path for him was well trodden. They completed the traverse uneventfully and gathered at the point from which they would summit.

"Nicely done so far, gentlemen," said Lew. He pointed out the path to the summit. All of their climbing so far had been over loose rock, or scree, as Lew called it. This path was a smooth granite slope with occasional seams and cracks. It was at least as steep as the slope they had just crossed. If footing on scree was treacherous, this slope offered almost no footing at all. The seams and cracks were sometimes not close enough together to offer a continuous grip. Between the seams, the climber would have to travel up the slope on smooth granite. It suddenly occurred to Jubil that if this slope looked intimidating going up, it would be even more difficult coming down. Surely it would be impossible for the major to climb up or down it with only one arm.

But even before he had completed the thought, Jubil was quickly proven wrong as Lew and Powell started up the stretch of granite to the summit. Just like everyone else, Powell placed his feet firmly before reaching up for his next handhold. But unlike the others, in order to secure a higher handhold, he had to let go of the wall completely to reach up, leaving only his feet securing him to the face of the mountain. This did not seem to faze the major in the least.

Once Jubil began this part of the climb himself, he paid attention to no one's technique but his own. Rationally speaking, the slope wasn't as bad as it looked; close-up, there were plenty of hand- and footholds. He took his eyes away from his hands and feet only long enough to glance ahead for another hold. When a hold was not within reach, he focused on maintaining a steady upward momentum across the smooth granite by placing his palms flat against the rock like a lizard on a wall and pushing up with his feet against the slightest ridge in the rock he could find. It was during these moments that fear threatened to paralyze him—in the periphery of his mind he felt the impulse to hug the mountainside and refuse to risk another move. *Keep your wits about you*, he reminded himself. Finally, he came to the top of the slope, climbed over the rounded edge, and looked out across a wide, flat, smooth expanse of granite, the summit of Longs Peak. He joined the other members of the party at the center of the summit plateau.

"Well done, gentlemen," said Major Powell. "Let's take a few minutes to enjoy our accomplishment before we make our way back down."

The men spread out to take in the view. Jubil felt as though he stood at the top of the world. In all directions the peaks and valleys of the Rocky Mountains spread out to the horizon. Carpeted in greenish-gray and splotched by white snowfields, the landscape rested in a pale blue mist under an azure sky. He recalled standing at the windows in Mr. Warner's office, wondering what the world would look like from atop the Rockies—and now he knew. He felt an expanding sense of achievement, but then he reminded himself he was only partway through the climb. He still had to get down. Jubil joined Lew, who was collecting rocks and had begun to make a pile of them.

"Congratulations on your climb," Lew said. "Well done. This pile of rocks has a fancy mountaineering name as well: it's called a cairn. It's used to mark a trail or a site. I brought along a baking powder can and a slip of paper and a pencil. We can sign and date the paper, put it in the can, and leave it in the cairn to mark our accomplishment."

"Fine idea, Lew," said Byers, the newspaper man. "I packed along a bottle of wine to celebrate the occasion."

Though Jubil had no experience whatsoever with alcohol, he doubted the wisdom of drinking it before climbing down a mountain, but he kept his opinion to himself. The other members of the party gathered to help finish building the three-foot cairn. Lew passed around the paper and pencil to get their signatures: Major Powell, Walter Powell, Lewis Keplinger, Samuel Garman, William Byers, Jack Sumner, Ned Farrell, Jubilee Walker. Lew put the document inside the can, but before he put the lid on, he reached into his pocket and extracted one of the major's biscuits, which Jubil would've bet was as solid as the granite on which they stood.

"I propose we also leave this biscuit," proclaimed Lew, "as an everlasting memento of Major Powell's skill in breadmaking."

Everyone laughed but Major Powell, who showed the slightest glimmer of a grin.

"I hardly think that befits the decorum of the moment," said Powell, feigning indignation. To underscore his point, the major removed his hat to make a speech as Lew, subdued, slipped the biscuit back into his pocket.

"We have now accomplished an undertaking in the physical field," the major intoned, "which had hitherto been deemed impossible, but there are mountains more formidable in other fields which are before us." The major put his hat back on, and Jubil resisted the urge to say amen.

Lew put the can, with their signatures, into the cairn and covered it with rocks. Byers opened the wine and anointed the cairn with a splash, then passed the bottle around. Jubil and Garman, who was a Quaker, abstained.

"We should make our way down, gentlemen," said Powell.

The men began to file toward the edge of the summit to start the descent.

Lew approached Jubil. "Do you plan to be the last in line?"

"I thought I would," replied Jubil.

"Good," said Lew. He removed the major's biscuit from his pocket and handed it to Jubil. "Wait until the others have started down, and then put this in the can."

Jubil broke into a grin. Lew winked at him and then went to lead the descent.

"Are you ready, gentlemen?" Lew asked. "Don't be shy about going down this stretch on your tail. That will surely be safer than trying to climb down facing the mountain."

One by one the men went over the edge, until Jubil was alone. He removed the baking powder can from the cairn, opened it and dropped the biscuit in. Then he replaced the can in the cairn and covered it with rocks. He looked at the cairn and smiled. It was a moment he would remember for the rest of his life.

CHAPTER 13

Once the climbers returned to the base of McHenry Peak where their animals were corralled, Major Powell made it known that he intended to explore the area, so they camped there two more nights before going back to Hot Springs. Despite Lew's initial concern, Walter Powell had been pleasant company. Jubil was surprised one evening when Walter serenaded them with a baritone rendition of the Civil War ballad 'Old Shady.' The song was sung from the perspective of a recently freed slave—Old Shady—saying a bitter farewell to Jefferson Davis and the south. Jubil wondered how much of Walter's time as a prisoner of war had been spent singing old ballads to try and lighten the mood.

Jubil socialized around the campfire but also took time alone to write a long letter to Nelly describing the details of the trip, especially the climb to the summit of Longs Peak. Hoping to put her mind at ease, he told her that the climb was the most dangerous part of the expedition and that he had come through it safely. He explained that Major Powell intended to camp for the winter about a hundred miles west of Hot Springs, on the White River. The major had selected the location for its milder winter weather and reports of ample grass along the river for the animals. There was also a band of peaceful and relatively prosperous Ute living nearby on a recently designated reservation, and Major Powell planned to spend the winter studying their language and culture. Jubil was committed to helping the major prepare for the winter.

He finished the letter without saying whether he would return home after the winter preparations were made, because he wasn't sure yet himself. Then he lay on his bedroll wondering what Nelly was doing while he was away. He hoped that he was not a worry for her every time she thought of him, but mainly he hoped she wouldn't forget him and what it was like for them to spend time together.

When Major Powell announced he was ready to move on, they broke camp and set out for Byers's trading post to rejoin the rest of the expedition party. When they came over the ridge around the Hot Springs, they saw a crowd down around the trading post. There were several dozen tents in the area that had not been there when the men had left for Longs Peak.

"Who are all those people, Major?" Lew asked.

"I don't know, Lieutenant," replied Powell.

"The Indian teepees are gone, Major," observed Jubil.

"Let's go find out what is happening," said Powell, leading the way down the hill. Mrs. Powell walked out to meet them.

"Oh, Wes," she said, "I'm so glad you're here."

"What is it?" said Powell.

"We've been warned that there may be Indian trouble," Mrs. Powell replied. "The band of Ute that was camped here decided to move to South Park a few days ago, but they ran into some Arapaho and Cheyenne and were killed. We were told some ranches have also been burned and some whites were killed. People have begun to gather here for security, hoping to find strength in numbers."

The major looked at the gathering, then turned in his saddle and surveyed the area.

"Thank you, Emma," he said. "I'll speak to the group."

They all rode in closer to the trading post, and Powell

called out to the group from his horse. "My name is Major John Wesley Powell. I am here conducting a scientific expedition, but some of my men and I have combat experience. If you are willing to follow my orders, I believe we'll be able to mount a strong defense, in the event of an attack." Hearing no objections, he proposed a plan. "All of the women and children should remain close to the trading post while it is daylight and be prepared to take shelter inside. The men should commence to digging rifle pits in the hillside, over there." He pointed. "This evening, we will barricade the women and children inside, and the men will take positions in the rifle pits. We should get at it, while we still have some light."

The crowd dispersed and began to execute Powell's orders, all except Reverend Wood. He complained that, as a man of the cloth, he would have no part in any fight with Indians. Jubil heard Powell tell the Reverend he could respect him not shooting Indians but doubted the Lord would mind if he dug a hole in the ground. Jubil chuckled and went to help dig. His run-in last year with the Indian raiders had educated him to the value of strong defensive positions. It was nearly midnight before Powell was satisfied with the preparations.

The night passed without an attack, but at dawn the quiet was broken by the barking of a dog. Major Powell, Walter Powell, Lew, and Jubil were positioned close to one another along the defensive perimeter.

"We need to conduct a reconnaissance to determine if we have intruders nearby," Powell said.

"I'll go," Jubil volunteered.

"No, I'll do it, Wes," said Walter Powell.

"I should go, Major," said Lew.

Powell surveyed them all.

"Jubil, you made the first offer. I'll honor that," Powell said. "We need to know what we are facing. Ride out and check our perimeter. See if there are Indians in the area. If so, estimate how many. Watch their movements. I suggest you start out along the river. Don't go further out than an hour. And most importantly, do not let them see you."

"Yes, sir," said Jubil.

He climbed out of the rifle pit, and adjusted White Dog's medicine bag on his hip.

"I hope that thing works," said Lew. "You be careful."

He saddled Diablo and set out along the Grand River with his rifle across his lap. About two miles from the trading post, the river turned west. Jubil followed it to where it was joined by a stream flowing in from the south. He heard the dog bark again. The sound came from the south. Jubil dismounted, hitched his horse, and started out on foot in the direction of the sound. He hoped Diablo would still be there when he returned. He came to a foothill topped with a rocky ridgeline and climbed it. Hidden behind a jumble of rock, he looked out over the ridge.

There was a lake below. Indians, maybe two hundred of them, were riding along the shore, heading south. He watched for a few minutes to be sure they were moving away. The dog barked again, but closer this time, from the south. Then the dog burst out of a line of trees at the base of the hill and ran straight up the hillside toward him. It stopped a few feet away, snarling, barking, and threatening to attack. Jubil ducked and watched through a narrow gap in the rocks. An Indian scout rode out from the cover of the trees, following the dog. The scout watched the dog for a moment, and then started his horse up the hillside toward it—and Jubil. Jubil put his rifle down and removed his hunting knife from the sheath on his belt. He could not risk taking a shot at the dog or the scout. It would alert the whole band of Indians, bringing them down on him and endangering the people camped at the trading post. He considered edging back down the hill and making a run for it, but he figured the dog would chase him.

The dog made a short burst forward, baring its teeth and snarling. A sudden flash of yellowish-brown fur appeared as the dog flushed a marmot from its hiding place in the rocky ridge Jubil hid behind. The marmot dashed across the hillside, and the dog gave chase. The Indian watched the dog chase its newfound prey, as he continued to ride up the hillside, his rifle butt on his hip, barrel pointed up, his finger by the trigger.

Jubil was not going to be able to stay in his position much longer. If the scout looked in his direction, he might see him. As if he had read Jubil's thoughts, the Indian turned his head in Jubil's direction and scanned the ridge. Jubil ducked down out of sight and flattened himself against the rocky ridge.

He was going to have to reconsider his defensive strategy. He wouldn't get a chance to use his knife. The Indian scout was on full alert, ready to fire. If Jubil leapt out of hiding to jump him, the scout would just shoot him down. He would just have to hope the scout didn't ride up the hillside and discover his position. If the scout did ride up on him, Jubil would have to use his rifle, regardless of the alarm it would raise.

He sheathed his knife and chambered a round into his rifle as quietly as he could. He listened carefully for the footsteps of the horse, but the barking of the dog made it difficult. Even above the sound of the dog, he heard his own heavy breathing and made an effort to calm himself. He needed to be totally relaxed and ready to shoot quickly and accurately if his position was discovered. Then he would have to get out of there fast and back to the trading post, to warn the others.

He stood with his back flattened to the rocks and held his rifle across his chest at the ready. He heard the clop of hooves and could tell the horse was very close. At the same time, the dog's barking changed into the growling and yelping of a life and death struggle. Jubil heard the Indian call out, "Shoon-kuh! Shoon-kuh!" He did not know what that meant, but he assumed it was directed at the dog. Whatever the scout said had no effect on the melee, which carried on for a while longer. In which time, the scout had ridden to the top of the hillside and his horse's head was now visible to Jubil over the top of the ridgeline. The scout shouted at the dog again. If the horse took one more step forward, Jubil would be exposed.

The horse turned its head and looked straight at Jubil, as the Indian called again to the dog. The fighting had stopped now, so the dog must have prevailed. The Indian called the dog once more, and the horse whinnied and nodded at Jubil, as if trying to alert his rider of Jubil's presence. Jubil held his breath and readied himself to fire.

The scout reined the horse's head to the left, away from Jubil, and turned him to back down the hill. Jubil saw the Indian's back, and then the horse's tail disappeared over the ridgeline. Jubil shifted his position enough to watch the scout ride down the hillside trailed by the dog, who proudly carried the dead marmot.

Jubil allowed himself to breathe freely again. As soon as the scout and the dog had disappeared into the trees, he retreated down his side of the hill. As he drew near to where Diablo was tethered, she turned her head to watch him approach.

"That's a good girl for staying here and staying quiet," Jubil said, patting his horse's shoulder. "That was a close call. Let's get out of here."

He mounted up and retraced his route to the trading post, where he described what he had seen and his close call with the scout. He assured Major Powell that the scout and the band of Indians were moving away from the trading post.

"Very good," said Powell, climbing out of the rifle pit. "I'm glad you made it back safely."

Lew nodded approvingly at Jubil.

Powell declared the emergency over and released the women and children from the barricaded trading post. That evening, he gathered his expedition party and made an announcement. He would be leaving the following day for the winter campsite. Those wishing to continue with him would need to be ready to depart the following day.

For Jubil, the prospect of helping Powell with the study and learning more about the Ute himself was appealing, but camping for the winter in the mountains was less so. That night he finished his letter to Nelly, describing the Indian scare at Hot Springs and telling her where they planned to camp for the winter. He did not say when he expected to be home. He was still not sure himself. He would enjoy staying for the winter, helping the major with his Indian studies and learning something himself. But he was concerned staying apart from Nelly for too long, she might lose her patience with him. Though Luke had insisted the decision was up to Jubil, he also did not feel good about leaving Luke without his help for that long. In either case, Nelly's first year of classes at Normal University would have begun by the time he got home, so he put off the decision for now and closed by wishing her well with her studies.

At the trading post, he bought her a pair of beaded deerskin moccasins and a fringed shoulder bag crafted by the Ute Indians. For Eli and Ike, he bought painted Indian tomahawks decorated with strings of feathers. He wondered if there might be a market for Indian crafts at home. Perhaps selling their art might allow Indians to turn reservations into small industries. He reminded himself to discuss it with Luke. In spite of the current Indian scare, he thought this would be a good place to bring Nelly. The area was usually peaceful and beautiful, and the hot springs was a delight. He'd mention the idea sometime, just to gauge her interest.

The expedition party would be smaller from here on. The three ministers, which included the irascible Reverend Wood and his hapless son Henry, had never intended to winter over with Powell, and were returning home. They would ride back to Denver and take a stagecoach on to Cheyenne. Byers would remain at the trading post. Heading for the winter camp were the major, Mrs. Powell, Walter Powell, and the seven students, along with Sumner, Farrell, Lew, and Jubil. Many of the students would stay at the new site just long enough to help the major prepare for the winter. Newly added to their ranks were two trappers who had been camped at Hot Springs, Gus Lankin and Billy Hawkins. Sumner endorsed the pair as skilled woodsmen and hunters. Jubil found Hawkins amiable, but Lankin struck him as shifty. Neither Jubil nor Lew saw any good reason for Powell to allow these men to travel with them, something they agreed on privately, but they did not question the major.

Jubil watched as Powell reviewed a map with Lew. Given his skills with the sextant, Lew was the best navigator in the group. Powell pointed out a trail leading out of Middle Park, scouted earlier in the decade by frontiersman Jim Bridger and surveyor Edward Berthoud. The trail led down Cedar Canyon and crossed over Gore Pass, perhaps fifty miles to the west. From there the trail continued on to Salt Lake City. Powell would follow it only fifty miles west of Gore Pass, to the winter campsite. On the map, it looked like a matter of staying on a course due west, but the mountainous terrain would make that nearly impossible.

The party's progress toward their new campsite was agonizingly slow. After two weeks of travel, they had covered only fifty miles. Just when Jubil was beginning to believe the trip had become an endless series of navigational challenges, they entered a region of dense but passable forest. They set up camp, but in the morning Jubil's relief turned to concern after checking on the animals, as he did each morning. He found Powell at breakfast with the rest of the party.

"Sorry to bring bad news so early in the day, Major," he said, "but two of the pack horses and one of the saddle horses are gone."

Before Powell could respond, Hawkins drawled, "I don't see Lankin around. I'm thinking maybe he lit out with them."

Lew rose and stepped away from the group.

"Which way would he head?" Powell asked.

"Well, I can't say for sure," replied Hawkins, "but my guess is he would stick to the hills rather than go back out onto those plains."

"Looks like he made off with a large portion of our supplies too, Major," said Lew, rejoining the group.

"We need those animals, and we need those supplies," said Powell.

Lew looked at Jubil and hooked a thumb in the direction of the forest. Jubil nodded.

"Jubil and I will go hunt him down, Major," offered Lew.

Powell nodded. "Thank you, Lieutenant. We'll wait here until midday."

Jubil and Lew saddled their horses and rode out.

"I don't think he'll be too hard to find," said Jubil. "The horses leave a trail, plain as day, in the soft ground."

"I'll keep an eye on the woods," said Lew. "You keep an eye on the trail."

Jubil followed the trail of the horses for about an hour. At one point, the trees thinned and the trail started up an incline, toward an outcropping covered with boulders.

"We're going to lose the trail over this ground," said Jubil.

A shot rang out and Jubil heard the buzz of a round fly past his head. He and Lew leapt down from their horses and took cover.

"He's in those rocks above us," said Lew. "Let's split up. You circle around and see if you can get behind him."

Jubil made his way around the hill, dashing from tree to tree for cover. Another shot was fired, this time in Lew's direction, and Jubil saw rifle smoke come from a position among the rocks. As he circled the hillside, Jubil spotted the two pack horses, still laden with supplies. They were at the base of the hill directly behind where Jubil had seen the smoke. Reaching the horses, Jubil heard another shot and heard Lew return fire. Jubil grabbed the lead rope and led the animals down the hill and back into the trees. Lew continued to fire.

"Lew!" Jubil shouted. "I've got the pack horses!"

Lew emerged from the rock outcropping.

"Looks like he snuck down the hill and got away," reported Lew.

"Let's clear out," Jubil suggested. "We've got the animals and the supplies."

Lew looked around behind him. "I hate to let that vermin escape," he declared as he scanned the area for some sign of Lankin.

"He's not worth the trouble of hunting down," Jubil said. "Come on, Lew. Let's go back. The others are waiting." Jubil watched as Lew continued to survey the area with a clenched jaw and fire in his eyes. Here it was again, he thought—that single-minded determination that sometimes seemed to go against Lew's own best interests.

"You know the major won't care about catching Lankin," Jubil urged. "All he cares about is the supplies and the horses for his mission. We've got those. Let's go. Even if we catch him, what'll we do with him? We can't take him with us. We can't just shoot him . . . so . . ."

Lew took a deep breath and blew it out. Jubil felt him wrenching his attention away from the hunt for Lankin. He put his hand on Jubil's shoulder and looked him in the eye. "All right," he said. "Let's go."

Lew and Jubil made their way back to the expedition party.

"Lankin escaped, Major," reported Lew, "but Jubil got the horses and supplies."

"Well, that's the important part. Thank you, gentlemen," said Powell.

After two additional weeks, they finally reached the White River and the area where Powell intended to camp. The party began chopping down tall grasses for fodder, cutting and stacking firewood, and building cabins. Jubil's experience helping Pete build his cabin made him valuable. Powell asked him to help supervise the students. Some cut and peeled logs while others built rock fireplaces. Jubil found them to be good workers. They raised two cabins and chinked them tightly. By the end of October the preparations for winter were complete. Major Powell and Mrs. Powell, now the only woman in the group, took one cabin. Walter Powell, Garman, Sumner, Dunn, Howland, and Farrell were left to share the other.

The next morning Powell would accompany the members of the party who were not spending the winter—most of the students and Dr. Wing—to the railroad depot at Green River Station, Wyoming, some one hundred fifty miles to the north. Lew and one of the students, were going back to Hot Springs to enjoy the area a little longer, before returning to Denver and home.

After supper, Jubil and Lew sat outside the cabin, tending the campfire.

"I've learned a lot from following you this summer," Jubil said.

"It's been my pleasure to travel with you," replied Lew. "You are a person a fellow can rely on, and you're easy to be around."

"Thanks," said Jubil.

Lew asked, "Have you decided yet about when you're going home—if at all?"

Jubil poked the fire with a stick, and sparks rose into the cold air. "I'm embarrassed to say I've put off making a commitment, but I'm going home. I've got responsibilities," he said, meaning Nelly, Luke, and the store.

"Good," Lew said. "You can head home with us if you like."

"Thanks," said Jubil, "but I think I'll ride with the major so we can talk about plans for the expedition next summer. I'm guessing I'll need to work on getting someone to build the boats."

"That's going to be a wild ride, down that river," said Lew, shaking his head. "I envy you a bit, I have to say. But I'll see you back in Bloomington well before then."

Jubil went to the major's cabin to inform him of his decision. Powell had no problem with Jubil's plans for the winter and appreciated his intent to start making preparations for the Grand Canyon expedition. Mrs. Powell, who had become an ardent supporter of Warner and Walker Outfitters and Nelly Boswell, praised his sound judgment for going home. He wished he had made his mind up before he had written his last letter to Nelly.

The next morning, Powell, Jubil, and the others departed the camp, leaving Mrs. Powell, Walter Powell, Jack Sumner, Ned Farrell, and Sam Garman there. The trip north was another trek across rugged but relatively flat terrain. Scarcity of good water in the arid high plains was their only real hardship, but they found enough to get by.

When Jubil could ride with Major Powell during the day and while sitting with him at the fire at night, he consulted with him about their next expedition, and their plans began to take shape. Jubil's experience with boats was limited to canoeing on the Mackinaw and Illinois Rivers, so he received a maritime education as Powell explained his sketches and specifications, which Jubil would take to the boatbuilder. The discussion also brought into clear focus how difficult the trip would be. Jubil hoped he was equal to the challenge.

The travel party made decent time and in mid-November reached Green River Station, Wyoming. The morning Jubil left for Bloomington, he carried out one responsibility he regretted having to do. He walked to the livery stable where they had boarded their horses and entered Diablo's stall. The sleek black horse turned her head to look at him.

"Well, girl," Jubil said as he patted her neck, "I hate for us to say good-bye, but I'm heading home. I'm sending you back with the major. He's a little set in his ways but not a bad sort. You've been a good friend." He hugged the horse's neck and walked away.

He and the others said good-bye to Major Powell at the depot. Jubil took some teasing from some of the students about being wealthy when he purchased a first-class ticket from Green River Station to Chicago, with a stop at Council Bluffs, for forty-eight dollars. But after months of sleeping outdoors, the comfort of a bed would be worth every penny, and he had few expenses at home these days.

On the second day of the luxurious train ride, Jubil entertained himself with thoughts of traveling in that fashion with Nelly. She was not overly dainty and could most likely endure the relatively harsh conditions of the Longs Peak expedition. However, he thought Nelly would undoubtedly enjoy traveling on the Union Pacific Railroad in a Pullman Palace Car. He passed the time pondering various scenarios in which he might make that happen.

He stopped for a few days in Council Bluffs. Even before the expedition to Longs Peak, Major Powell had charged Jubil—and Warner and Walker Outfitters—with finding a boatbuilder capable of producing craft tough enough to withstand the Colorado River yet light enough to portage around rapids when necessary. Mr. Warner had been making inquiries to identify the best craftsman for the job, and Jubil was eager to find out what he had learned. After reviewing the information, they agreed that the best candidate was Thomas Bagley, of Chicago. Jubil would plan a visit to consult with him after the new year.

In turn, Jubil provided Mr. Warner a report on the performance of the clothing and equipment used on the trip, and the performance of various suppliers. Jubil enjoyed these aspects of the outfitter business. It was sitting in the store that made him restless.

Before he left Council Bluffs, Jubil sent a telegram to Nelly telling her when he would be home.

CHAPTER 14

When Jubil's train pulled in to the Bloomington station, Eli and Ike were there to meet him. They waved dramatically as Jubil stepped off the train and welcomed him home with big handshakes.

"Hello, boys. It's good to see you. Is Nelly all right?"

"Yes, she's fine," said Eli. "She's sorry she couldn't meet you, but she had an examination today in one of her classes, and she couldn't miss it. She said she'd be finished by three o'clock."

"I see," said Jubil, tamping down his disappointment. "Well, thanks for coming to pick me up. Did you boys burn anything to the ground while I was gone?"

Eli pulled a face. "Very funny," he said. Ike looked at the ground and fidgeted.

"You were gone a long time," Eli said as Moses pulled the carriage up Front Street. "Do you have any Indian stories?"

"In fact, I do," Jubil laughed. "I'll tell you all about it later. Say, by the way, happy sixteenth birthday, boys. I'm sorry I missed it."

"Thanks," said Eli. "Luke bought a cake, and we shared it with the customers. It was fun."

"Luke is a good fellow," declared Jubil. "Is everything all right with him and the store?"

"Yes, everything is fine," said Eli.

Ike gave Eli a nudge with his elbow. Eli shook his head and tried to ignore him. But Ike persisted. "Tell him, Eli," Ike said under his breath. Eli stared daggers at his brother.

"What is it?" asked Jubil.

"It's nothing," replied Eli, giving Ike a shove. "It's none of our business."

Jubil frowned at the twins until Ike turned to address him.

"Some fellow has been calling on Nelly while you've been gone," reported Ike.

Jubil was stunned. "Who?"

"William Brown," Ike said.

"The Willy Brown we went to school with?" Jubil asked incredulously. Surely she was not seeing the fellow Jubil had trounced many years ago for teasing her at school.

"Yes," said Ike. "He's going to Normal University with Nelly."

Surely Ike and Eli had the wrong idea. "What did you mean, when you said he has been 'calling on her'?" inquired Jubil with a sense of growing dismay.

"He came to the house," said Ike, "more than once."

Jubil stared straight ahead, struggling to overcome his shock, as Eli drove the rest of the way to the Boswell residence. Surely Nelly wouldn't consider someone else without even talking to him about it first. Then again, why wouldn't she? She had told him that she didn't dare let herself care too much for him, and he had let it go at that in order to protect their friendship.

"What class was Nelly's examination in?" asked Jubil when they arrived at the house.

The twins looked at each other. Ike replied, "Latin."

"I'll get my pack later," said Jubil, climbing down from the carriage. "If you go back to the store, tell Luke I'll be along in a while."

Jubil went to the Boswells' stable to retrieve Star. She saw him coming and began to whinny and prance. "Hello, Star," said Jubil, hugging the horse around the neck and patting her shoulder. Star pressed her head against his chest. "I missed you, too." Jubil saddled her and mounted up. "Come on, girl. Let's go find Nelly."

Jubil rode to Normal University's campus and hitched Star to one of the newly planted trees around Old Main, the university's central building. Old Main was much larger than Wesleyan's North Hall, and the cupola atop the building was proportionally larger, with clocks on each face. Jubil had ridden past the building countless times but had never been inside. He stepped through the main entrance and asked the first person he encountered where to find the Latin classroom. Climbing the stairs to the third floor, he waited outside the classroom until a student emerged.

"Is this the classroom with a Latin examination under-way?" Jubil asked.

"Yes," answered the student.

"Is Nelly Boswell still in there?" he asked.

The student nodded.

"Thank you," said Jubil, and stepped back to wait for her. After a few minutes she emerged.

"Jubil!" shouted Nelly, as she threw her arms around him. He thought this was a good sign, and he couldn't help hugging her back unreservedly. It felt unbelievably good to hold her in his arms.

"I'm so glad you're home!" she said. "I'm sorry I couldn't come to meet you at the station. What are you doing here?"

"I came to see you," he said.

"How nice of you," Nelly said sincerely. "Is anything wrong?"

"Is there somewhere we could talk?" asked Jubil.

"I suppose we can sit in any of these open classrooms," she said. "Will that do?"

Jubil nodded. Nelly led the way into a lecture hall in which the seats looked like pews and the lectern at the front of the room looked like a pulpit. They entered and sat side by side in the front row.

"What is it, Jubil? You're worrying me," said Nelly.

"The boys met me at the station," Jubil said. "Ike told me that William Brown has been calling on you."

Nelly looked at Jubil and then looked away. She sighed. Jubil knew she was about to deliver some hard truth, and he prepared himself for it.

"I wouldn't say he's been 'calling on me,'" said Nelly.

Jubil remained quiet.

"Billy is in my Latin class, here at Normal," Nelly began.

"Billy?" Jubil parroted.

Nelly frowned slightly. "Yes, that's what he prefers these days."

Jubil wanted to remind Nelly what a dumb brute William Brown had been in their earlier days. How he had teased her about her real name, Cornelia, calling her 'Corny' until Jubil stepped in and pounded some sense into him. He wanted to say it, but he didn't. He knew he was being childish, so he held his tongue.

"He's a good student, Jubil. He's been helping me with my Latin verb conjugations," Nelly explained. "He asked if he could call on me at home, and I told him yes. He's someone to study with. He's a perfect gentleman."

"Perfect?" Jubil said, with a hint of disbelief.

Nelly narrowed her eyes at him. "You know what I mean."

Jubil looked away, ashamed for feeling so possessive. He had no right to be. There were no commitments between them.

"I'm sorry, Nelly," said Jubil, looking at her. "I'm not accusing you of doing anything wrong." He struggled to find the right words. "It's just that, I think about you a lot while I'm away."

"I certainly know that feeling," Nelly said. "I think about you a lot while you're away too. I do my best to be strong and tell myself that all the worry in the world about you will not stop fate.

But it is so hard, Jubil. Sometimes it's nice just to have someone to pass the time with—someone who is here to talk to."

Tears welled up in Nelly's eyes.

"I'm sorry, Nelly," he said, again. "It's just that I . . ."

Nelly reached out and took his hand.

"I know, Jubil," she said. "I would never ask you not to follow your heart. I'm proud of the person you are . . . but still . . . it's hard to be here without you."

Jubil watched a tear roll down Nelly's cheek. He put his arm around her. She laid her head on his shoulder.

"I understand," he said. "I want to make you happy, but I can't do that by pretending to be someone I'm not."

"Neither of us can," Nelly replied.

He was very aware he might have delayed too long in confessing his deepest hopes for their relationship.

"I love you, Nelly . . . I think I always have . . . and if you'd have me, I'd like us to spend our lives together."

Nelly took one of Jubil's hands in both of hers. "Are you asking me to marry you?"

"I am," he said, and waited with dread for her response.

She leaned toward him, put her hand on his cheek, and gently kissed his lips. A surge of heat flushed his face, and he felt lightheaded. He had dreamed of this moment for years, and wanted the kiss to last forever. After a long moment, she leaned away.

"I told myself I wouldn't do that," she said, looking at him with a sad smile. "I love you too, Jubil, but there are many types of love. There is love for family, for friends, for nature, for our life's purpose. I don't think either of us is sure yet which of those is driving us most."

"Are you saying you won't marry me?" he asked with a sinking feeling in his stomach.

"I'm saying I'm not ready to be married," she said. "And I don't think you are either . . . not really. I want to finish my education and find a job as a teacher. I'm so weary of having my life dictated to me by someone else. I want to make my own decisions."

"I would never prevent you from that," Jubil said. Though he had never given this a great deal of thought, he felt what he was saying was true.

"I appreciate that, I really do," she said, patting his hand, "but I'm just not ready. Maybe someday . . . but not yet." She fixed her gaze on his and waited for his response. He remained silent—considering what she had told him. She continued, "And if I'm totally honest, I'm still concerned about losing you. I don't want to become a widow, Jubil. I don't want to be viewed as a sad shell of myself and have to contend with pity and proposals from every bachelor in town. That may sound selfish, I know, but there you have it."

He was disappointed, of course, but it gave him hope to hear her say that she just wasn't ready 'yet.' But then there was the matter of her concern about his adventures. He had yet to tell her of his plans for next summer.

"I may as well go ahead and confess that I've committed to next summer's expedition with Major Powell."

"What a surprise," Nelly said sarcastically. "How are you planning to defy death on your next trip?"

"You know Major Powell," Jubil said, attempting to deflect the blame. "He wants to do something no one has ever done before. We're going to follow the course of the Colorado River all the way through the Grand Canyon."

Nelly's jaw dropped. "You can't be serious."

Jubil searched for words to reassure her that the trip would not be as dangerous as it sounded, but there were none— because it was as dangerous as it sounded. His stomach tied itself in knots as she frowned at him.

"When were you going to tell me about it?" she asked pointedly. "After I'd accepted your marriage proposal?"

"I didn't see any reason earlier to worry you—or anyone

else—so far in advance. I haven't even talked to Luke about it yet."

She narrowed her eyes at him, a sure sign she was angry. "Very thoughtful of you to tell me before telling Luke."

"I'm making a mess of things here, I'm afraid," Jubil said in frustration. How had the conversation gone from confessing his deepest feelings to apologizing for his plans?

Nelly studied his face as she absentmindedly refolded the handkerchief she had been clutching. Her tears seemed to have dried up in the heat of her anger.

"Welcome home from your expedition, by the way," she said coldly. "I'm glad you survived. Congratulations on being one of the first explorers to summit Longs Peak. It's quite a feather in your cap, and a boon for Warner and Walker Outfitters as well. Luke and my brothers are very excited. You would think they had all climbed that mountain with you."

"Thank you," he said. He was at a loss for words otherwise.

"I'm sorry, but I have another class now," Nelly said, and she stood up.

Their conversation had not yielded the result he'd wanted, but it hadn't dashed all of his hopes either. She would not have kissed him like that if she did not love him. That gave him hope that over time he'd be able to convince her to marry him. But while he saw and longed for a future with her, he was not sure she would ever feel the same. They stepped out of the lecture hall just as William Brown stepped out of the Latin examination classroom.

"Hello, Walker," said William Brown, offering Jubil a handshake. "Welcome home."

"Hello, Brown." Jubil did not want to shake the other man's hand, but he did.

"Will you be in town long?" Brown asked.

"Yes, for a good while," replied Jubil, with an air of warning.

Brown nodded. "Well, I have another class. Good day, Nelly. Good day, Walker."

"Thank you," said Nelly, smiling at Jubil. "You were very gentlemanly."

Jubil gave her a courtly bow.

"I haven't seen Luke yet," said Jubil. "I'm going back to the store, and then up to the farm. When will I see you?"

"Come have Thanksgiving dinner with us Thursday," said Nelly. "Invite Luke too."

They all lent a hand putting the finishing touches on dinner at the Boswells' on Thanksgiving Day. As they enjoyed their meal, the room was filled with the buzz of joyful conversation. After dessert, Jubil presented the gifts he had bought at the trading post. Nelly loved her shoulder bag and the Indian moccasins, which she immediately put on. They fit her perfectly, and Jubil thought they made her even more beautiful, if that was possible. The tomahawks put Eli and Ike into a swoon of gratitude, though Mrs. Boswell questioned the wisdom of arming the boys with axes.

"I have one more gift for you," Jubil said to Nelly. "In the form of an invitation. To celebrate your upcoming eighteenth birthday, I'd like the honor of escorting you to supper at the Ashley House...with your parents' blessing, of course."

Nelly looked surprised, and stared at him for a moment. Luke smiled at him and gave an approving nod. Ike and Eli, surprisingly, held their tongues and waited for the drama to unfold. Nelly's parents were waiting for her response.

"That's very thoughtful, Jubil," she said, and turned to her parents. "Mama?"

"You're old enough to decide for yourself who you are seen with, dear," Mrs. Boswell said with a smile.

"I see nothing wrong with it," Mr. Boswell said. "It certainly won't be the first time you two have been seen together."

"Thank you," Jubil said to her parents. He appreciated their easy acceptance, considering everyone knew that being seen on a formal evening out was not the same thing as walking home from school together.

"I'll pick you up the evening of your birthday then?" he asked Nelly.

She nodded and smiled.

On the evening of December 11, he picked Nelly up in a hired carriage and drove them to the Ashley House. They were seated at a table by the window looking out on the courthouse square. It had begun to snow lightly, beautifying everything with a downy white blanket.

"This is very nice," Nelly said, after they had ordered.

"I'm pleased you were willing to be seen in public with me," Jubil said with a grin. Nelly smiled at him and rolled her eyes.

"How are you enjoying your studies?" he asked. "Is university living up to your expectations?"

"It is, yes," she said enthusiastically. "Especially my class in English Literature. My professor makes studying the works and lives of the Brontë sisters enlightening and inspiring. They were so talented and did so much to further women's place in literature, and the world. I'm enjoying it very much."

Jubil enjoyed hearing her be so passionate about her studies. He was pleased that her determination and persistence had won her this opportunity. Somewhat selfishly, he also hoped her studies would fill her days while he was away, rather than worry about him.

Warner and Walker Outfitters did a brisk business during the Christmas season. No other store in town sold anything like their heavy-duty but stylish clothing. Even more unique was their harsh weather gear, especially slickers, parkas, and furs. Sales were also robust in camping gear, but competition from other local stores cut into their sales of firearms and fishing gear. Jubil worked longer hours in the store than usual to help with the heavy sales, but the holiday atmosphere made it a pleasure. Luke, Eli, and Ike boasted to customers of Jubil's mountain climbing accomplishment and of his firsthand experience with many of the store's products. Jubil had not yet tired of talking with people about being one of the first to summit Longs Peak, but his story was becoming shorter with each retelling.

In mid-January, Jubil set off for Chicago to meet with Thomas Bagley at his shop on Clark Street, on the banks of the Chicago River. They reviewed Powell's diagrams and notes: Powell wanted four boats. Three of them—at twenty-one feet long, four feet wide, and two feet deep, each capable of carrying two tons of cargo—would carry the expedition's freight. They were to be constructed from oak, with double-ribbed hulls and double posts on stem and stern. Fore and aft, there would be storage compartments, decked over and sealed watertight. The fourth boat would be smaller and lighter: sixteen feet long and made from pine. Powell intended it to be a pilot boat to lead them through the more treacherous passages, so it had to be fast, maneuverable, and light enough to portage easily. The design, Bagley said, was a customization of a Whitehall harbor boat, often used as a ship's tender. Bagley had built many of them.

Once the boats were under construction, Jubil spent the remaining winter months ordering the provisions and equipment listed on the manifest, and having them shipped to Mr. Warner's warehouse in Council Bluffs. His level of anxiety about the expedition rose during this time as he attended to the many details that would contribute to a successful trip. Each item on the manifest caused him to review how it would meet their needs, which required him conjuring up possible scenarios—best case and worst. He did not by nature focus on negative outcomes, but thorough planning required it. And thinking things through improved his confidence that he was ready for what he would face.

When Jubil returned to Chicago in April to verify that the boats were ready, he found there had been a humorous misunderstanding about one of them. Powell had instructed that the pilot boat be named the *Emma Dean* and that two of the freight boats be named *Kitty Clyde's Sister* and *Maid of the Canyon*. When Bagley had asked the name of the third freight boat, Jubil had said, "No name." When he arrived and saw names painted on all of the boats, including the third freight boat, he laughed, for Bagley had painted *No Name* on her hull. Jubil began to mention it to Bagley, but then he decided to leave it as it was.

He and Bagley tested the boats on the Chicago River. Though much larger and heavier than any canoe or rowboat Jubil had ever handled, the boats were more manageable and responsive in the water than he had expected. Still, he was concerned that his limited skills would be an embarrassment to him in the company of the rest of the expedition party.

Throughout the spring, Nelly was working on her studies at Normal University. Jubil enjoyed spending evenings quizzing her on her course material from notes she had prepared. One warm evening in April, they sat on the porch swing, working on Nelly's Latin.

"Do you mind going over the verb conjugations one more time?" she asked.

"Not at all," he said. In truth, he would rather not, but he would not disappoint her. "I'm glad you let me help. Considering I'm not the scholar William Brown is."

"Well, I'm much more at ease in your company," Nelly said with a smile.

"Thank you," he said. "Is that out of habit or affection?"

"Some of both, I suppose," she said and patted his hand.

He had not brought up marriage again, though he had been tempted. He would like to get some form of commitment before he left for the expedition, but he didn't want to force her hand and risk pushing her away. And tonight, again did not feel like the time to mention it.

They made another review of Nelly's Latin lesson.

"You did very well that time," he said. "Very impressive. Last summer I listened to Major Powell and Lew rattle off Latin names for specimens and none of those words stuck with me. I may never be much of a scholar."

"Oh, you could do it if you put your mind to it," Nelly said. "You just don't see it as important to you right now."

"I appreciate the vote of confidence," he said. He hoped she was right.

"Will there be much science on your Grand Canyon trip?" she asked. "Or is it all about exploration and adventure."

"I believe there is science done everywhere the major goes," Jubil said.

"I have to be honest," she said, furrowing her brow. "I have a bad feeling about this trip. I understand your desire to explore the wilderness, but do you have to put yourself this close to death to enjoy life?"

He considered his answer carefully.

"I set out to follow Major Powell, and he's counting on me now," he said. "I have to meet the challenges I'm given in life, Nelly—and I want to go. I'll admit to being nervous about this trip, but I won't refuse to go just because I'm afraid. That's not the person I want to be—that's not the person I am."

Nelly held his gaze for moment, then her hard attitude fell away. "I know," she said. She took his hand and laid her head on his shoulder. "And I'm proud of you for it."

"It's not all danger, you know," he said, gently. "I see a lot of wonderful things on these trips. Some of it I think you would enjoy yourself. I read the essay you wrote for English class. I loved it." She had been assigned to write an essay about a favorite gift she had received, and she had written about the Ute moccasins he brought her from Colorado. "Especially the part about how the soft leather connects you to the Earth, rather than being held apart from it by hard boots—that was beautifully done. Last summer when we were camped at Berthoud Pass, I thought of you, and again at the Hot Springs trading post. You should go see some of these things for yourself and write about them. It's so beautiful and peaceful. I'd do everything I could to make it as comfortable as possible for you."

She raised her head from his shoulder and smiled. "I'll not say that I won't."

"Good enough for now," he said, happy the conversation had ended on a positive note.

In early May, Jubil made his final preparations to leave Bloomington. Due to the limited space in the boats, he took only a small knapsack containing a few personal items, his bedroll, and his slicker. He rode Star to the Boswell residence and said his goodbyes to the boys and Nelly's parents. Then he and Nelly stepped out onto the porch and took a seat on the swing. She seemed unusually distant, which made him uneasy.

"I'll be home before you know it," he said, trying to be optimistic and cheerful. "If I can find somewhere to post a letter, I will."

Nelly nodded.

"What's troubling you?" he asked.

"I'm just concerned for you," she said, her eyes tearing up.

"I'll be as safe as I can be. I'll be back," Jubil said. "We'll get this behind us, and then we'll come to some kind of reckoning about the future."

Luke pulled up in front of the Boswell residence in his carriage and waved to them.

"Luke's going to take me to the depot," Jubil said, not wanting to let go of Nelly's hand.

As they rose from the porch swing, Nelly surprised him by wrapping her arms around him and pulling him close. He wanted badly to kiss her, but this embrace would have to suffice. And he was grateful for it. He just hoped she would welcome him home in a similar fashion after another long summer apart.

CHAPTER 15

In Chicago, Jubil supervised the loading of the boats onto a flatbed rail car, and then he rode the train with them to Council Bluffs, thinking the whole while of how painful it had been to leave Nelly behind this time.

In Council Bluffs, Mr. Warner met the train with wagonloads of supplies for the expedition. Powell did not know how many months the expedition would take, and had ordered the maximum food rations the boats could carry. Mr. Warner had hired a couple of men to help Jubil load the goods onto a freight car—flour, rice, sugar, bacon, beans, dried apples, and coffee adequate for ten months, along with tents, ponchos, bedrolls, rope, gold-panning gear, axes, hammers, saws, nails, and caulk. Jubil then continued west that same day.

They would set out from Green River Station, Wyoming, where Jubil had ended his adventure in the fall. He arrived there on May 18, and found the bulk of the expedition party—which would consist of eleven men, total—waiting for Powell and his brother Walter, who would not arrive for another week. Jubil and the men unloaded the boats and supplies from the train and hired a wagon to take them the short distance downriver to their campsite. Jubil organized their gear and checked it against his manifest, then checked it again, hoping to have everything in good order for Powell when he arrived.

Jack Sumner was among the adventurers again this spring, and he introduced Jubil to the other men. Jubil already knew Billy Hawkins, one of the trappers who had traveled with them from Hot Springs to the winter camp the previous year, and an acquaintance of Gus Lankin, the man who had stolen the horses and supplies on that expedition. Hawkins told Jubil he had never seen Lankin again after that episode. Sumner had recruited a few other men to serve as the designated hunting party for the expedition. Oramel Howland was a printer by trade, though his long hair and beard gave him the appearance of a mountain man, which was the manner in which he presented himself. At thirty-six years of age, Oramel was the oldest member of the party. Ten years his junior was his brother Seneca, who was quiet and shy and accepted his older brother's orders stoically. Bill Dunn was another trapper. His long hair fell down his back, his beard was waist-length, and he wore buckskins weathered to a greasy shine.

Powell had recruited the others in the party. Frank Goodman was a good-natured Englishman who had met Powell while adventuring the previous summer and had offered his services. George Bradley was a soldier so weary of military life he said he would volunteer for the expedition if Powell could arrange a military discharge for him, which Powell did. Andy Hall was a freckle-faced, gap-toothed, happy-go-lucky wanderer and sometime mule-tender who was one year younger than Jubil. Powell had spotted Andy the previous summer rowing on the Green River for his own recreation, and had recruited him for the trip.

While they waited for Powell, they divided and stored their supplies and equipment in the sealed compartments of the three freight boats and familiarized themselves with the vessels. Andy Hall gladly shared with Jubil what rowing experience he had, and in turn Jubil helped Andy improve his swimming skills. Sumner and his men also passed the time in Green River Station's saloons. Jubil became aware during this time of the differences between the two distinct groups in the party, those recruited by Sumner and those recruited by Powell. So far, he got along with everyone, although listening to Sumner pontificate about anything under the sun, he sometimes smiled to himself remembering how, the previous summer, he had scooted across the narrow ridgeline in the Rockies on his tail.

With all the preparations behind him, Jubil was finally able to let go of his anxiety about the trip and enjoy it. As his worry faded, he felt a level of enthusiasm for the expedition that surpassed anything he'd felt before in his life. He was doing what he was meant to do. He was willing to risk his life to be one of the first explorers through the Grand Canyon. If he met his end, then fate had simply taken its toll. There were worse ways to die, but no better way for him to live. He felt fortunate to be a part of the expedition, but he also felt he had earned his place there. And while he was traveling, he would come up with a plan to persuade Nelly to accept his life's purpose and agree to be his wife.

Major Powell and his brother arrived in Green River Station and were ready to leave the next day. There would be two major legs to their journey. First, they would follow the Green River south to where it met the Grand River and formed the Colorado River. It would take several weeks to even reach the Colorado. During the second leg, they would follow the Colorado through the Grand Canyon. How long that would take was anyone's guess.

By the time Powell and his brother arrived, the expedition's plans had become common knowledge in town, due to Sumner and his men frequenting the saloons. The novelty of the boats attracted the curious, and on the day of their departure, a small party of townspeople turned out to wish them well and wave them off as they launched.

The major rode in the pilot boat, the *Emma Dean*, along with Jack Sumner and Bill Dunn. Powell sat in the middle, navigating. Walter Powell and George Bradley were in the *Maid of the Canyon*. Jubil, Andy Hall, and Billy Hawkins manned the *Kitty Clyde's Sister*. The Howland brothers, Oramel and Seneca, and Frank Goodman crewed for the *No Name*.

Jubil sat in the center of the *Kitty Clyde's Sister*, Billy Hawkins took the propelling oars in the stem, and Andy Hall manned the steering oars in the stern. Jubil faced forward in the direction of travel while the oarsmen rowed blindly with their backs turned. It was Jubil's responsibility to direct his oarsmen. Given the practice he and Andy had gained before the expedition left Green River Station, Jubil thought his abilities were equal to anyone else's on the expedition except maybe Jack Sumner's. Sumner was the only one of the men who claimed any notable skill as a boatman, but that remained to be proven.

Within a mile of their departure, Jubil learned that facing forward was not a full defense against the river's obstacles. He thought the *Kitty Clyde's Sister* had settled into the flow of the current when she crunched to a halt, having run aground on a hidden sandbar. Jubil was thrown forward, while Hawkins and Hall, facing the other way, were thrown backward off their benches. The river current pulled the boat sideways as the men tried to recover.

"We've got to free the boat!" shouted Jubil, jumping over the bow onto the sandbar.

Hawkins joined him, and they struggled to free the boat. When it drifted free, the current pushed the stern around, and the boat began to float sideways downriver. Jubil and Hawkins jumped back in, and Hawkins and Hall tried to regain control. As Jubil and his crew struggled, the other boats made an effort to wait for them by rowing against the current. In the process, the Howland brothers and Goodman in the *No Name* drifted into a rocky area and broke an oar.

They lost control of their boat for a few minutes but mounted a spare oar and recovered. Only a few minutes into the expedition, Jubil and the other men were already on notice: the river was unpredictable and powerful.

They managed the remainder of the day without incident and made their first camp under an overhanging cliff among a cottonwood grove. Throughout last year's expedition Powell and his brother, Walter, had spent most of their evenings mingling with other expedition members, though the major occasionally went off alone to read or write. Jubil didn't notice that the major was sitting off by himself with his brother until Billy Hawkins, the designated camp cook, took a plate of food to Powell and left after delivering it. Jubil thought it rude of the men to shun Powell and took his own plate to join him.

"Mind if I join you, Major?" Jubil asked, preparing to sit on a log near Powell.

"Actually, I do," said Powell, looking up at Jubil and then glancing at the other men. "My role on this expedition requires me to comport myself as a commanding officer, not as a peer. I'll keep my distance from the men to give them an opportunity to grumble about my decisions. Several of these men were soldiers who didn't like taking orders while enlisted, and now that they are civilians, they have even less use for authority. But I must exercise authority, Jubil, to protect the expedition."

"Well, I don't expect to be grumbling about your orders, Major," said Jubil, "but if that's the way you want it, I'll go along."

Jubil had mixed emotions about Powell's comportment. He could see these were harder men to manage than the students and professionals on last year's expedition, but Powell placing himself apart seemed more likely to hurt his cause than help it. On the journey to Fort McPherson, General Sherman had never separated himself from his men—quite the opposite—and his men admired him for it. Jubil also felt personal rejection because Powell had included him, a family friend, in the group that he needed to remain aloof from. Once again Jubil recalled Lew's observation that Powell never let anyone's feelings deter him from his mission, but Jubil wondered if this determination might be a weakness rather than a strength.

For the next few days, it rained. Powell insisted on taking time at each campsite to go on his scientific forays. Occasionally, Jubil and others were invited to accompany him. Other times, Jubil went hunting with Sumner and his men or went fishing with Andy Hall. He enjoyed listening to the tall tales spun by Billy Hawkins, the camp cook. Jubil also enjoyed George Bradley's company. His stories about dissatisfaction with military life added to Jubil's conviction that the life of a soldier would not suit him either.

As the Green River approached the Uinta Mountains, the cliff walls rose higher, and the river began to tumble over the rocky riverbed. It was the first canyon of their journey. Oramel Howland was creating a map of the route they followed and labeling locations with the names Powell agreed to for areas with special features. The men named the canyon Flaming Gorge for the rusty red color of the rock walls. The channel narrowed and cut back on itself, forming a horseshoe shape.

The boats picked up speed, and, at first, Jubil gripped the sides of the boat with unease as they raced along the channel, but he soon felt excitement overtake him and was whooping along with the other men as they flew down the gorge at railroad speeds. The boats bucked and swayed but stayed reasonably under control. Shifting his weight and holding onto the boat in order to stay aboard reminded Jubil of staying on Diablo's back when he was breaking her. The wind in his hair, the cold spray off the prow as it dove into the channel, the bob-and-weave of the boat as it rolled with the waves—it was the most exhilarating experience of his life.

As the gorge widened, the river flattened out, and the rapids died. Powell's pilot boat, leading the way, had pulled in to shore, and Powell stood waving at the other boats to pull over.

"We were fortunate none of the boats hit any obstructions on that run," said Powell. "From this point on we will scout each stretch of rough water. The lookouts, sitting center position in each boat, will keep a sharp eye out for these flags," explained Powell, holding up two small red flags. "Waved right, then left, then down, indicates land at once. Waved right, indicates your boat should follow to the right of the pilot, waved left, follow to the left. Are we clear on the signals?"

Soon an opportunity arose for Powell to test his signal communications. Just past a rock the men named Beehive Point, for its dome shape pocked with holes where scores of swallows nested, they encountered the worst rapid so far. The channel was filled with large boulders, and the river dropped twenty feet over the next two hundred feet downriver. Midway through the rapid was a ten-foot waterfall. Here, Powell signaled them to land, and the men made the first of what would be innumerable portages.

Emptying the boats of their contents, they made multiple trips to carry the cargo along the rough banks of the river. Once the cargo was moved downstream, they lined the boats down, which required securing both the bow and stern with ropes. The bow rope was tied off downstream, while the stern rope was held fast by a crew upstream. The crew then let out the rope and eased the boat down the rapids, until it reached the falls. There the stern line was released, and the boat shot over the falls and was caught by the secured bow line. The crew then reeled it back in to shore, repacked the food and supplies, and set off down the river again.

The next day, the canyons opened up on a wide, lush valley. Powell said this area was known as Brown's Park, named after a Hudson's Bay Company man who came here decades ago with his Indian wife. The party rowed the boats through these still waters until they approached another canyon. Hearing the roar of another rapids ahead, they pulled in to rest. Powell went off on a scientific exploration of the area, and the hunters went in search of fresh meat. The hunters had no success, but Jubil and Andy Hall managed to catch a few bony fish to add to the party's stores.

Jubil missed traveling with Lew, but he was coming to enjoy Andy Hall's company very much. The son of Scottish immigrants, Andy had left home at thirteen to make his way in the West. He had no advanced knowledge or skills, but he was likeable and willing to work hard, and these traits gave the impression that he was a good man to have around.

As the trip progressed, Jubil reassessed Powell's insistence on maintaining his distance from the rest of the party. Every evening, Sumner and his men found something about the major's conduct to criticize. Their main complaint was his manner, which they found needlessly authoritarian. Perhaps it was authoritarian, Jubil thought, but maybe not needlessly. Without someone to make quick, firm decisions in the situations they faced daily, Jubil thought this lot would never survive.

On the twelfth day of the trip, the party finished their breakfast and made their preparations to navigate through the canyon ahead, into the Uinta Mountains. Powell, Sumner, Jubil, and Andy Hall stood looking toward the light purple cliffs that rose two thousand feet on each side as the river entered the narrow passage. The roar of the rapids was never-ending.

"Something about this place puts me in mind of a poem I recall from my school days," said Andy Hall. "It was called 'The Cataract of Lodore.' I can't recall who wrote it, but it was about a spirited river."

"That it was, Mr. Hall," said Powell, looking at Andy with astonishment. "It was written by Robert Southey. I know the piece by heart, but I'll spare you the recitation. It does express an apt sentiment for this place. We'll call this Lodore Canyon, in the poem's honor."

"Nah, that name don't suit me," said Sumner. "Using musty old poems to name new discoveries don't seem right."

Andy gave Jubil a gap-toothed smile and shrugged.

But the name Lodore Canyon stood, a testament to the authority Powell still maintained over every aspect of the journey.

Seneca Howland approached Jubil and asked shyly if he would mind switching boats with him for a time. Jubil agreed, thinking that Seneca might be anxious to escape his brother's criticism. That put Seneca in the center seat on the *Kitty Clyde's Sister*, with Andy Hall and Billy Hawkins rowing, while Jubil took the center seat on the *No Name*, with Oramel Howland and Frank Goodman rowing. They set off into the steep canyon, the steepest they had traversed yet, and the two-thousand-foot cliffs loomed over them on either side and blocked out the sun. The high walls allowed only a dim dawn-like light to reach them, and a chilling gloom fell over them. The goosebumps on Jubil's arms were as much a product of uneasiness as they were of the suddenly cold air.

The lighter and faster pilot boat soon moved ahead of the group, and Jubil, in the *No Name* at the back of the group, lost sight of it, which was not unusual. The pilot boat's function was to reconnoiter. The distance between the three freight boats increased as they entered a curving passage. The *Maid of the Canyon* was out of Jubil's sight now, and the *Kitty Clyde's Sister* was rounding the curve ahead. As Jubil and the *No Name* rounded the curve after them, the roar of the river rose ominously. Downstream, he saw the pilot boat pulled over, and Dunn waving a flag signal indicating that they should stop. The *Maid of the Canyon* complied, and the *Kitty Clyde's Sister* was angling for shore as well.

"Signal ahead to stop!" Jubil shouted. Howland, sitting backward to the flow of the river and facing Jubil, heard the order and pulled his oars to head the bow toward the shore.

But Goodman, in the steering position, sitting with his back to Jubil, did not hear it. Jubil turned to shout to Goodman again.

"Goodman! Pull over! Stop! Goodman! Stop!"

Goodman nodded his head to indicate he heard the order, but by then it was too late. The *No Name* was caught in the speeding center channel of the river. Jubil's heart leapt into his throat as their boat shot past the others and went over the edge of a line of water. He clutched the side as the boat flew into the air, dropped three feet, and then raced down a twenty-foot-long incline of boiling rapids. They dropped again into a flat stretch, and Howland and Goodman pulled frantically for shore. But they only had a few seconds, and a few seconds wasn't enough. The boat dropped into another stretch of rapids, longer and steeper than the last, and ran headlong into a huge boulder. The oars flew into the air, and the boat spun around.

Jubil began to experience the world in slow motion. He tried to keep his wits about him as he and the others sat helplessly clinging to the sides as their boat ran sideways down the rapids, directly toward another boulder. The boat smashed into the rock and broke in two. The men were thrown forward into the remains of the bow and clutched it as they were swept down the river. The shattered bow careened off another boulder, and Jubil lost his grip on it. The water encircled him and forced him under. He tried to swim for the surface, but the current keeping him underwater was too strong. The slipstream whipped him around a boulder and pushed him even deeper. His lungs began to burn as he fought the instinct to gasp for air. Time stood still, and he felt himself sliding into unconsciousness. Suddenly he was violently thrown over the top of an underwater boulder, bounced off the river bottom, and thrown upward again. He broke the surface and gasped for air. The remains of the bow passed nearby, and he grasped it but was thrown off again when it hit a rock. Still racing downriver but now able to keep his head above water, he saw

Oramel Howland ahead, standing on a sandbar in the middle of the current.

"Walker! This way!" Howland shouted, as Jubil swam hard in that direction. He beached himself on the sandbar as Howland grabbed his arm to keep him from being pulled downstream.

Jubil and Howland stood on the sandbar. *I nearly drowned,* Jubil thought. *And here I am, alive, but only by dumb luck.*

"Where is Goodman?" Howland asked.

"There!" Jubil shouted as Goodman flew past them, clinging to the remains of the bow.

Goodman saw the men and let go of the bow. Grabbing a barrel-sized boulder at the edge of the sandbar, he clung tightly.

"Hold tight, Goodman!" called Jubil. "Hold onto me!" he shouted to Howland. "I'll pull him in." He and Howland locked forearms as Jubil waded into the river and pulled Goodman onto the sandbar.

The three men stood on the sandbar, watching as the rest of the party lined the *Emma Dean* down the rapids toward them. Once the boat was beyond the rapids, Sumner brought the *Emma Dean* into the river and rowed for the men's small island. In an impressive show of boatmanship, he beached the *Emma Dean*. The three men held the boat fast, and Howland and Goodman jumped in.

"Leave the oars to me," Sumner ordered the others. "Lie flat in the bottom of the boat."

Jubil pushed the *Emma Dean* off the sandbar and leapt in. She caught the current, and Sumner rowed successfully for shore. Finally safe, the men waited for the remaining two boats to be lined down to meet them.

Beyond that point, the river flattened out. A few miles downriver, they spotted the remains of the *No Name*. It had run aground on another small sandbar near the canyon wall. Opposite the wreckage was a pool of calm water with a small beach. The boats pulled in to shore to attempt a salvage operation. Sumner again proved his worth as a boatman by rowing across the current, along with Andy Hall, to the shattered bow of the lost freight boat.

The *No Name* had held one-third of the expedition's food, gear, and scientific instruments, most of which was now gone. Fortunately, all of the party's personal belongings were stowed on the *Kitty Clyde's Sister.* Jubil felt overwhelmed by regret and shame as he and the rest of the expedition party watched Sumner and Hall pull out the remaining cargo. He had gained an intimate understanding of the river's power: it could turn a misstep or a second's hesitation into a deadly situation. Jubil heard a whoop as Sumner and Hall both held pieces of cargo above their heads. Sumner held a box, Hall a small keg.

"Your barometers survived the ride, Professor," called Sumner.

"That is some comfort, at least," said Powell.

"The whiskey made it too," shouted Hall gleefully. Jubil was surprised to see such cargo was among their supplies. He certainly hadn't packed it.

"I was not aware we carried any," said Powell. "Oh well, it may improve everyone's spirits . . . temporarily, at least."

Sumner and Hall made their way back across the river. Powell declared the beach a decent campsite, so they collected driftwood for a fire.

"Since we are in the business of naming landmarks," Powell said, looking back up the river at the rapids. "We'll call this area Disaster Falls." He turned and walked away.

Later that evening as the men sat around their campfire, Major Powell and his brother approached the group.

"Jubil, you were riding center on the *No Name,*" the major stated accusingly. "Why did you not heed the signal to stop?"

Jubil was surprised by Powell's tone.

"I did see the signal, Major," explained Jubil calmly, "but the men couldn't hear me shout over the roar of the rapids. By the time we saw what was happening, the current took us down."

Powell stared at Jubil for a moment and then turned on Goodman.

"The other oarsmen had no trouble against the current, Goodman," declared Powell.

Goodman just looked at Powell and shrugged.

"And you, Mr. Howland," Powell said, continuing his rant. "I understand you managed to lose the maps we've been creating." Powell turned his attention back to the whole group before Howland could respond. "Any more displays of such incompetence and the expedition will be lost." Powell then stormed off, leaving Walter Powell glaring angrily at them.

Jubil was shaken by Powell's criticism. Surely the major did not think whenever something went wrong, there was someone to blame? Surely he did not think everything that happened on this river would be under their control? Jubil thought a more appropriate response would have been to show relief that the men were not lost and to confer with the group about how to prevent such an accident in the future. Did Powell really care so little for Jubil's and the other men's lives? It wasn't the first time Powell had confirmed Lew's description of him: he did whatever he thought necessary to accomplish his goal without considering anyone's feelings. Jubil supported the goal wholeheartedly, but this was one instance in which Powell's approach was making a bad situation worse.

Andy Hall gave Jubil his signature smile and offered him the whiskey keg. "Take a pull or two on this, Jubil. It'll ease the pain of Powell's tongue lashing." The other men laughed.

Walter Powell, who had continued to stand on the periphery of the group, growled, "You deserved every word of it. We're lucky one of you damned fools hasn't killed anyone yet."

"Now, Walter," Sumner said condescendingly, "you seem to

be a little hot under the collar. Go have a soak in the river . . . it'll cool your head."

Walter clenched his fists and made a move for Sumner. Bill Dunn stood up and put himself in Walter's path. "No need to get all violent about it, Walter," Dunn said, calmly stroking his waist-length beard. "The major has made his point, and you've had your say too. . . . Let's all just let it go, and tomorrow will be another day."

Walter took another step forward and squinted into Dunn's face. Then he waved dismissively at the group and joined the major.

Andy Hall held up the whiskey keg. "I believe this is where we were before we were interrupted . . . Jubil?" Andy said offering the keg to Jubil again.

Jubil had never tasted alcohol in his life, but if it would give him some relief from thinking about what had happened that day, he thought the time might be right. He accepted the keg from Andy and poured a swallow of the whiskey into his mouth. It tasted terrible, and the fiery trail it burned down his throat and into his stomach was almost too much to tolerate, but he would not risk the men's taunts by coughing or spitting it out and being accused of wasting their valuable elixir. So he sat there, choking in silence, and felt sorry for himself. By the time the keg came around the fire a third time, Jubil's head was swimming, and his guts were churning. He retreated to his bedroll, hoping to sleep off the day and the whiskey, but he had a restless night.

The next several days were spent laboring down the river. Jubil was now back in the *Kitty Clyde's Sister* with Andy Hall, Billy Hawkins, and Seneca Howland. In one section, they faced three sets of rapids too rough to run. Powell named this area

Hell's Half Mile. The first set of rapids was too rough to line the boats over, so the first portage of both equipment and boats was required. The oak freight boats required six men to haul them over the rocks along the shore.

The boats were lined over the next two sets of rapids but not without incident. The *Maid of the Canyon* broke free as she was being lined down the final rapids. She spun into a boulder that smashed a hole in her bow. She stayed afloat and miraculously drifted into a calm pool, where they retrieved her. The men performed a quick patch job, and they moved on. A few days later a similar incident left the *Kitty Clyde's Sister* with a damaged bow, which soaked the men's personal belongings and the food rations. With both their freight boats leaking, the men needed to camp and make more thorough repairs. Jubil was wearied by these near-disasters, but at least Powell had not made matters worse by assigning more blame. Jubil was particularly glad that Goodman was not singled out for any criticism. Ever since the loss of the *No Name*, and Powell's rebuke, Goodman's mood had been much more subdued than usual. Jubil was ready to put the whole unlucky episode behind them and move on—they still had a long way to go.

Three weeks into the trip, they floated around a gentle bend and came to a forested beach about a quarter of a mile long and fifty yards wide, lying up against the canyon wall. It was an unusually welcoming campsite, covered with willows and cedar—which they could cut to make replacement oars— and pine trees, from which they could extract sap to caulk the leaky hulls. The understory was thick with sagebrush and dried grass, which would make comfortable bedding, and the beach was littered with driftwood for a campfire.

Powell went off to explore as the men unloaded the boats and made camp. They took off their outer layers and hung their wet clothes in the bushes to dry while Billy Hawkins began to work on supper. He set his campfire in a little alcove, tucked in among the brushy undergrowth. As Jubil and Andy were gathering more firewood, a strong gust of wind arose which blew embers from Hawkins' campfire into the sagebrush and dried grass. Jubil was amazed at how quickly the whole area was ablaze as the flames rapidly spread into the brushy understory. There was nowhere for them to run but into the river.

The scene was chaos. Jubil and Andy Hall ran for the *Kitty Clyde's Sister* and launched the boat into the river. Frank Sumner, Frank Goodman, and George Bradley bolted for the *Maid of the Canyon*, waded into the river and hung onto the side of the boat. Oramel and Seneca Howland attempted to pull their burning clothing from the blazing bushes as Bill Dunn flailed at the sleeve of his burning shirt and his smoldering beard. Billy Hawkins grabbed two nearby bedrolls and ran into the water. He unrolled the blankets, soaked them in the water, draped them over his head and shoulders, and went back into the burning camp. He gathered as much of the mess kit as he could carry and hurried to the *Emma Dean*. The fire reached the boat before Hawkins and burned through the rope tethering it to shore, setting it adrift in the current. Hawkins waded into the river, laden with gear, to catch the boat. A few steps from shore, the bottom dropped off sharply, and Hawkins went under. He came up empty-handed, having lost two blankets, a bread pan, a frying pan, spoons, tin plates, cups, a pickax, and a shovel. Sumner and Goodman were able to catch the *Emma Dean* before she was swept away.

Jubil and Andy came to rest in a pool below the rapids, where they were soon joined by the other men in their boats. They all pulled to shore and waited for Powell to join them. When the fire died out, they returned to the beach upriver to salvage what little they could find. They were now left with only the gold-panning pan in which to bake bread, a bake-oven with a broken lid, a kettle, a frying pan, one large spoon and two teaspoons, three tin plates, and five bailing cups. This mess gear had to support eleven men for the rest of the trip.

That night, the bedraggled crew made camp on a small sand beach. Jubil realized he was in for some cold nights. He had lost his bedroll and slicker in the fire. The only personal possessions he still had were in his knapsack—his money belt, White Dog's medicine bag, a shaving kit, and his hat.

He expected Powell to begin a court of inquiry and critique everyone's performance. To his surprise and relief, Powell was philosophical about the loss and blamed no one. The other men seemed to take the whole situation in stride.

After the whiskey keg had been around the fire a few times that night, Sumner observed, "You know that fire wasn't all bad . . . I'd say the trim it gave Bill Dunn's beard makes a sharp improvement to his looks."

The men roared with laughter, including Dunn. Oramel Howland caught the spirit of the moment. "Hawkins learned something too . . . you don't need to go in so deep, Billy, to wash the mess kit."

At first Jubil saw nothing funny about the situation, but their laughter was contagious, and soon he was laughing along with them, his mood lifting. He imagined the whole experience might seem more amusing if he accepted the whiskey keg when it came around, but he passed it along to Andy Hall, who was sitting next to him at the fire; if he was going to laugh in the face of death and disaster, he would do it sober. All of the other men—except maybe Andy—had much more experience in the wilderness than he did, but he wondered if, even after years of adventuring, such a reaction would ever come naturally to him.

After thirty-five days on the Green River, the men reached a major crossroads, the mouth of the Uinta River, where it flowed into the Green. The wagon trail from Denver to Salt

Lake City crossed the Green River here. Forty miles upstream on the Uinta River was an Indian agency, located on the Ute reservation. Powell thought they should take the opportunity to resupply the expedition before continuing on.

The party set up camp on the bank of the Green River, and the next morning Major Powell, Walter Powell, Billy Hawkins, Frank Goodman, Andy Hall, and Jubil set out to hike to the Indian agency. They were able to buy three hundred pounds of flour there, which would help prevent starvation, but they found nothing to replace their lost food or gear. Powell bargained the services of a pack mule, and an Indian boy to lead it to the camp and back, into the terms of the flour purchase.

The men camped at the Indian agency for a few days, and Jubil took the opportunity to write Nelly the first, and likely the only, letter he would send this summer. He did not conceal the dangers of the trip, as Nelly knew better by now, and while he told her about the events at Disaster Falls, he did not disclose how close he had come to drowning. He described the hard work of portaging and lining the boats, the exhilaration of successfully riding a rushing river, and the monotony of camp life. He told her of his pride at taking part in the expedition and expressed his confidence that, in spite of the hardships, this was the work he was meant to do.

On July 5, as the men prepared to return to their campsite on the Green River, Frank Goodman called an end to his participation on the expedition. He would stay behind at the Indian agency, he said, to wait for the next stagecoach to anywhere. Jubil was not surprised at his departure.

Two days later Jubil, Powell, and the others rejoined the expedition. The other men were waiting impatiently on the riverbank, anxious to get on with the trip. The expedition continued down the river, and soon they were in a wide canyon with thousand-foot walls on either side and a bare, deep shoreline bracketing the river channel. Powell was fascinated by the rock that made up the canyon walls.

"Sort of a desolate area, wouldn't you say?" Powell asked rhetorically. "We should call this Desolation Canyon."

One morning in early July, in spite of the men's desire to move on, Powell proclaimed, "I am going to have a closer look at these rock cliffs," waving his arm at the canyon walls. "They are almost bare of vegetation, with an uncommon pattern of striated grays and browns. Would anyone care to come along?"

Jubil looked around as the men sat silently.

"I'll go, Major," said George Bradley, the ex-soldier.

"I'll go too, sir," volunteered Jubil. He didn't want to sit with Sumner and his men, listening to them gripe about Powell. Bradley was usually good company, and Powell might be today. His invitation was a good sign.

"Excellent," said Powell. "I want to measure overall canyon height, Mr. Bradley, so we will need to take a barometer."

"Should I carry anything along, Major?" Jubil asked, looking up at the cliffs. "Some rope?"

"Not necessary," replied Powell. "It will only be an encumbrance."

They walked about five hundred feet from the camp toward the canyon wall, and when they reached it, they found the face was not a sheer cliff, as it appeared from a distance, but instead was made up of tiers of ledges and smaller cliffs. Each ledge, Powell explained, was a different type of rock which had eroded at a different rate than the adjacent rock: sedimentary layers that were deposited during the Cretaceous period; sandstone and shale layers deposited during the first half of the Tertiary period. While Jubil couldn't be certain that he would remember the geologic names, he was fascinated by Powell's explanation and the way the rocks so clearly illustrated stretches of time he had never considered before.

The ledges were like a gigantic uneven staircase up the face of the canyon wall. The distance from the base of one ledge up to the next was generally no more than fifty feet up over large ragged rock, making for strenuous but safe climbing, and Jubil enjoyed it. The base of each ledge butted out several feet from the cliff face, so even though they climbed up several hundred feet, the exposure was only the distance to the ledge below them rather than to the floor of the canyon. Jubil knew the cliffs were still nothing to be trifled with. A broken bone out here could be a death sentence, and a slow and miserable one at that.

The climb went along well until they reached about eight hundred feet. There, the broad ledges disappeared, and the remaining two hundred feet between them and the top of the canyon wall was a vertical face of rough rock. Jubil thought they had gone far enough and should just climb down, but Powell was intent on gaining the summit. Jubil was accustomed to Powell proceeding into situations not normally attempted by a one-armed man, but going up this sheer rock face seemed impossible for him.

"I plan to measure the height of these cliffs for my scientific journals, Mr. Bradley," insisted Powell. "We'll need the barometer when we reach the summit. To get it up there, we'll share the burden of carrying it. I'll lead up a few steps, and you pass the barometer to me. You climb up a few steps, and I'll pass it up to you. We'll proceed in that manner to the top."

Jubil did not see how this would be possible when Powell had only one hand, but he watched as they set off up the cliff. Powell tucked the barometer under the stump of his right arm and waited for Bradley to climb up a few steps past him on his left. To hand the barometer over to Bradley required Powell to let go of his one handhold. Even without the barometer, this type of climbing for Powell was risky, and juggling the barometer under the stump of his right arm made it even more risky. Bringing the rope would have made the situation much easier—climb up carrying the rope, drop it down, and pull up the barometer. He did not bother to suggest returning to get the rope. He knew if Powell wanted rope, he would order someone to get it. More critically, for Powell himself to be on this cliff face without being secured by a rope was foolish, but Jubil knew Powell was not interested in his opinion.

Powell had not invited Jubil to be a third set of hands in the barometer-passing brigade, so he climbed up, staying below Powell and Bradley as they scaled the wall. This type of climbing was different from scaling Longs Peak. The exposure here was much greater, but, for reasons Jubil did not fully understand, he was not petrified today. There was a slow-motion calmness he was finding in these dangerous situations. He knew from past experiences that if he could keep his wits about him, he would make sound decisions at each step of the journey and, in that way, survive.

The climbers reached the last few feet before the summit, and Bradley took the barometer from Powell.

"I'll take it on up, Major," said Bradley.

"All right, Mr. Bradley," said Powell.

Bradley moved up the wall, switching the barometer from hand to hand, depending on the holds he could find above him. Soon, he gained the top and looked down over the edge to Powell and Jubil below.

"Straight on up, Major," encouraged Bradley, "only a few more feet."

Powell moved a few feet up the cliff wall and stopped before he reached the route Bradley had followed to the top. Jubil watched him from below.

"Mr. Bradley," said Powell, "I have a problem. I can't move. I made a step up with my right foot, without a hold for my left. I have a hold above with my hand, but I fear letting go to drop back down to my left foothold. If I miss it, I will fall. I am stranded, Mr. Bradley."

Jubil was shocked. Powell was only three feet from the top of the cliff. It was unimaginable that he could have scaled one thousand feet only to find the last three feet impassable, but Powell was not a man to freeze from fear. If he said there was no good hold, then there was none.

"Hang on, Major," said Bradley. "I'll throw the leg of my britches over. You grab them and I'll haul you up."

Jubil's mind flashed with an image of Powell falling, pulling Bradley along with him, and the two of them knocking Jubil off the wall on their way down.

"Wait, Bradley!" called Jubil. "I'll help you pull the major up."

"All right, Walker," shouted Bradley, "but make it snappy."

Jubil angled left to follow Bradley's route, climbed past the major, and reached the top. He found Bradley in his long underwear, one leg of his pants wrapped around his forearm, the other leg of the pants dangling over the cliff edge. Bradley knelt and peered over the edge. Jubil sat behind Bradley with his arms locked around Bradley's waist, his feet braced against the rocks embedded in the top of the cliff.

"All right, Major," said Bradley. "Reach out and grab the pants, and we've got you."

Jubil felt Bradley's whole body tighten as the major's weight hit the pants leg.

"Pull us up, Walker!" said Bradley. "Hold tight, Major."

Jubil pushed with his legs against the rocks and scooted backward, pulling Bradley and Powell along. He found a new foothold, first with one foot and then the other, and scooted backward again. The major's hand, clutching the pants leg, showed over the edge. Jubil kept scooting backward until Powell was pulled fully onto the summit. The major released the pants leg, and the men lay on their backs, panting with relief.

"Thank you, gentlemen," Powell said.

Jubil and Bradley exchanged a glance.

"You're welcome, Major," Bradley said.

After Powell took his altitude reading, they walked along the summit plateau and found a much safer route down than the one by which they'd come up. They descended in silence with Powell stopping from time to time to search the rock face for fossils. By late afternoon they were back in camp. Powell separated himself from the men, and Bradley said nothing to the other men of the climb or the rescue. Jubil told Andy Hall only that they had had an invigorating day.

That night, Jubil lay on his back as close to the campfire as safety would allow. Without his bedroll and his slicker, nights were uncomfortably chilly at best and miserably cold when he was wet. He was grateful for the small comfort of a dry night as he lay looking up at the stars. He pondered Powell's performance that day, unsure how he felt about it. Powell's nerve, strength, stamina, and commitment were beyond reproach. Jubil admired him greatly for those traits. However, his insistence that he always knew best, as in insisting that they leave the rope behind, and his willingness to put himself and others at risk doing things beyond his limitations, which he would not admit he had, was dangerous and selfish. Powell ordered men into situations in which he could not do his part, and then ranted at them when they did not perform to his expectations. Yet here they all were, following a man down a wild river who could not row, or portage, or line the boats, and yet he demanded perfection from them in doing so.

Jubil went to sleep wondering if Uncle Pete or Lew Keplinger had ever had such doubts about following Powell.

CHAPTER 16

The next few days brought brief periods of riding the current downstream and a seemingly endless repetition of portaging and lining the boats. Morale among the men was growing worse as they became increasingly disgruntled with the major's decisions and his manner of making them known. What Powell took to be prudent, the other men saw as over-cautious. What the men thought of as bold, Powell considered reckless. A particular rapid that might take a few minutes to run in the boats took hours to portage or line the boats past. Powell never asked anyone for his opinion about whether to run a rapid or go around; he simply gave orders and expected to be obeyed. This habit was irritating enough, but the fact that Powell was not much help portaging and none at all lining the boats was an added insult. It was clear he cared only about his boats and his mission, and nothing for the men's opinions or their rope-burned hands. Jubil's morale suffered along with the rest of the group's, and he found himself agreeing with the men more often than with the major.

During these days of tedious manual labor and slow progress, Jubil often turned to daydreaming of Nelly. He missed her company and the easy way they had of passing the time—talking about her studies, playing checkers in the parlor with her brothers, conversing while sitting by the woodstove at the store, and even going to church occasionally. But too often he found himself wondering how she was spending her days and worrying she might be perfectly happy in the company of William Brown or some other fellow. The only way to shake those worries was to turn his mind to something other than Nelly, which left him little to focus on but his discomforts.

Then Powell found another set of canyon walls he wanted to inspect, and Oramel Howland went along to help with barometer readings. Jubil chose to stay in camp that day and fish with Andy Hall. By late afternoon, Powell and Howland were still not back in camp. There was discussion about going to look for them, but no one knew where they had gone. With dark approaching, it would also add to the expedition's problems if the search party got lost. Late that evening, Powell and Howland returned to camp. Powell took his leave of the men and went to sit with his brother, and Howland aired his grievances to the rest of the men. Powell had spent the whole day taking his readings, insisting they remain high on the cliff as dark fell. This, Howland said, was in spite of his urging that Powell accept the readings he had and climb down in favor of safety. Powell ignored him. Howland could see no sense in Powell taking great caution with the boats but ignoring his own safety and that of others when on the cliff walls. Jubil could not disagree, but he resisted adding his own opinion for fear of dragging the mood even lower. He and Bradley exchanged a solemn look across the fire, but Bradley also remained silent.

The next day, they reached yet another set of troublesome rapids, but Powell decided it could be run. The boats navigated the first section successfully, but then the river veered left and hit the cliff face. Powell's boat, the *Emma Dean*, swept around the bend, out of control, missing a huge boulder by inches. A large wave rebounded off the boulder and flipped the boat. Jubil watched as Major Powell, Sumner, and Dunn flew into the river and the *Emma Dean* rolled, over and over, but did not sink.

Powell and his crew struggled to stay above water and managed to grab their swamped boat. The *Emma Dean* was heavy with water and difficult to control as the crew struggled to swim it to shore. They succeeded by effort and by luck: the *Emma Dean* ran into a snarl of driftwood near the shore and was caught, keeping it from plunging into the next rapid. The freight boats safely ran the same stretch that had capsized Powell's boat and pulled over to regroup.

Powell and his crew dragged the *Emma Dean* ashore and dumped the water out. The guns in the boat had been lost, along with one of the barometers and some blankets. None of the food was lost, but it was soaked, again. The major's design for watertight compartments was largely effective, but nothing could keep the water out under these circumstances. Some of their provisions could tolerate the water, but the flour was a sodden mess. The prospects for the bacon, already beginning to turn rancid, were not good. They camped there for the night, and by the next afternoon, they managed to exit Desolation Canyon without further trouble.

On the afternoon of July 13, Jubil's twentieth birthday, he received an unexpected gift: they arrived in an area where the river flattened out into a swiftly moving but manageable flow. This part of the canyon was cut from gray sandstone, so Powell named it Coal Canyon. These soft sandstone cliffs eroded easily and did not form the rapids created when hard rock such as granite or basalt accumulated in the channel. The men made eighteen miles that day. Camp that evening was the most pleasant since their departure, forty-nine days before. Jubil mentioned that it was his birthday to Andy Hall, who thought the occasion warranted breaking out the whiskey keg. No one objected. Jubil had a few pulls to celebrate, laughing and joking with the other men, but the next morning his pounding headache told him he would never become a problem drinker.

The river was so placid that, for the first time, they needed to row to make progress. As they were rowing, they passed within sight of another channel on their left. The sight piqued Jubil's curiosity, but when one of the men called out to Powell to ask if they should explore it, Powell ordered them to continue downriver. Soon they reached a horseshoe bend in the channel, and within the hour Jubil spotted another channel nearby—which, he realized by a unique rock formation nearby, was the one they had just come down. The river had looped around and come right back, almost crossing itself. What would have been a few minutes portage across the gap had become a long, hard row downriver that had only led back to their starting point. Soon enough, they reached another horseshoe bend and another, prompting Powell to name the area Labyrinth Canyon. Powell did not think it worth the effort to portage across these cutoffs, so the men were left to row their way through this section of the canyon.

After three days of following this meandering path, they reached the end of the first leg of their journey, where the canyon opened up and the Green River met the Grand River. It was July 16, and they had arrived at the head of the mighty Colorado River and the entrance to the Grand Canyon. The confluence of the two rivers was not at all what Jubil had expected. Instead of a raging cataract of colliding rivers, the waters met calmly—the Green River muddy and brown, the Grand River clear and clean—and then flowed side by side down the wide channel of the Colorado for half a mile as it led into the Grand Canyon. Powell ordered the boats to pull over, and the men made camp. They needed to rest, dry out, and patch the boats. Powell took sextant readings to mark their location. The point of confluence had never been accurately mapped, and Powell would not leave until he was positive he had correctly identified their position.

Here, the weather was more than warm, it was hot. A thermometer reading indicated one hundred degrees, and there was no shade to be found. Jubil decided to review their food rations to see what might need to be aired out. When he opened one of the flour bags he was shocked. The flour had become a mass of moldy green lumps. Opening the other bags, he found several in the same condition. Sumner helped Jubil spread the remaining flour on a tarp to dry in the sun. They fashioned a sieve from mosquito netting and set about trying to sift out the worst of the mold. When they finished, only half of the flour remained, about two hundred pounds. The bacon had developed a rancid taste. It was still edible but would not last much longer. Most of the beans and dried apples were intact. Powell estimated they had rations adequate for two months, but he had no idea how much longer the trip would take.

That evening, after another dismal meal, Jubil sat looking at the stars. He chided himself for his naiveté about what the conditions would be on this expedition. Last year's adventures in the Rocky Mountains, with plentiful game, fish, and berries, now seemed like a dream of paradise. In his planning for this expedition, not once had he worried about being reduced to eating spoiled rations, and he certainly had never thought they might starve. Possibly the hunters would provide, though the prospects for that were dim. They had been largely unsuccessful so far, and the presence of game in the Grand Canyon was likely to continue to be sparse.

As the men sat around the campfire, Powell came to join them.

"We've faced our challenges adequately so far," Powell orated. "We have had some misfortunes and made some mistakes but suffered no casualties. We can be proud. We will be remembered well for our efforts so far. From this point forward we go down the great unknown."

No one spoke. Jubil watched his companions as they sat staring at either Powell or the fire. His own attitude toward Powell was not generous enough at the moment to receive the speech well. Powell probably thought he was making a grand gesture to show the men his patience and vision. Reminding them they were making history and inspiring them to stand up to the challenge. What Jubil felt at the moment was tired, sore, hungry, wet—and haunted by Nelly's question, *do you have to put yourself this close to death to enjoy life?* But he was fully invested in the expedition, and he would not give up to weakness and despair. When they had first set out, he had told himself he was willing to risk his life for this achievement, and now he could see how real that possibility was. But there was no turning back. However, if he got out of here alive, he would consider Nelly's question from a different perspective than when she had first asked it.

Billy Hawkins broke the silence. "Say there, Jack," he drawled to Sumner, "let me borrow that sextant for a bit."

Sumner, who had been helping the major with readings, handed it over. Hawkins turned his back on the men and took a step away, then began to aimlessly scan the skies with the sextant. Everyone watched him for a few moments before Powell finally spoke up.

"Mr. Hawkins," said Powell politely. "I was not aware that you knew how to use the sextant. I'd be happy to help you. What is it you are looking for?"

Hawkins turned to Powell.

"Well, Major," said Hawkins, "I was hoping to find the longitude and latitude of the nearest apple pie."

Everyone else collapsed with laughter. Jubil, clutching his belly, realized he was coming to appreciate these men in spite of their griping. When all else failed them, their sense of humor survived, even under the worst circumstances.

It became commonplace to declare each new set of rapids the worst yet. The ones they reached on July 25 were no exception. They faced a stretch of river with three sets of rapids, the third with a drop of seventy feet. Powell chose to run the first rapid, but the *Emma Dean* struggled and lost an oar. They lined the other boats down. The next two rapids were too steep for lining, so the men made a hot, difficult portage and camped for the night. Powell named this area Cataract Canyon.

The next day, Powell and his brother, along with Bradley, Sumner, and Jubil, went to search for pine trees to harvest pitch for the boats. During the search, Powell separated himself from the others, as he often did. Jubil and the men returned to camp to find that Powell was still gone. When he did return, his clothes were soaked through, and he urged the men to secure the boats and haul the gear to higher ground. He had been caught in a violent rainstorm earlier, he said, and he feared a flash flood might result. The men in camp had not seen or heard any evidence of rainfall upriver.

Jubil and Andy went to lash the boats down tighter while the other men carried their supplies to a ledge about one-hundred feet up the canyon wall. Just as Jubil and Andy were finishing securing the last of the boats, the channel of the river began to fill alarmingly quickly. They scrambled back up the canyon wall to join the others with no time to spare as a flood of rusty red water, sand, and debris rushed down the channel. If Powell had not chanced into the rainstorm, the boats, supplies, and possibly the men themselves would have been swept away. Much to Jubil's surprise and relief, none of the boats or supplies were lost.

The following day Dunn and Bradley finally bagged two mountain sheep. That night, for the first time in weeks, the men ate their fill of good fresh meat. The meal did a great deal to bolster their spirits. A few manageable rapids followed, and then, just past where the San Juan River merged with the Colorado, the men again got a brief respite. No difficult rapids presented themselves for miles, and the wide swift channel moved them along effortlessly. Powell named this area Glen Canyon, for its tranquil nature. They reached the mouth of the Little Colorado

River on August 11. Powell took sextant readings and concluded they were at the furthest point south they would travel. From here, the river ran due west, or would if it were to flow in a straight line. They were now in the vicinity of Callville, Nevada, a small Mormon settlement that offered the last safe escape from the Grand Canyon. From here, the only known landmark was the point where the Colorado River exited the canyon.

Over the next four days, the men fought the most difficult section of river to date. For the first time on their journey, the canyons walls were solid granite. The other canyons they'd been through had presented shoreline to walk along and, often, wide beaches. Here, they came across stretches of sheer cliffs lining the river with no shoreline at all. In these stretches, the channel closed in to a narrow passage, the rate of flow increased, and fallen boulders created raging rapids. Scouting ahead for waterfalls was difficult, requiring a climb up the canyon walls to look downriver, but even then, with no shoreline, portaging or lining the boats was impossible. Their only choice was to run the river. The most formidable of these rapids they named Sockdolager, slang for a knockout punch. During this run, Oramel Howland was thrown from his boat and, for the second time, lost the maps he had been charged with creating. In camp that night, Powell did not let it go unmentioned but did not create a scene as he had previously done.

Stretches of granite cliffs occasionally gave way to softer rock, where the river would calm and they could camp, which was welcome but meager comfort. Rations were perilously low now, and the condition of the bacon was worsening. The temperature was now more a factor in the condition of the rations, as temperatures regularly measured over one hundred degrees.

Late one afternoon, as the men were lining the boats down one of the rapids and Powell was supervising their effort, Bill Dunn stood downriver on the shoreline taking a barometer reading for the major. For each reading, he noted the exact time on the gold watch Powell had given him to carry in his pocket for that purpose.

Upriver from him, the men released the stern line and let the *Maid of the Canyon* run downriver, to be caught by the bow line. As they came down to retrieve the boat, they found Dunn standing on the beach, drenched.

"You appear to have fallen in the river, Mr. Dunn," said Powell.

"Well, it ain't the first time I got wet this trip," grumbled Dunn. He explained that he had not realized the bow line was secured to a rock spire behind him, and as the boat came downstream, the bow line had pulled him into the river. He had struggled to avoid being swept downstream into the rapids. Finally he had managed to catch the bow line and pull himself back to shore.

He reached into his pocket and removed Powell's watch. Jubil could see that second hand was no longer moving.

"I'm afraid the river put an end to your pocket watch though, Major. Sorry."

Powell stared at Dunn. Jubil watched as Powell shook his clenched fist at Dunn, his face twitching with anger.

"Being sorry, Mr. Dunn," Powell snarled, "is not adequate. That watch is not only a critical piece of our scientific equipment, it is worth thirty dollars. I'll have thirty dollars from you, right now, or you are dismissed from the expedition."

Jubil could not believe what he was hearing. Making a threat like that, over a watch, was beyond unreasonable. What did Powell think would become of Dunn if he were forced to leave the expedition? Jubil did not want to accept the answer.

Dunn scowled back at Powell, both of his own fists clenched.

"Major, I don't think a bird could get out of these canyons," Dunn said carefully. "I reckon this was just another accident along the way, like many before it."

"Bill's seeing it right, Professor," said Sumner, putting Powell on notice.

"This weren't no fault of Dunn's, Major," added Billy Hawkins. "We've lost all manner of things to this river. Lucky we ain't lost our lives."

Powell looked around at the men sternly.

"You owe me thirty dollars, Mr. Dunn," said Powell flatly, and then he walked away.

Sumner and Dunn looked at one another and shook their heads. As the men prepared to move downriver, they were delayed as Oramel Howland could not locate the maps he had been drawing. He had left them in the *Maid of the Canyon*, but they had apparently blown away while the boats were being lined downriver. Powell scowled, but said nothing. After running one more rapid, they came to the mouth of a swiftly flowing creek. Where the creek entered the Colorado, it formed a sandy shoreline that supported a large willow tree. The beach and the shade offered a luxurious campsite. Powell ordered Howland to mark the spot on the maps he was charting as Bright Angel Creek, in honor of its sparkling clear waters.

Bread, dried apples and coffee would have to do for supper, Billy Hawkins, the cook, declared. He poured coffee for the men as they came to the campfire to eat and told them that he had had to discard the bacon—it was too spoiled now to eat. Powell sat with his brother apart from the other men, as usual, and waited for Hawkins to bring his food. When Hawkins sat down with his own plate, it became obvious he was not going to serve Powell.

"What about the major?" Jubil asked Hawkins.

"What about him?" Hawkins challenged. "He can come get his grub, like the rest of the boys."

Jubil considered taking Powell his food, but then he decided Hawkins was correct. There was no reason Powell could not take a few steps to the campfire and collect his own food. He thought back to his trip to Fort McPherson two years ago in the company of General Sherman. Not once that Jubil could recall had Sherman made a point to his men of his superiority. He had done the opposite. Sherman had taken time every evening to visit with the enlisted men around their campfire. Not to give orders but simply to show interest in them. Sherman earned his men's respect by being one of them; Powell simply demanded it.

Walter Powell came to collect the major's supper and returned to sit with his brother. Those around the campfire were too tired and angry with Powell to complain. As they ate their meager rations in silence, they looked up to see Major Powell approaching them.

"Mr. Howland, once again I understand you've lost the maps we have been laboring to create," Powell stated, addressing Oramel Howland. "By my count, this is the third time— once at Disaster Falls, once at Sockdolager, and now here. I am disappointed, to say the least."

Jubil wondered why Powell would feel compelled to bring this up tonight, when nerves were already on edge.

"Yes, Major," said Howland. "You have made that very clear, on several occasions. I can't see what's to be done for it now. Frankly, I'm just happy to still be alive, maps or no maps."

"With the likes of you and Dunn along," Powell said, glancing scornfully at Bill Dunn, "the scientific value of our efforts is threatened. This is not some adventure trip. It is a scientific expedition, and I intend to have it operate like one."

Jubil was angry at Powell for once again criticizing the men for accidents that seemed unavoidable. Powell was wrong about the expedition too . . . it was in fact an adventure trip, at least for everyone but Powell.

"You know, Professor," Sumner said, "the war is long over, and your time of ordering everyone around is over right along with it. You can't come down all military on us. We won't stand for it."

Bill Dunn stood up. Jubil felt violence brewing and stood up to intervene.

"Sumner's right, Powell," Dunn said bluntly. "If you weren't a cripple, I'd thrash you good for the aggravation you've caused us all."

"Well, I'm no cripple!" shouted Walter Powell, rushing at Dunn. "I'll kill you!"

Hawkins tackled Walter as he ran at Dunn, and the two men went into the river. When they came up, Hawkins had Walter by the hair and pushed him underwater.

Jubil ran into the river to pull Hawkins off of Walter.

"For God's sake, Hawkins," shouted Dunn. "Don't kill him!"

Hawkins released Walter, who staggered out of the river and ran to his boat.

"I'll shoot you both where you stand!" screamed Walter. As he bent over to retrieve his gun from the boat, Andy Hall came up from behind and slugged him. Walter wheeled around to find Andy with a rifle trained on him.

"You make a move for that gun, Walter," vowed Andy, "and I'll take your head off!"

Jubil's frustration exploded. "Andy, put that gun down! What is wrong with you men! All of you! Isn't it enough we have the river and rotten food trying to kill us? Now we're set on killing each other too?" He turned to address Powell directly. "I'm sorry to say it, Major, but I think you're doing more harm than good with your discipline." Then, turning back to the others, he said, "You men may be frustrated, tired, and hungry, but killing each other is not going to improve our situation, and you know it! Can we just settle down here and do our best to come out of this whole thing alive? All of us?"

Andy lowered his rifle, and Walter looked surly but kept quiet. The others looked at Jubil for a moment and then stared into the fire. Major Powell turned and went back to his spot isolated from the other men.

Life became a miserable routine over the next two weeks: float on the river for a brief period, run a rapid and hope to survive, line the boats down a dangerous rapid, and portage around impassable areas. Powell named a few of these, for mapping purposes, Grapevine Rapid, Hermit Rapid, and Crystal Rapid and one treacherous area Lava Falls. They were cautious to avoid swamping the boats now, because the food supply was so low. This meant more lining, which slowed them down and taxed their rations further. A new misery developed as their gear began to deteriorate or was lost. No one had a full suit of clothes any longer; tent canvas was moldy, and the seams were rotting; blankets, for those who still had them, were never completely dry. Adding to the discomfort were the temperature variations. Several times in the past two weeks, the thermometer had indicated one hundred fifteen degrees. Then, in the evenings, the air cooled and made wet clothes and bedding feel frigid. As if that were not enough, when the canyon walls were made of granite, the men were forced to camp on small beaches, which did not accumulate driftwood, so campfires were sometimes not possible. When rain began pouring down on a night with no fire, no tent, skimpy clothes, wet blankets, and no food, their misery was complete. On these nights they beached the boats and huddled beneath them for some meager relief. The cold, wet, sleepless nights were enough to drive Jubil to consider giving up on the expedition, but there was no giving up now—there was no safe escape route. There was no way out of the canyon that was any less risky than going forward down the Colorado.

If the men had faced only physical challenges, Jubil thought they might have a chance of getting through this, but he was not sure they could survive the animosity. The fight initiated by the loss of Powell's watch ended without deadly violence, but the anger was only repressed, not forgotten. Much to

Jubil's dismay, Powell still maintained his imperious ways and further irritated the men. He would sometimes go off exploring while the men lined or portaged the boats, and often they would finish before he returned, forcing them to sit idly waiting for him rather than moving on down the river. Other times Powell supervised the lining or portaging, shouting out commands the men found unhelpful and unnecessary. The open griping about Powell was replaced with a silent resentment that permeated the whole day, every day. Jubil considered trying to speak with Powell again about his demeanor, but Powell had ignored him before. Jubil did not think he could influence Powell's behavior.

Then they reached a point in the river where they could see the rapids ahead but could do nothing to avoid them. The granite walls on both sides of the channel allowed no riverbank, and the cliffs overhung the river so that it was impossible to see any farther ahead. Without a riverbank, lining and portaging were impossible. The entry to this rapid was also particularly daunting. The rapids began where two smaller canyons entered the main canyon, one from the left, one from the right. The canyon on the right was several yards further downriver than the one on the left. Water gushed in from the canyon on the left and slammed against the right side of the main channel wall, creating a huge swell and a wave that moved downriver. The canyon on the right did the same from the opposite direction. Straight ahead, all the men could see was a zigzag channel of roiling water. They had no way to tell what was beyond it. If they made it through the rapids only to find there was a huge waterfall on the other side, they were doomed.

There were two options: run the rapid blindly or give up and climb out of the canyon. They camped for the night to consider their next move. After their paltry meal, Oramel Howland approached Powell.

"Could I have a word with you Major," Howland asked, "in private?"

Powell and Howland walked a short distance from the camp. Though Jubil could not hear them, he could see that Howland was animated as he spoke to a stoic Powell. Howland returned to the camp, followed by Powell, who picked up the sextant and went off to take a reading. Jubil followed him.

"Can I have a word with you also, Major?" Jubil inquired.

"Have you decided to abandon the expedition too?" Powell asked.

"Is that what Howland said?" Jubil replied. "He's giving up? Who else?"

"Oramel and Seneca Howland and Bill Dunn," Powell said. "The others, Howland says, are undecided."

Jubil watched the river roll by and considered what to say. "Are you determined to go on," Jubil asked quietly, "no matter what?"

"Honestly, I am undecided myself," Powell turned to look at Jubil. "What about you? What do you think?"

Jubil thought carefully about what he wanted to say and then replied, "I don't want to quit, but I don't want to drown or starve either. For tonight, I'll say I'm undecided as well."

Powell nodded. "I'm going get a fix on our position. We'll take it up tomorrow."

"Yes, sir," Jubil said. "Thanks for talking with me."

Jubil went back to camp as Powell took his reading. He lay down on the ground and used his canvas knapsack as a pillow. As he lay looking up at the stars Andy Hall joined him.

"The Howlands and Bill Dunn are leaving tomorrow," Andy said. "The other boys are still on the fence."

"I heard," Jubil said. "What do you want to do?"

"I come over to ask you," Andy said, flashing his ever-ready smile. Jubil thought he would remember Andy's goofy smile for the rest of his life. He had come to really enjoy Andy's company, but he doubted that after this expedition he would ever see him again. Andy was even more itinerant than Uncle Pete had been, and far from ready to settle down.

"What I want is to get out of here alive," Jubil said. "If all we had to do was turn around and walk away from this, I'd be tempted to do it, but we can't. Climbing out of here and hiking through the desert around the edge of this canyon for God knows how long seems like an even stupider way to die than letting this river kill me. And even if I lived, I'm not sure I could sleep ever again for constantly questioning myself for giving up." Jubil found that he was making up his mind as he talked to Andy. "I came here to run this river clear through the whole Grand Canyon . . . even if it kills me," he said. "That's what I'm going to do."

"I'm with you," Andy said without hesitation. "If we don't make it through, it's been a pleasure knowing you, Jubil."

No one got much sleep that night. Jubil could hear the other men turning restlessly as he lay awake. In the morning Powell addressed the group.

"I took a reading on our position last night," explained Powell. "We are no more than forty-five miles from the mouth of the Virgin River, the known end of the Grand Canyon. Of course, that is in a straight line. If we find the rapids ahead to be runnable, we are only a few days from our destination. If we lose no more supplies, we should be fine."

"Those are some mighty big ifs, Major," Oramel Howland pointed out. "Me, Seneca, and Bill Dunn are for climbing out of the canyon and hiking to the Mormon settlement upriver on the Virgin."

"If you are worried about food, Mr. Howland," Powell reasoned, "you have no idea how many miles you must hike around the rim of the canyon to reach that settlement. You will also go from an overabundance of water to a shortage your first day out. There is an inhospitable environment above this canyon and perhaps unfriendly Indians as well. My point, Mr. Howland, is that climbing out is no guarantee of survival."

"Lesser of two evils," Howland said, without hesitation. "Running that rapid is suicide."

Powell looked at Howland, shook his head, and then turned to the others.

"What about the rest of you?" Powell asked.

The men looked at each other in awkward silence. Jubil looked at Andy Hall, who returned Jubil's gaze and flashed his indomitable gap-toothed smile. Jubil cleared his throat.

"Major, I'm surely not anxious to get myself killed on this river," he said, "but after all the effort we've put into making it this far, I'm not anxious to give up either. If fate decides my life is over out here, I'd rather it be at the hand of this river than by some other cause. I hope to have a long life ahead of me, and I don't want to spend it regretting I gave up on the expedition. I'm going on ahead, regardless of what everyone else does."

"I'm going too," Andy said and beamed his smile out to the group, shoring up Jubil's declaration. The other men quietly considered Jubil's words and murmured to one another. Powell stared at Jubil and then spoke.

"If even one of you is willing to go on," Powell said softly, "I'm with you."

Jubil was astonished to see a tear run down Powell's face. In that moment, Jubil felt a new compassion for Powell. The major did have feelings, strong feelings, but they were for accomplishments, not for people. Powell could not help being emotionally crippled, any more than he could help being physically crippled. Every man there had shortcomings, but every one of them was there because of Powell. It was Powell's passion and commitment that drove men to historic achievements. Powell was hard to love, but he still deserved respect.

"I see it the same as Walker, Professor," said Sumner. "I ain't come all this way to quit."

Bradley and Hawkins spoke up in agreement.

Powell nodded gratefully as he fought to contain his emotions.

"Will you reconsider, Mr. Howland, Mr. Howland, Mr. Dunn?" Powell asked.

"We're climbing out," said Oramel Howland, shaking his head.

Powell nodded.

The men began to make preparations to go their separate ways. Howland, recognizing the men's dire food situation, would not take any of the rations. Instead he took two rifles and a shotgun, expecting they could hunt once they were out of the canyon.

"We'll take the two freight boats the rest of the way down the river and leave the *Emma Dean*," said Powell. "If you change your mind, or find you can't climb out, you will still have a means to move on."

"We'll do fine," said Howland. "We're not running that rapid."

Jubil watched as the men bid one another farewell. Each thought the other group was signing its own death warrant. Sumner and Hawkins wept, as did Oramel and Seneca Howland. Jubil was surprised to see tears on the dirty faces of these hard men who were so quick to laugh at their own misfortune. Major Powell wept but stood apart from the group, while Walter Powell and Andy Hall looked on dry eyed. Jubil's tears also welled, but not from sorrow. He felt pride and sympathy for these rugged souls he had lived with and, more than once, nearly died with.

"Walter, Sumner, and I will take the *Kitty Clyde's Sister* down first," said Powell, addressing Jubil. "You can learn from our experience."

"Yes, sir," Jubil replied. "Before you launch, I want to say thank you, Major, for allowing me to be a part of your expeditions. I've learned a lot about the world from following you. Thank you, sir, and good luck."

"It has been a pleasure to have you at my side, Jubil," said Powell. "You are a good man, just like your uncle Pete and your father. Your family would be proud of what you've become."

Jubil, Hall, Bradley, and Hawkins stood by the *Maid of the Canyon* and watched. The Howland brothers and Bill Dunn stood a few feet away.

The *Kitty Clyde's Sister* entered the river and found the main channel. The boat was swept to the right wall of the canyon then veered sharply left and went over a small waterfall, vanishing from view. Jubil and Andy looked at one another.

"How tall do you reckon that waterfall is?" Andy asked anxiously.

"I don't know," Jubil said, holding up his hand to silence Andy. He listened intently for any sound that might give him an idea what was happening—the crash of wood against rock or shouts from the men. His stomach was so taut—and empty—that he felt nauseated. The waiting was worse than just pushing into the river and being done with it. He and his companions stood silently waiting as seconds felt like minutes. Then a shot rang out.

"They made it through!" exclaimed Jubil, and then turned to Oramel Howland. "Are you sure you fellows don't want to follow along in the *Emma Dean*?"

Howland shook his head.

"All right," Jubil said to Howland, and then turned to address Hall, Bradley, and Hawkins. "You fellows ready?"

They settled into the *Maid of the Canyon* and drifted into the current. Hall and Bradley manned the oars as Jubil and Hawkins lined up in the center to keep the boat as stable as possible. The men pulled for the center of the river and entered the rapid. The boat tore along the right-hand wall of the canyon, sideswiped a boulder, flew over the small waterfall, nosed into the waves, and filled with water. They were now moving quickly toward a huge boulder downriver. Hall and Bradley pulled on the oars to move across the channel, but the swamped boat was too heavy to control. All the men could do was hold on. The waves built up in front of the boulder, creating a huge swell. The boat caught the swell of the standing wave, swept around the boulder, and flew straight at the left-hand wall. There it met another standing wave pushing against the wall. The boat caught that wave and veered away from the wall, heading downriver. To their amazement, their boat was now past the rapid and bobbing along in the choppy water. It had taken perhaps a minute to run. It was far from the worst rapid they had ridden. In calmer, shallower waters now, they pulled the boat in to shore. Sumner fired another shot to signal the *Maid of the Canyon* was safely through the rapid, in case the other men might change their minds.

Powell wanted to wait for a while before moving on, in case the other men decided to continue with them down the river. While they waited, they emptied out their swamped boats and spread their meager belongings out to dry. Jubil retrieved his soaked knapsack from the sealed compartment in the bow of his boat and examined its contents. He left his oilcloth money belt in the bag, although it was wet and the bills inside were damp. He set his hat out on a rock to dry. White Dog's medicine bag was soaked, but the deerskin would dry. The teeth, claw, rock, bones, and arrowhead inside were intact, but the tiny pine cone was a sodden mass. Whatever spirits possessed that token had been forced to relocate.

They waited an hour for the Howland brothers and Dunn, but they did not appear, and Powell and what was left of the expedition party moved on.

The rest of the day they continued to fight their way downriver in the routine to which they had grown accustomed. Only one rapid that day was worthy of naming, a treacherous section Powell called Lava Cliff Rapid. Just beyond it, the men camped for the night.

In the morning they set off downriver again and soon noticed a change in the river and the surrounding walls of the canyon. The channel still ran swiftly, but the rapids were all navigable. As they sped downstream, the canyon opened up. The boats floated around a bend, and the men beheld a vista of low rolling desert.

Powell stood up in his boat, his arm extended above his head. "Thank God, Almighty!" he shouted jubilantly. "We've made it! We have run the Grand Canyon!"

Jubil felt a sense of relief beyond words.

Powell estimated it would take another two or three days to reach the mouth of the Virgin River. The Mormon settlement was twenty miles up the Virgin. The men rowed to hasten their progress down the smoothly flowing river. Their rations remained meager, but the knowledge that starvation was now unlikely made the situation tolerable.

Around midday the following day, Jack Sumner stood up in the *Kitty Clyde's Sister* and peered through Powell's telescope.

"There's three men downstream!" he exclaimed. He opened the sealed compartment in the front of the boat, pulled out a small Stars and Stripes, and set it waving from the bow. They rowed downriver to meet three men and a boy, fishing at the mouth of a muddy stream.

"Is this the Virgin River?" Powell asked.

"Yes, sir, it is," replied the oldest of the fishermen, taken aback to see this small flotilla coming from the direction of the canyon.

"Thank goodness," declared Powell. "I am Major John Wesley Powell. These men and I make up the Colorado River Exploring Expedition. We've just come down the length of the Colorado River through the Grand Canyon."

The fishermen stared at the expedition party.

"Yes, sir," said the eldest fisherman slowly, "we know who you are. We were asked to keep an eye out for signs of you . . . and we did until we heard that you were dead."

The statement hit Jubil like a punch to the stomach.

"Where did you hear it?" Powell asked.

"It was in the newspapers," the fisherman explained. "Your party drowned in the river."

"We come close often enough," cracked Sumner, "but apparently, we survived."

Jubil thought of Nelly, the whole Boswell family, Luke and his parents, and what they must have been through this summer, thinking Jubil was dead.

"We'll set that record straight soon enough," vowed Powell. "Can we get your assistance in getting home?"

"Yes, sir," said the eldest fisherman. "My name is Joseph Asey. I'll send my boy upriver to St. George to get help. You're welcome to stay the night here, by my cabin. I'll fry up some fish."

Camped next to Mr. Asey's cabin, the expedition party was in paradise. They were safe, comfortable, and well-fed, and they had other people to talk to. The next day, the bishop arrived from the Mormon settlement of St. George with a wagonload of flour, cheese, bread, butter, and melons, and the offer of a ride back to the settlement.

Powell and his brother, along with Jubil, accepted the bishop's offer of a ride. Andy Hall, Billy Hawkins, Jack Sumner, and George Bradley chose to take the supplies and follow the Colorado to the ocean, then see which way the wind blew them.

Jubil and the Powell brothers spent a few days at St. George, where Powell saw to it that news of their safety was dispatched to Emma Powell, the Boswells, and the Warners. Jubil took the opportunity to take a proper bath, get his hair cut, and purchase a new set of clothes. While they were at the settlement, much to their dismay, they learned that the Howland brothers and Bill Dunn had indeed climbed out of the canyon but had been killed in the desert by Indians. According to the story related by a friendly Indian, three men were found and fed by some Shivwit Indians and sent on their way. The men then supposedly came across a squaw gathering seeds and proceeded to rape and kill her. The Shivwit men tracked them down and killed them. Powell was outraged at this story, declaring the Howlands and Dunn would never have committed such an act. Jubil agreed. These were hard men, but he could not imagine them ever being that senselessly violent and evil.

Finally, rested and fed and eager to get home, Jubil accompanied the Powell brothers when they caught a ride on a mule team bound for Salt Lake City. He had never felt such a longing for home and a longing to see Nelly's face again. He only hoped she could forgive him for giving her such a scare.

CHAPTER 17

The leisurely ride to Salt Lake City gave Jubil time to ponder a variety of subjects. The mental anguish he had surely caused Nelly weighed heavily on his mind. He was proud of what he had done, two historic expeditions and one memorable trek to his credit, but each one had nearly cost him his life. He could not promise he would never make another expedition, but he could promise to not risk his life so routinely. As he pondered a way to balance these factors, an idea occurred to him that struck a chord. Perhaps there was a way to satisfy his wanderlust that would not trouble Nelly and would benefit Warner and Walker Outfitters in the process. He was anxious to discuss it with the Warners and, if they agreed it was a good idea, with Nelly when he got home.

He had also decided he would not speak openly about Powell's dangerous behavior during the expedition. He would talk to Lew Keplinger and to Nelly about how Powell had put other people's lives at risk, but to no one else—not even Powell himself. He wondered whether his uncle Pete would agree with his assessment of Powell. Powell's assessment of Pete was that he was directionless, but Jubil thought Powell had not recognized Pete's true skill. Pete followed his heart from one adventure to another and made each one a success by being there, which was what Jubil was trying to do as well. Success achieved by dominating people and having no concern for their feelings was not the kind of success Jubil wanted. He was proud to be like his uncle in that regard, but his feelings for Nelly and commitment to the outfitting business perhaps gave him more direction than Pete.

When they arrived in Salt Lake City, Jubil went directly to the Western Union office and sent three telegrams. The first was to Nelly telling her he was alive and would telegraph again when he arrived in Council Bluffs. The second was to Luke Warner, asking him to come to Council Bluffs to discuss a business proposal. The third was to Mr. Warner, telling him the date Jubil planned to arrive in Council Bluffs.

Before Jubil and Major Powell parted ways, Powell told Jubil he was planning a return expedition to the Colorado River and invited him to join. Jubil listened to the major's plans but didn't feel his usual sense of excitement. He thought of how exhilarating that opportunity once would have seemed to him. He told Powell that Warner and Walker Outfitters would be happy to handle the logistics but that he was hoping to pursue other business opportunities with the Warners and so would not be available to make the trip.

Powell was staying in Salt Lake City to give a lecture on the expedition, but Jubil elected to catch the Union Pacific night train to Council Bluffs. They said their good-byes without fanfare or emotion, agreeing to reconnect once they were both home again. If Major Powell regretted the ways he had contributed to the hardships of the expedition, he gave no sign of it. Jubil guessed that the major was simply not capable of regret. Everything Jubil had seen suggested that the major would willingly pay with his own life, not to mention the lives of others, to be known as a pioneer.

Jubil hired a carriage to take him to the Union Pacific depot, and when the 11:15 p.m. train arrived, he found his section in one of the Pullman Palace Cars. It was comically lavish after the deprivation of the expedition, but he wanted the bed at night and the sofa during the day. When Jubil entered the car, he found the steward had his bed ready, the curtains drawn back, and he fell asleep immediately to the rhythm of the train.

The next morning, as they passed Cheyenne, Jubil looked out from the Palace Car and thought about his first train ride. A little over two years ago he had set out for Chicago, on his way to Council Bluffs to impress Major Powell and get away from the farm. He thought about how those goals had changed his life for good.

Striving to be found worthy to travel with Major Powell had brought many good things into his life. Without this effort, he never would have met the Warner family, whose members, as a result of their trust and support, now seemed part of Jubil's own family. His friendship with Lew Keplinger, and everything he had learned from following him, was a blessing. Lew was the most competent person at the widest variety of things of anyone Jubil had ever met, and good company as well. The places Jubil had been on his adventures, the things he had seen and done had marked him indelibly and made him who he was.

He thought about Nelly's first response to his desire to go adventuring: *You could get yourself killed.* She had been correct from the start, and he had known it, but he had still been willing to chance death in favor of living fully. He had been willing to do it again this year, but the Colorado River had taken him to his limit. In the past months, he had tempted fate nearly every day, week after week. Yes, he had made it through alive, but most of the credit for his current existence stood with fate, not his own efforts at survival. This expedition had changed him. Having seen the real possibility of his own death at close range, he no longer felt a need to come so close to death in order to feel the thrill of adventure. Powell might need the public glory and adulation that accompanied being the first to climb mountains and run rivers, cheating death at every turn, but Jubil had realized he did not need that extreme experience to be happy. He looked forward to sharing these conclusions with Nelly, to promising her that he would no longer tempt fate so rashly in his future travels.

Arriving in Council Bluffs, Jubil found Luke Warner waiting for him at the station. They hugged spontaneously, without any sense of self-consciousness, and Jubil's feeling deepened of having found a brother. Luke stepped back to survey him.

"You look fairly decent for a dead fellow," Luke joked.

"It's true that I came close, more than once," said Jubil. "It was a wild ride. Thanks for coming to Council Bluffs."

"I was anxious to see you with my own eyes." He grew serious. "We've been worried, of course." He reached out and squeezed Jubil's shoulder and then brightened again. "What a feather in the cap of Warner and Walker Outfitters. You're a celebrity, Jubil."

"I hope you aren't thinking of trotting me out on some kind of speaking tour," Jubil said, frowning.

"I know you're not the boastful type," Luke said, to Jubil's relief. "But will you talk about your travels if people ask, maybe address groups if invited?"

"I guess I don't mind doing it if folks ask," Jubil said, "but I don't want to go out beating the bushes for attention." Powell had already begun doing exactly that.

"That's good," said Luke. "Pa is home today, waiting for your arrival. Let's collect your things and be on our way."

Jubil held up his knapsack. "I'm ready."

When they reached Luke's carriage, Jubil saw the strong gray horse pulling it. Were his eyes playing tricks on him? "Is that Rocky?" Jubil asked.

"It is," Luke declared. "Pa said the army never called for him, so he just kept him. He's a good carriage horse."

"Hello, old friend," Jubil said. Rocky turned his head to Jubil and nudged him in the chest with his nose. "It's good to see you. Our Indian fighting days are over aren't they? Thank goodness."

Jubil enjoyed the ride from the depot to the Warner's house. It felt like coming home. Mr. Warner came out of his study to greet them. "Jubil!" he said animatedly.

Mrs. Warner came into the foyer from the kitchen and hugged him, "It is so good to see you, Jubil. We were very worried."

"Yes, ma'am, it's good to see you too," said Jubil. "I'm sorry to have caused everyone such trouble."

Mrs. Warner nodded. "We're just happy you are safe."

"Blasted newspapers," swore Mr. Warner. "Printing rumors for news. We're glad you're home safely." Mr. Warner shook Jubil's hand and then, uncharacteristically, embraced him. Jubil did not mind.

"Let's go into the study and discuss this business proposition of yours," said Mr. Warner, rubbing his hands together. "I'm anxious to hear what's on your mind."

Jubil walked into Mr. Warner's study and looked around at the collections. Then he reached into his knapsack and removed a fist-sized chunk of rock.

"I brought you something, sir," said Jubil. "This is a chunk of granite from the last rapid we ran on the Colorado River before we left the Grand Canyon. I thought you might want it for your collection, to commemorate the expedition."

Mr. Warner took the rock and looked at it as if it were as precious as a diamond.

"I will treasure it, Jubil," said Mr. Warner as he placed it on his desk.

"As far as this business proposition goes," Luke said, "I have a question. If we all agree that it's a splendid idea, can we implement it right away, or is there someone else who would need to approve it?"

Jubil was confused by the question. "Well, if you mean bankers and lawyers and such," he said, "you would know that better than I would. Of course, I'll have to talk to Nelly about it, to make sure she approves."

"That's what I figured," said Luke, walking to the door of the study.

Luke opened the door, and behind it stood Nelly and her mother. Jubil couldn't believe his eyes. He was speechless as Nelly ran to him. He opened his arms, and suddenly she was in them, as if he had wished her there.

"I'm so happy to see you," said Jubil, overcome and at a loss for more sophisticated words. He held Nelly tightly. He had spent so many nights camped by the river, dreaming of this moment. This was what he wanted from life, to hold Nelly and feel the love between them. Not spend months away from her, dreaming of how much he wanted to be with her. Certainly not putting himself in serious danger daily, chancing he might never see her again, all for the sake of adventure, or science and history's record books. With Nelly's love, he could have an exciting life without being driven to risk everything just to feel alive. He wanted to kiss her, but he couldn't do such a thing in front of her mother and the Warners.

Nelly looked up at him, her blue eyes filled with tears. She reached up and brushed away his own tears with her thumbs. He hadn't realized he was crying.

"I thought I had lost you," Nelly said softly and then clutched him to her again. After a moment she stepped back and surveyed him closely. "Good heavens, look at you—you are skin and bones and sunbaked as leather."

Jubil shrugged. He thought of the last days of the expedition when he had been so hungry, he would have eaten spoiled bacon or biscuits made from moldy flour—one of Major Powell's rock-hard biscuits would have been like a feast. He would not trouble Nelly with an awareness of how desperate those days had felt.

"Why don't we leave you two alone for a while," Mrs. Warner suggested. "You can talk, and then we'll have supper."

Mr. Warner and Luke moved out into the hallway. "Take

your time," Mr. Warner said, closing the door.

Once the door closed, Jubil kissed Nelly for a long while. Her mouth was soft and warm, and he felt more tears fall down his face as he channeled all the longing he had felt into the gesture. When they finally parted, Nelly's cheeks were bright pink, and her eyes were sparkling. Jubil expected he looked the same. He stared at her, searching for the right words. "I'm so sorry I put you through such terrible worry," he apologized. "I don't know where the papers got the idea we were drowned."

"If it weren't for Lew Keplinger," Nelly said, "well, I don't know what I would have done."

"What do you mean?" Jubil asked.

"He heard the stories about the expedition—everyone did—but he wrote a letter to the *Pantagraph* refuting the rumors of disaster. He pointed out several statements in the report he found suspect. Even before the newspaper printed his letter, Lew came to see me to offer his assurance that the stories were wrong. He visited a few times afterward, to check and see how I was doing. His confidence that the stories were unfounded gave me the strength to remain hopeful, to not be . . . despondent. He is a good person, Jubil, and thinks very highly of you. You are fortunate to have such a loyal friend."

"I do appreciate him," Jubil said sincerely. "I'll thank him when we get home."

He took her hands in his. "I love you, Nelly. I thought about you every day while I was gone. I knew you would be worried. And I knew your worry was justified. This expedition made a big impression on me. I won't lie to you—I am fortunate to have made it home alive. I can't promise I'll never venture into the wilderness again, but I can promise you from now on that I will not give fate such an easy shot at me."

Nelly took his face in her hands. "I love you too Jubil. I'm so glad to hear you feel that way. This expedition made a big impression on me as well. When I heard your party had drowned, I was stricken with grief and regret. I especially wished I had made better use of the time we had together. You were right when you said we can't hold back love because it will hurt too much to lose someone. When I learned you were alive, I vowed to not keep making that same mistake."

Nelly stood on her tiptoes and pressed her lips to his again, and he wanted nothing more than to stay in the study and spend the evening kissing her. Finally, she sighed dreamily and stepped back out of his embrace and patted her hair.

"Will you marry me?" he asked.

Nelly looked into his eyes and grinned, but rather than answering his question, she went off in a different direction. "When we arrived last night," she said, "Mama and I talked late into the evening with Mrs. Warner. She has helped me see our situation in a whole new light."

"Mrs. Warner?" Jubil asked, wondering what she had to do with the question at hand.

"Did you know she is originally from Nantucket?" Nelly asked. "It's a small island off the coast of Massachusetts."

"Yes, I did," he admitted, patiently waiting for Nelly to get to the point.

"Seafaring is a common occupation in that area," Nelly said. "Gentlemen make their living going to sea for long periods of time. It is common to find women living independently of their partners, fully in charge of the family's affairs. Many women enjoy this independence and even find it helps them accept the dangers inherent to their partner's way of life. It strengthens them to go on living if their partner never returns. She encouraged me to see our situation in that light. Doesn't that make us sound heroic?" Nelly smiled radiantly.

"You are a piece of work, Nelly Boswell," Jubil said. "Can I ask your parents for your hand?"

Nelly's smile faded to a look of concern. "Before we agree to marry, we need to talk about some things. I need you to consider some feelings I have about my future."

"Certainly," Jubil said. He knew she had strong convictions about her independence. He admired that and would never stand in the way.

"Do you know that if I am married, I cannot be hired as a teacher? A stupid law made by men to control the lives of women," Nelly said scornfully. "I don't regret not becoming a teacher, but I don't like losing it as choice for a career. I want to do something with my life besides be a housewife and mother, Jubil. I'm not saying I'll never want those things, but not for some time to come."

"I'm not at all surprised at that," he said, half truthfully. They had never discussed their feelings about having children, and he found that he was fine postponing fatherhood for the time being. The idea of going adventuring and leaving not only her behind, but her *and* their children did not sit well with him. And he wasn't entirely ready to give up adventuring. "Do you know what you want to do instead of teaching?"

"Not exactly," she said, with a frown. "I have a notion about being a writer, but I'm not sure I have the talent for it. I want to finish my university education no matter what direction I choose. Illinois Wesleyan is accepting women next year for the first time. I may apply there, since I no longer need the teacher training."

"As you've always told me," Jubil said, "I'm sure you can do whatever you set yourself to."

"Thank you," she said, giving him another light kiss. "Also, it's a big world out there, and I want to see some of it. Maybe you can even show me some of the sights you've seen?"

This idea sent a tingle of joy through Jubil, and he nodded enthusiastically.

Nelly threw her arms around him and they shared another passionate kiss. At the moment, he would have agreed to travel anywhere on earth to continue kissing her.

"You'll marry me then?" he asked.

"Yes," she said with a smile. "But I'd like to announce our engagement without setting a date yet," she said. "I want to take a real honeymoon, and I won't be able to take the time away from school until next spring."

"I'd rather do it tomorrow," Jubil said with a grin, "but I won't miss my chance whenever you're ready."

"I love you," she said. "You know, Papa will want his say, but you can ask Mama tonight."

Jubil was elated. "I wish I had my mother's ruby ring—it's locked in my trunk in the cabin. She'd be thrilled knowing it will be yours."

Nelly hugged him again.

"I suppose we should rejoin the Warners and your mother," Jubil sighed. "We've got a big announcement to make. And I've got a business proposal I want to talk with you and them about."

"Well," said Nelly, "you sound like a much better marriage prospect than the lovable but aimless fellow who left me this spring."

Jubil smiled sheepishly.

They found the Warners and Mrs. Boswell in the parlor, patiently waiting for them. Mrs. Warner suggested the group move to the dining room.

"Let's fatten you up," Nelly said, pinching Jubil's lean side.

"It is such a pleasure to be together," said Mr. Warner once Mrs. Garcia had served the soup. "We're all very anxious to hear about the expedition."

Jubil gave an account of riding downriver, lining the boats through the rapids, and portaging around them. He admitted to periods of boredom punctuated by periods of terror. He told how rations became sparse as they lost things to the river and to the heat.

"All in all," he said as he concluded his tale, "I would not recommend it to anyone, but it was an exciting accomplishment, and I'm proud to have done it."

"And an historic one, at that," said Mr. Warner. "Congratulations."

"Thank you, sir," said Jubil.

"I'm ready to hear about this business proposition of yours, Jubil," said Luke. "What do you have in mind?"

Jubil looked at Nelly. She held her fork aloft, waiting for him to speak.

"A lot of good has come into my life from following Major Powell the past three summers," he said, "but it has also routinely put me near death's door. I've finally heard what Nelly has been telling me from the start—I could get myself killed out there. I don't want to do that. I want to be with Nelly and you all for a long time to come. At the same time, I want to do adventure travel. But in the age of the transcontinental railroad, a person does not have to skirt death to experience the wonders of the outdoors in America. I think Warner and Walker Outfitters should start offering guided adventure travel expeditions, led by me, to take people to see the natural wonders of America. I focus on adventure tours, and you all get relief from my restlessness. Warner and Walker Outfitters can sell the travelers the gear they'll need for the journey, and we can charge a fee for the trip. Our customers will mostly be well-to-do folks, but more of those are made every day in America. What do you think?"

Nelly beamed at him.

"What do I think?" Luke slammed his palm down on the table, rattling the china and startling everyone. "I think it's genius! Adventure travel expeditions outfitted by Warner and Walker and led by Jubilee Walker himself—a member of the Powell Expeditions and one of the first men to summit Longs Peak and run the Colorado River through the Grand Canyon. Whooee! We can charge a handsome fee for that!"

Mr. Warner sat back in his chair, smiling and nodding. "I think this is an excellent idea," he said. "You and Luke draw up the plans, and let me know what I can do to help. This fits well with something I wanted to talk to you about. We've been paying you a salary for your part in operating the store, but from here on, I think you should consider yourself a full partner. You deserve a full share of what the business earns. Your knowledge of expedition outfitting, your experience with the products we sell, and ideas like the one you just proposed make you as much a part of this business as Luke or me. What do you say, Jubil—full partners?"

"Nelly?" Jubil said.

"Oh yes, it sounds wonderful to me," said Nelly.

"Yes, sir, thank you," said Jubil. "It would be an honor to be partners with you."

"Excellent!" exclaimed Mr. Warner. "Let's have a toast." He rose and went to the sideboard.

"Mr. Warner," Jubil called, "if I could have a moment before we celebrate . . . there's something else I'd like to say." Jubil looked at Nelly and smiled. "I have declared my love to my dearest and best friend Nelly Boswell, and I'm happy to say she feels the same for me." Jubil turned to Nelly's mother. "Mrs. Boswell, with your permission, ma'am, and Mr. Boswell's, Nelly and I would like to marry."

Mrs. Boswell reached over and took Nelly's hand. "I'm sure Theodore will be as thrilled as I am," she said. "We won't tell him that we've already celebrated tonight."

Mr. Warner poured glasses of wine for everyone, including Mrs. Garcia, who smiled and accepted a glass.

"I propose a toast," announced Luke, standing and holding his glass aloft, "to Jubilee Walker, Nelly Boswell, and Warner and Walker Outfitters."

Jubil lifted his wine glass as well. "To the future," he said.

ACKNOWLEDGEMENTS

I would like to thank my editor, Heidi Bell, for her indefatigable efforts in helping me shape this book. Her patient coaching and insightful comments have turned my framework of a story into something I am proud of. I am also grateful for the proofreading by Regina McCaughey-Silvia. Without her meticulous review of the manuscript, some embarrassing mistakes would have haunted me. Any shortcomings in the finished product are mine alone.

My thanks also to Meg Miner, Archivist & Special Collections Librarian at Illinois Wesleyan University's Ames Library in Bloomington, Illinois, for providing access to the John Wesley Powell Special Collection, and for directing me to other valuable reference materials.

The McLean County Museum of History and the online archives of Bloomington's newspaper, The Daily Pantagraph, provided colorful insights into community life in the period covered by the book.

I might never have completed the book without the help and encouragement of my daughter, Lori Kaufman. She served as my editor before Heidi took the wheel, as my beta reader supreme, and as my unflagging moral support. Many thanks also to my patient friend, Rich Teegarden, for his critical reading of and comments on early drafts, and to all of my friends and family who took the time to read and comment on the book.

For readers interested in a historical account of Powell and the expeditions described in the book, I recommend the following works: *A River Running West: The Life of John Wesley Powell* by Donald Worster; *Down the Great Unknown: John Wesley Powell's 1869 Journey of Discovery and Tragedy through the Grand Canyon* by Edward Dolnick; *The Professor Goes West* by Elmo Scott Watson.

ABOUT THE AUTHOR

Tim Piper retired from a career in information technology, and has been a lifelong hobbyist musician. He lives in Bloomington, Illinois, with his cat Maggie, who was no help at all in the writing of this book, but is a grand companion nevertheless. This is his first novel, and the first in a series of planned *Jubilee Walker* novels. Book two in the series, *The Yellowstone Campaign*, will be released later this year.